D1572666

Neon Hemlock Press
www.neonhemlock.com
@neonhemlock

© 2022 Neon Hemlock Press

We're Here: The Best Queer Speculative Fiction 2021
Edited by L.D. Lewis and Series Editor Charles Payseur

Cover Illustration by Paul Kellam
Cover Design by dave ring

Paperback ISBN-13: 978-1-952086-54-0
Ebook ISBN-13: 978-1-952086-55-7

WE'RE HERE
THE BEST QUEER SPECULATIVE FICTION 2021

Neon Hemlock Press

We're Here
2021

EDITED BY L.D. LEWIS & CHARLES PAYSEUR

2021 WAS CERTAINLY...a year. One that saw renewed and widespread anti-LGBTQ+ legislation and energy across the United States, and indeed across the world the fight for queer rights continues to be hard fought and often disheartening. Even in the realm of publishing, book banning and censorship in the name of "family values" has been a rapid and virulent push from those who consider conversations and education about gender and sexuality better off silenced. I can only take heart that, despite the hate and discrimination finding new footholds, queer expression and art has continued to flourish. Do I worry that this very book might be banned and withheld from the hands of readers who desperately need it? I do. But I also know that the only way to counter organized hate is organized defiance. And in the face of intolerance, it's important to shout it to those all over the world, to all those needing to hear a voice of solidarity.

And of course we affirm that even as we acknowledge that some people pass, some publications close. *Prismatica Magazine* joins other queer-centered speculative publications who have shuttered in recent years. With *Glittership* becoming dormant as well, it means that outside of anthologies or yearly efforts like *Decoded Pride*, the number of publications focusing on LGBTQ+ stories has dwindled. *Anathema* still publishes works by authors who are LGBTQ+ as well as BIPOC. And *Baffling Magazine* publishes quarterly issues packed with queer flash fiction. And I do still list dozens of LGBTQ+ short speculative fiction a month on my Patreon lists. So it's not expressly accurate to say that, overall, queer stories are being published less frequently than in years past.

It was, after all, a very good year for queer-authored collections. I had my own *The Burning Day and Other Strange Stories* out at Lethe Press. 2020 *We're Here* contributor Charlie Jane Anders's *Even Greater Mistakes* came out from Tor, Isabel Yap had *Never Have I Ever* from Small Beer, and

Kelly Robson's *Alias Space and Other Stories* was released by Subterranean. Brian Koukol put out a collection of his work independently with *Handicapsules: Short Stories of Speculative Crip Lit*. And queer speculative novellas were all over the publishing world as well, from Aimee Ogden's *Local Star* to Nino Cipri's *Defekt*, from Arula Ratnakar's "Submergence" to Shingai Njeri Kagunda's *& This is How to Stay Alive* (indeed, Neon Hemlock once again put out a flight of four queer speculative novellas).

Queer-focused anthologies are still coming out with some regularity as well. Speculatively Queer, a relatively new press, published *It Gets Even Better: Stories of Queer Possibility* in 2021, and ran a successful crowdfunding campaign for the 2022 plant-themed follow up, *Xenocultivars: Stories of Queer Growth*. Lethe Press, long a stalwart of queer publishing, put out *Burly Tales: Finally Fairy Tales for the Hirsute and Hefty Gay Man*. From the Farther Trees published *Queer Blades: A Queer Sword and Sorcery Romance Anthology*. And Neon Hemlock whetted many an appetite for queer short speculative fiction with *Unfettered Hexes: Queer Tales of the Insatiable Darkness*. And, as briefly mentioned before, QueerSpec returned for another year of *Decoded Pride: A science fiction, fantasy, and horror story-a-day anthology for Pride month*. I definitely don't want to minimize those amazing contributions to the queer speculative fiction scene.

It's possible that queer stories are simply reaching a level of saturation across the speculative fiction field. Certainly memorable examples from prestigious publications have been nominated for and won the field's highest honors. In many ways this very book is a testament to how widely queer stories are published, as works in this volume come from fourteen different publication. And we again received hundreds of submissions for this volume of *We're Here*, which combined with my reading from the field in general, means that I probably considered over 600 stories for this volume.

That's fantastic, and certainly a sign of the enthusiasm and passion for queer speculative fiction. But a large number does come from the special projects listed above, and though having queer stories appear across the field is definitely a good thing, I still mourn the loss of publications who keep queerness explicitly in their vision and mission.

Which is another reason why I am so happy to be a part of *We're Here*, to shine this light on stories and put them into the hands of people who might have missed them otherwise. To celebrate these works from a diverse array of authors and publications and not shy away from saying that they are explicitly queer. They say that part out loud, and in a time when more and more people are trying to silence queerness, to stifle and legislate away the truths of so many, that's vitally important.

I am especially happy to be joined in this work by this year's guest editor, L.D. Lewis. She is an award winning writer and editor, and currently the publisher of Fireside Fiction. She is a founding creator, Art Director, and Project manager for the World Fantasy and Hugo Award-winning *FIYAH Literary Magazine*. She has done foundational and transformational work through her role as the founding Director of the Hugo-nominated FIYAHCON. She also acquires novellas for Tor.com and researches for the LeVar Burton Reads podcast. Her short fiction has appeared across the field, including the amazing "From Witch to Queen to God" at *Mermaids Monthly* in 2021 and "The Currant Dumas," originally in *Glitter + Ashes*, which appeared in *We're Here 2020*.

As a writer, editor, and organizer, L.D. has done so much to push speculative fiction as a field in a better direction. To show what's possible when people step away from systems that only work for some and try to be as inclusive as possible while also getting great things done. I am so honored that she took the time amidst all the other things she's doing to edit this volume of *We're Here*. We are all very lucky.

In writing this introduction to the second volume of *We're Here*, I'm struck that I've already done the work last year of defining what I think queer speculative fiction is and making the argument for why there should be a Best Of anthology dedicated to it (and technically I argued that there should be *more* Best Ofs devoted to queer speculative fiction). And rather than lay that out again, I think it's important to recognize that the work of pushing for recognition and celebrating queer stories doesn't become less vital over time. The origins of our title is a chant, and part of the power of a chant is that it repeats. Hopefully, it grows. And as the chant spreads from person to person, from place to place, ideas travel with it. A kind of magic happens. So that even as some voices fall silent, others fill in, and more, and more until there is no ignoring it. No avoiding it. No banning it or censoring it.

The stories in this volume once more justify their own prominence with their beauty and their defiance. With their charm and their compassion. With their centering of queer characters and themes in remarkable and remarkably diverse ways. They are the voices raised against the efforts to erase queer stories, saying...*We're Here.*

Charles Payseur
May 2022
Eau Claire, WI

A Note From the Editor

I've had this tab open for maybe a month now. The problem, you see, is I can't quite remember where 2021 began and ended. I'm only vaguely certain it isn't still 2021 right now.

What I've learned about myself over the pandemic years is that my stress response is: work. When in doubt, another project is always good medicine, the busying of idle hands leaves them unavailable as a devil's playthings, et cetera. Create a convention. Create an awards series. Create a writing contest for LeVar Burton. Take a job administering some queer awards. Co-edit a queer lit anthology.

Between researching for LeVar Burton's podcast and selecting material for this latest iteration of *We're Here*, I have been drowning—in all the best ways— in rich, diverse, gorgeously executed short fiction.

There is something specific about queer speculative literature. In much the same way as any marginalized storytelling, there is an insistence in envisioning ourselves in every conceivable universe with every kind of power, in every quiet and cacophonous environment, every moment of vulnerability or righteous violence. I love the rebellion of it, especially now. The guerilla nature of writing and publishing defiantly with these identities is a tangible, palpable concept. Every story in a world where throngs of people want your voice and history silenced for no other reason than because your existence highlights the emptiness of their own, becomes a taunt, a battle cry. There is so much now that needs defying. Our queer fantastic is where we've made and unmade and remade ourselves so often now that when we say "we're *here*" as queer authors, it's both a promise and glorious threat that should be heard as "we're everywhere."

And with that, I am thrilled to co-present some of the best queer speculative storytelling 2021 had to offer. Rest assured that these selections represent a drop in an ever-growing sea's worth of us.

L.D. Lewis
June 2022
Atlanta, GA

We're Here 2021

TABLE OF CONTENTS

A Note From the Series Editor by Charles Payseur
A Note From the Editor by L.D. Lewis

❖

❖

About our Contributors
Story Acknowledgements
About the Editors About the Press

The Captain &
the Quartermaster

C.L. Clark

COMMANDER MAEB LEN knows that, more than anything, an army needs hope in order to struggle onward. They need a vision to fight for and faith that the future will be better than the past. Better than the present.

The People's Army itself is one such hope. The fall of the Tyrant is one such vision.

Commander Len also knows that people find hope in other, smaller things.

In the laughter that replaces the moaning of the wounded after a quiet winter of healing and souls put to rest.

In the green shoots of grass, wildflowers blooming in the untrampled fields around the army's camp.

In the unwavering dedication of Commander Len and Quartermaster Omopria to each other, and to The People's Army. Their teasing romance. The brilliance of their successes. Together, they can do anything.

Anything to remind the army that the world will go on, and that perhaps, they will, too.

❖

COMMANDER LEN CLASPS arms and grips shoulders with the other officers as they gather in the command tent one last time before the final campaign against the Tyrant begins. (No one has said out loud that it is the final campaign. No one would dare.)

Captain Dhissik, the new leader of Len's old company, gives her a fierce hug. High Commander Aulia does not. She nods gravely, warily. Lately, Len has been keeping her distance from her old sparring partner.

The new season brings new promotions, and it will take time to see how they fit.

Once they are all seated on the circle of blankets, High Commander Aulia raises a hand for quiet.

"Officers of The People's Army." Aulia looks at them each in turn, and Len feels the strength in Aulia's certainty spread from officer to officer, commander and captain alike. "We've been fighting against the Tyrant for six years. He's stolen our youth. He's stolen our good looks." She smiles, and the scar that splits from below her right eye to the left side of her sharp chin stretches. She sobers immediately, though. "He's stolen the happier lives we might have lived, and the loved ones we might have spent them with."

Solemn nods from all. Len isn't the only one whose grip tightens around a sword hilt or into a fist. Here in this stuffy tent, they are the same. The People's Fist. The Hand That Would Open the Cage.

"It's time we steal from him." The officers cheer Aulia's words. "This spring, when the flowers bloom and the trees fruit, so do we." They cheer again.

But as the high commander details the plan for the campaign, Len's heart sinks. They will need the best quartermaster in the world for such a risky campaign. The Army's standing supply caches had been targeted early in the war. Their quartermaster had worked without sleep to decentralize what remained. From then on, each unit became responsible for carrying a portion of the Army's stores so the Tyrant couldn't destroy them with a single blow. It is a delicate balance; one overlooked shortage or faulty supply line, and the entire Army risks slaughter or starvation.

And unlike everyone else in the room, Len knows in her bones that the best quartermaster in the world wants to leave The People's Army and go home. She doesn't think Quartermaster Omopria will last another full campaign.

The worst part about it is that Len can't blame her, won't blame her, if she leaves.

While the other officers leave the command tent feeling determined, Len finds herself drifting. Instead of convening with her captains, she stands outside of the tent and watches the camp shake off winter's slumber. There, in the eastern corner, is the sparring square, bright with the clack of wood, the grunts of effort and laughter.

There, toward the center of the camp, the supply wagons, where Quartermaster Omopria and her staff would be, counting and loading, loading and counting. Someone is cooking the beans for lunch.

Then she looks to the north, toward the city where the Tyrant waits, not knowing he has rats in his larder, stealing hope for The People.

"Is everything all right?"

Len jumps at High Commander Aulia's soft voice beside her. "Fifth," Len greets her with her old company's name.

Len knows that the smile she gives doesn't pass muster. Aulia's expression softens with understanding. Somehow, the scar on her face only makes the expression more tender.

"I know it's none of my business, but the soldiers talk and—"

Len walls up her expression, and she looks balefully at the high commander of The People's Army.

Aulia crosses her hands awkwardly behind her back, leather armor creaking. "Just. If you need anything, I'm here. I was married once, too."

"Oh?" Len turns sharply, hungry for someone else's answers. Someone else's sorrow to show her what to do with her own. "What happened?"

"A little thing called a civil war." A complicated grief crosses Aulia's face.

Cold fills Len's belly as realization dawns. "We're fighting them."

Aulia nods solemnly. "We're fighting them."

"I'm so sorry."

"So am I."

❖

A LONG TIME ago, when The People's Army was first born from the spark of rebellion against the Tyrant, Captain Maeb Len of the Third Company trudged back into camp on her own sore feet. Agno, her horse, had fallen, stabbed behind one of his legs, and she'd jumped from the saddle, praying for mercy and so much blind luck. She hadn't even had time to cut his poor throat before she had to face the onslaught of the enemy. Maybe the very ones who'd brought down Agno.

The rage of the battle gone, her company limped into the marching camp after her, their faces drawn in pain or shame or exhaustion—likely a combination of it all. Truth to tell, Len felt more than a twist of shame herself. And not just because she hadn't given Agno the mercy he deserved after faithfully carrying her for so long. But the battle was done, and ahead of her was a meal and her first bath in weeks, if she could make the walk to the stream. A dry scrub if she could not. But first, she would ki— No, she wasn't sure that was true, that she would kill for a decent meal. Not right now. The memory of running her bloodied sword through another thick body, scraping it back out of a bone-caged heart, coating her hands in sticking blood—it made her want to bring up food instead of shovel it down. Luckily, she'd lost all the food she had to spare on the field amid the corpses. Many of her soldiers had. The sick still tasted sour in her mouth.

Water. A drink of water first.

She lined up at the officers' soup queue, among other young captains and senior captains without the colors of distinction on their coats. Well—no color of distinction but the deep arterial red of close combat.

A woman, the quartermaster's assistant, doled out the soup in carefully measured ladles, making sure each was equal. So careful, even here with the officers, to make sure that precious goods lasted. The sergeant wore her hair in a tight braid, but curls sprang free at her wide brow; some of them clung in sweat there. She looked thin, as if she should have her own rations doubled.

"Come on, missy, you cannot give me more than that?" A senior captain shook his bowl expectantly at the woman, stalling the entire line of weary and aching soldiers. The soup's scent reached Len. Beans. Again. Thank the gods. Better than nothing at all, and though beans could wreak havoc in the communal tents, they would hold to your guts and keep you full. At that moment, Len could not have stomached meat.

"No, *sir*, I can't." And when he refused to move on, the quartermaster's assistant shoved past him to the next officer with the next carefully measured bowl. That officer had the sense to move along quickly.

The senior captain did not. He pushed his way back in front of the assistant. "Excuse me? Do you not think you're out of line?"

The quartermaster's assistant met his glare with hers. "No, I do not, but I would be *most* glad if you were out of this one." Then she beckoned the next person to the pot.

Captain Len stifled a smile as she watched the woman pour, watched the irritation creep into the set of her jaw. This close, the captain saw a streak of gray climbing through her hair. Surprising, as she didn't look a day out of her second decade, cheeks round, skin unlined. Likewise, Len could smell the blood on the senior captain's coat. Could trace the tension in his shoulders through the fabric, the bunching before a blow.

Captain Len reached up and placed a hand on his shoulder. "Sir! Sir, you were brilliant on the field today. I hope I'm half as good as you before I'm promoted. You'll have a high commander's cloak before we're done here."

The senior captain looked at her, disdain in his gaze for the interruption but courtesy toward a fellow winning out over it. The higher-ups looked on mentoring as favorable for promotions.

"Thank you, Captain...?"

"Len. Maeb Len. Do you want to share a drink?" She leaned close to his ear. "I've been hiding a stash of 798, if that interests you."

His mood perked up instantly. "Now that I cannot turn down." And Len led him away, past the other cookpots with other men and women on the quartermaster's staff and around to where her company would pitch her tent.

Later, when the senior captain had gone, a slight stagger in his step, Len lay under the stars, stomach growling, still dirty and unwilling to sully her tent with her own filth. That was where the quartermaster's assistant found her.

"You forgot your dinner." The woman smiled, with a bowl of soup in each hand, and lowered herself down.

"Thank you." Len sat up, taking the offered bowl. "I'm sorry he was an ass."

The quartermaster's assistant waved the apology away. "It comes with the post. The People's Army welcomes all people, and so on. Thank *you* for getting rid of him."

"It took almost an entire 798. Well worth it, I'd say." Len waved the squat-bottomed bottle by its short neck, but the stars spun and her soup sloshed at the bowl's rim.

"Steady on," the quartermaster's assistant said with a chuckle, easing the bottle from Len's hand. "I'm Jissia Omopria."

"Maeb Len."

From the beginning, Jissia had taken care of Len.

❧

FOUR YEARS LATER, Captain Maeb Len knelt by Quartermaster Jissia Omopria's side in her own tent. It was bigger than the quartermaster's tent, and Len didn't have to share it with subordinates like Jissia did. Still, it smelled sour with sweat and sick.

Jissia burned with fever. Her hand was clammy in Len's, and she muttered to no one, delirious and barely conscious. Half the camp was.

The People's Army had been fucked for four years, but this day had been an exceptionally bad day.

"Captain!"

Her lieutenant's voice was frantic outside the door. She startled upright, out of her almost-doze.

"What now, Balissen?" Len tried to shout it, but her voice was too hoarse. She'd been screaming retreat after retreat for weeks. The Tyrant wasn't letting her people rest. That was the point. Harry them, and when they stopped to catch their breath, harry them again, until they collapsed from exhaustion. If Len let herself go to sleep now, she would never wake up, and she would be glad for it.

It wasn't Balissen who came in. Len blinked blearily in the dim candles lighting the tent. Oh. Right. Balissen had taken an arrow through the throat three months ago. She hadn't been the one to find his body or she would never have forgotten. So she told herself.

"What is it?" she croaked.

This new lieutenant's name was Dhissik. Lieutenant Dhissik first handed her a small cup of what Len already knew was dirty water masquerading as coffee. Jissia had stretched the rations as far as she could so that the soldiers could keep moving, over and over again, but now the officers were hoarding it jealously. Jissia hadn't approved, but how was Len supposed to make the decisions that would save their lives if she was more than half asleep?

Len sipped, to make the cup last.

"Captain Aulia found out what's wrong." The lieutenant swayed with exhaustion, but fear made her eyes wide. "It's the water. They're dumping corpses upriver. It's running straight to us."

Len's eyes went down to her coffee. "Shit."

"Not that water."

The lieutenant didn't leave.

"What else?"

"The Tyrant's moving again. Not to chase us," Dhissik said quickly, to forestall Len, "but something else. The Fourth and Fifth just arrived. They want to speak with you."

Len turned back to Jissia. The fever hadn't broken, but the murmuring had stopped. She didn't once think of sending Dhissik in her place. Dhissik had been a corporal three months ago. She wouldn't even have sent Balissen, who had been her lieutenant for three of the five years.

Four years. She turned Jissia's right forearm over. The inked marriage mark matched the one on Len's, so that when they clasped forearms the images made a whole.

There was duty, and then there was *duty*. Len heaved herself clumsily to her feet. Though the young lieutenant had to grab her by the arm to steady her, Len didn't spill the coffee.

"Tell me where they're meeting," Len said. "You stay here with her."

"Sir," Dhissik said with a sigh. Her voice cracked. "I can't. I have messages to run to the other two captains."

"Why do they have my lieutenant doing everyone else's job?" Len growled as she pulled her leather armor back on and buckled her sword belt.

But she knew the answer. Everyone else was dead.

And The People's quartermaster lay alone in her sickbed.

❖

HOW DIFFERENT THAT was from the beginning.

With her hand in Deputy Quartermaster Omopria's, sneaking away from the army's camp, Captain Len felt like she could climb the clouds. But the sky was clear and blue, and the quartermaster's smile was bright and warm, and the captain was sinking hopelessly into it.

Back when the war was new and hope was sweet on the tongue. Freedom from the Tyrant. Rule by The People.

Len tugged Jissia's hand again, smiling slyly. "They'll be fine without us for ten minutes."

"Ten minutes?" Jissia raised an arched eyebrow. "Is that all?"

Len blushed but, even so, pulled Jissia close. "I'm happy to draw this out longer if you are."

Jissia's body melted into hers as they kissed, delighting in the sensation of eyelashes on cheeks, noses nuzzling, hands holding tight at the wonder of it all. Len wanted it to last forever.

And so she asked, after they peeled apart and lay in the soft grass of the clearing they had claimed. Amid their strewn clothing there was even someone else's jacket— neither of theirs but another lover, perhaps, who had forgotten it because they were too flush with the warmth of their own kindling. Len would bring it back to camp and tease the owner mercilessly, knowing she would be teased in return. But that, too, was the joy of it.

"What are you doing in a few months time?" Len rolled over to walk her fingers gently up Jissia's sternum before tracing the lower curve of her right breast. "When this is all over?"

Jissia rolled over, tangling her boots with Len's. She'd pulled her uniform trousers back up but they were still unlaced, and Len gave them a playful tug. "You think this will be over that soon?"

"No civil war on the entire continent has lasted longer than two years! We're close. Look how easily we've routed them." She met Jissia's gaze and held it earnestly. "We have the people on our side. The Tyrant can't stand against his own nation."

Jissia raised both of her eyebrows this time and snorted. "The folly of youth."

"You weren't complaining about my youth a few minutes ago." Len used their tangled legs as a lever to roll back on top Jissia and kiss her deeply. But when Jissia sank her hands into Len's long braids, Len stopped. She stroked the thin streak of gray in Jissia's dark hair. "Would you make a life with me, when it's all done?"

Jissia's face softened in surprise and then tenderness. "Are you sure you'd be happy? You're a fighter. Even off the field."

"I've had enough of trouble." Squads of soldiers lost, the roughness of sleeping in cold tents, waking up knowing so clearly that the day could be her last. Len could walk away happily and never look back. "Let's have something simple and easy."

"And when you get bored, Maeb?"

Len bent down and kissed her on the forehead, then the nose, then the lips. "No one can fight forever."

❖

MUCH LATER, CAPTAIN Maeb Len will remember that day with the fever as the day it all broke because it was the day many things broke.

It was the day that she learned she would fail again and again and again. It was the day she learned that she never wanted to fail those she loved but she loved too many.

It was the day she truly felt in her bones that war is not kind to love. She had loved Lieutenant Balissen like a brother and had not even looked for his body after the report came in. She had tried not to let the deaths become rote, to force herself to feel disgust instead of numbness at bloody leathers, because that, too, was a failure of love.

Love was the only thing that held any of them together. The People's Army went to fight for love of their neighbor, who the Tyrant would have let starve in the street. For love of the mothers, who died in childbirth rather than give birth in the fine hospitals that became debtors' prisons. For love of the teachers, who starved rather than let their students go hungry.

War brought the captain and the quartermaster together, because they believed in love over the Tyrant. They had to love each other more than the war would have torn them apart.

It would not be one crack but many, and still Len would always try again.

❖

AFTER SIX YEARS of civil war, Len sits at her travel desk to draft a letter to a potential ally recently freed from their own queen. That is the first task High Commander Aulia has given her. The words don't come out right. If she sounds too desperate, they might balk; what use in sending troops to fight for a lost cause, no matter how just?

But The People's Army *is* desperate. Six years. Even Len can see that there won't be a year after this. Not with this army. Not these leaders.

Len looks down at the embroidered crimson fist on the breast of her jacket. She is a commander now. Aulia is counting on Len's intelligence for the new campaign.

She feels a warm hand on her shoulder. Jissia hands her a cup of coffee that smells strong, black as pitch. Len's eyes watered. It smells like hope.

"Where did you—"

Jissia shakes her head and kisses Len gently on the cheek.

"This is it, isn't it?" Jissia asks softly. "Either we win or..."

Or. They both know the other would finish that sentence differently.

Len takes Jissia's hand and kisses the knuckles gently.

❖

LEN ALSO REMEMBERS a time, in the middle of the war, the third year, maybe the fourth? They had already been fighting longer than The People's Army had prepared for. Longer than Len had prepared for. Still, Len thought they had turned a corner in the war. She'd had an idea for a new, more devastating munition.

"Jissia!" she called happily when she found the quartermaster in her domain. The unit's supply wagons were nestled within the camp so that they couldn't be easily picked off by the Tyrant's raiders. Even though the ground around them had been trampled, green grass had begun to shoot up in tufts between the wheels.

Jissia pecked Len on the cheek, and Len caught one of the junior quartermasters hiding a smile. Len smiled tentatively at Jissia in turn.

"Yes?" Jissia said suspiciously.

"We've had an idea," Len said, now almost shy. "We need to melt all of our extra iron into some kind of heavy impact projectile."

Jissia's face darkened immediately. "*Extra* iron? We don't have any iron left."

"Wait. What do you mean we're out of iron?" Len pursued Jissia around the supply wagons while Jissia checked this thing and that thing in her inventory ledger. "Jiss, we've been doing shit-all for a whole season! What do you mean we're out of iron?"

Jissia pressed the ledger to her forehead before enunciating slowly, as if Len were stupid. "I mean that between the reinforced shields, the re-shod horses, and the new wagon axles that you'll need to start moving your army again—we're left a bit short." Jissia lowered her voice so the underlings couldn't hear. "Besides, we don't have the facilities for casting iron. If you stopped playing games and paid attention to the actual war, you'd know this."

"Playing games?" Len was almost tempted to throw her sword into Jissia's arms, to make her swing it. It would show her just how easy these games were. "This is why we *have* you. You help us make this possible. *My* job is to coordinate the ground strategy within the army. That includes knowing my soldiers and training them, too."

She didn't understand why Jissia begrudged her the time in the sparring square even though it brought Len some of the only peace she ever felt.

Jissia's own outlet had soured. At first, she had painted, carrying small scraps of canvas and painting until she tired of the same dull colors, the same dull scenes. Len wondered if Jissia saw the same things she did, over and over again. Brown mud, grey-brown corpses, red-brown dried blood.

"I saw you with the captain of the Fifth." Jissia didn't look at Len when she said it.

Len didn't look at her either. She felt the need to protect something small inside of herself. She dug the toe of her boot into the dirt.

"That wasn't the vow we made."

"She understands me. That's all."

"Good for her. I'm glad someone does."

❖

AND THE SILENCE. Cold, lonely silence.

❖

LEN HAD ALSO struggled to find her place, though Jissia
perhaps hadn't realized it. By the third year, Len finally
understood the cycle of war: the wintering camps, the spring
thaw into movement. When spring came, the fighting would
start over again without care for those who needed time
to catch their breath or whose legs and back had become
too weak to carry the weight. She was still not used to the
death, not exactly; she would regret the day the dead were
nothing to her. Her body, however, could learn to tolerate the
exhaustion.

And yet, she no longer thinks of Balissen. There are the
living to think of.

One day that third winter, the sparring square was full of
soldiers trying to keep themselves sharp. And by sharpening
herself here, Captain Len thought that, perhaps, she could
forge herself into something better for Jissia.

Len pulled a practice blade and arced it across her body.
Already she was able to replace thoughts of Jissia with the
natural flow of her own body.

"Third!" A cheerful voice interrupted the flow. Captain
Rix Aulia, of the Fifth. She was tall and narrow, with sharp
eyes and a sharper chin. Her face was smooth and unlined
despite a few sporadic gray hairs amid her cropped black
curls.

"Fifth!" Len tapped Aulia's bare blade with her own in an
invitation.

They crashed together in a joy of panting. Each near miss,
a curse tinged with laughter. In the end, Len slipped within
Aulia's longer reach to disarm her. They fell to the ground.
She ended up weaponless beneath Aulia, whose forearm
rested on her throat.

Aulia of the Fifth smiled, showing crooked eyeteeth.

Len left the sparring square with the flutter of finding cherished jewelry that she thought she'd lost.

❖

FOUR MONTHS BEFORE High Commander Aulia gave the army its commands for the final campaign, Len and Jissia lay awake in the pitch-black tent. The candles were snuffed. Outside, the early winter wind howled like the hungry coyotes dogging the supply train. The Tyrant was pulling back for the season.

Len felt the hands-breadth of space between them like a wall. The effort it took to keep themselves distinct. And still, she could have drawn the shape of Jissia's body beside her.

"I want you to go," Len whispered. "I can't do this anymore."

Saying it felt like siphoning poison from her blood.

"What?" Jissia's voice cut through the quiet.

"I know you want to leave. Go. There's still time to live the life you dreamed of. I won't steal it from you, like the Tyrant."

"You have no idea what I've dreamed of. What I've given up for this war. Do you?"

"The same things we've all given up."

"No. You've found glory. You've found friends. People who think and act like you. I've grown more and more isolated, with each passing year."

"Your assistants—"

"They're not my friends any more than an unranked soldier is yours."

"Some of them are my friends."

"Then I'm not like you. It's not easy for me."

"You're right. And it doesn't have to be. You can go."

"I stayed here for you. I'm not leaving now. We'll see this through to the end. Together. Like we promised."

Silence stretched, full of Len's doubts. Jissia's hand snuck over, hesitant. Len remembered times that the two of them had been as tightly laced as fingers, able to support more together than apart.

"You're sure?"

"Of course."

◈

DURING THAT AUTUMN campaign season, the captain and the quartermaster worked miracles together, even when they thought they couldn't.

"There's no way to get an extra two weeks' worth of food all the way to a company you've stationed on the ass-end side of the world." Jissia ran her hand through the snarl of her curls, a riot of gray and brown. She rounded on Len. "You've stationed them too far from us."

"I know. I'm sorry. We didn't mean to let it get like this, but it was our only option. They knew the risks and—"

"An army marches on its stomach. And its gear. You've stripped away my ability to provide for either. That is my *job*." Jissia about-faced and strode away, leaving Len to trail, limping, after her.

"I know. Of course, I know." Len searched for the words to soothe her quartermaster, but, as happened more and more often these days, she found herself at a loss. No matter how much she explained, it was never quite enough—or perhaps, never quite right. When they ducked into their tent, she added, "It's my job to make sure this war is won."

"And then we can stop, yes? Isn't that what you said four years ago?" Jissia didn't bother to light a candle. They were running low, and she limited them to strategy meetings only now. The officers needed to read missives and see the maps. Letters from home—such that they were—could be read by daylight or moonlight or not at all.

Len didn't need a candle's flickering flame to see the severe set of Jissia's mouth.

"Part of me feels like you'd be fine for this to keep going forever," Jissia said. "You thrive on this. I don't."

The remark stung. "No? You don't thrive on the satisfaction of keeping our soldiers alive?" Len snorted. "I know the way you get when you solve a problem we couldn't figure out." Smug and beautiful with the sheer brilliance of her mind. Jissia had saved them more times than Len could count. The two of them could do it again, but only together.

Len could see Jissia gathering breath, like a snake coiling for a strike. As if granted a vision of the future, Len knew what could happen: they would strike and parry until there was nothing but silence between them. Tonight of all nights, she didn't want that.

Len held up her hands in surrender. "I'm sorry." She reached out to clasp Jissia's forearm. Though their clothing covered it, their marriage marks lined up and reminded Len why they had bound themselves together.

Jissia clasped back, tentatively at first, as if she wasn't sure she was allowed. "Me too."

They slept together that night for the first time in many months, but it wasn't until after Jissia rolled away that Len admitted to herself what she couldn't during the act. Jissia had either forgotten how to touch her, or didn't want to. The captain turned her back to the quartermaster. Her core felt hollowed out.

❖

Two DAYS AFTER receiving High Commander Aulia's orders and one day before The People's Army marches, Quartermaster Jissia Omopria requisitions all of the sugar in the army. She calls it hope.

With her help and The People's cooks, every soldier has one sweetened biscuit to eat.

It shouldn't be enough to cry over, or enough to set a field army to carousing happily through the rows of tents as if at festival.

But it is. Jissia is right. Sugar is hope, and that's what The People's Army needs after six years of attrition. That's what they need for one last push.

Commander Len and Quartermaster Omopria eat their biscuits with their closest friends. Captain Dhissik of the Third. The First. High Commander Aulia and the new captain of the Fifth. Deputy Quartermaster Chessian.

Len's knee bumps Jissia's, and when Jissia cups Len's knee with her hand, Chessian giggles. He has a sweet laugh and dark doe eyes, and he idolizes Jissia. Len feels Aulia's eyes on them.

"How long *have* you two been together?" Chessian asks. "Longer than the war?"

Jissia tears up a clod of dirt and tosses it at him as she laughs. It sounds as forced as Len's own strained smile.

They share a knowing look before answering.

"We're as old as the war."

"We started because of the war."

Chessian mock swoons, but when he recovers, he looks at them with a sugar-shine in his eyes. "It's nice to know that something good can come out of this, after all."

❖

AND BEHIND THE forced smiles, the silence still; now scalding to the touch and swollen, like a blister.

But a blister must be lanced before a march.

❖

AND IN THE morning, The People's Army is on the move again.

Len helps Jissia saddle her placid horse and kneels to offer her a vaulting step onto its back. It is the horse least tempered for war that Len has ever seen. Jissia strokes its neck from the saddle.

High Commander Aulia rides over. She looks anxiously at the sky, judging the position of the sun, which has not even crested the horizon. The deep black of night is only just turning gray. It's time to go.

Aulia sees Jissia's saddlebags. They don't have the familiar waxed ledger cases to keep the inventory books safe from rain and blood and whatever war would throw at them. "What's going on, Commander?" Her eyes flick between Len on the ground and Jissia, on her horse. "Quartermaster?"

"Quartermaster Chessian has his orders," Jissia says. "He's more than up to the task."

"We have a plan in place," Len adds.

And though something inside Len is asking *are you sure are you sure are you sure that you will not break without each other*, Len knows that she has never been more sure of anything.

She sees the same certainty in Jissia's face.

She expects Aulia to balk at losing the best quartermaster in the world; expects her to try and convince Jissia to stay.

Instead, Aulia turns her horse. She nods to Jissia in farewell and says to Len, "We move out in ten." She leaves them their privacy.

"I always knew—"

"You know, I thought—"

They stop. They laugh. It feels as if they should weep.

Len holds her arm up one more time, and Jissia clasps her elbow. Len's bare arm, her sleeve rolled up, shows one half of the marriage mark, tattooed in black.

"You're my best friend."

"We'll be okay."

There is nothing else to say, and their efforts to find the right words, the right *last* words, feel futile.

Nothing else to say but: "Thank you, Jissia."

As Len looks up at Jissia, her face finds it hard to smile, even though it is all she wants to do, for Jissia's sake.

Jissia squeezes Len's arm. "Thank you, Maeb."

They stay like that, arms linked, for eight more minutes, even though Jissia's back must be straining and Len's shoulder aches.

Then, when the former quartermaster is gone, the commander reaches for the reins of her own horse, pulls herself up, and rides after the high commander.

❖

THE NIGHT BEFORE, after the celebrations, they sat on their shared blanket amid their shared pillows. Years of words unspoken sat with them.

"That was well done, Jissia," Len said. "Genius."

Jissia smiled. "An army marches on its—"

Len rolled her eyes and gave the quartermaster a playful shove. "Len?"

Len looked into Jissia's eyes, startled to see them shining. Outside, the revel continued. Firelight and starlight crept in through the cracks of the tent.

Suddenly, it was as if there wasn't enough air in the tent. Len could only say, "Mm?"

"Chessian is ready to take over." Jissia let the weight of her words sink in.

"What happened?" By which Len meant, *why now, how did you change your mind*, **are you sure**?

"We've been the captain and the quartermaster for so long. I thought we couldn't be anything else." Jissia shrugged. "Tonight... I realized that may not be true. But if I stay, I won't find out."

And instead of pain and fear, Len felt the salt tears of relief.

For the first time in too long, the air felt truly easy between them.

"Here." Jissia smiled through her own tears as she pulled out a tiny paper parcel.

Len knew what it was the moment she held it in her hand. She laughed. She pulled out her own small package for Jissia, this one wrapped in admittedly dingy cloth.

They opened them at the same time. Each parcel held the slightly crumbled half of a sweetened biscuit.

❖

WHEN THE QUARTERMASTER and the commander go separate ways, no one will understand why. Commander Len will assure everyone that the Jissia is still a dear friend; they will exchange letters—when the war ends, when Jissia opens a school, when Len takes a seat on The People's Council.

They will both remember things that they had forgotten, like how to walk on two legs instead of four, or how to take enough food just for one, not two. They will both love again; other people, other ways.

Len doesn't weep until The People's Army is riding away from their winter camp and her quartermaster is just a speck on the road, heading the other direction.

Life goes on. In their own corners of the world, they will go on, too.

A Study in Ugliness

H. PUEYO

UGLY GIRLS WILL NEVER be happy, insisted Ms. Leocádia, standing in front of the blackboard. *Simply put: never, ever, ever.* And ugly, they knew, could mean a number of things: too short or too tall, too thin or too fat, too square or too round, with a big nose or a line for a mouth, a chin pointing forward, slouching shoulders, crooked legs, hairy arms. *But we can fight nature with effort*, she added after a pause. *Even the ugliest girl in the world can be pretty with a little effort.*

Everyone looked at Basília.

She had eyes like slits in a sharp face, a long body that towered over everyone else, a flat chest, a sallow complexion, a rat's nest, a masculine gait. Basília, who wore pants under the skirt of her uniform, who cut her dense black hair short (*it was lice, miss, I swear it was lice!*), who had a scar in her jaw, who smoked as much as she could in the confinements of their boarding school. *Well*, Ms. Leocádia continued, looking at her, *some cannot be saved.*

And maybe she would not have been saved indeed, not from ugliness, but from boredom, if a pair of polished red shoes had not appeared on the other bed of her room the next day. Two leather slingbacks, high-heeled, four sizes smaller than her feet, with a little ribbon on each.

Basília thought it was a prank. The second bed of her room had been empty for years, as other students were afraid of her and she didn't want company. *Basília is coming*, whispered a twelve-year-old as she walked down the corridor. *We need to get out, hurry, hurry.* The younger ones were so little that they looked like children close to her, and Basília felt a wicked pleasure in confirming their fears. *Watch out*, she slammed one of the walls with a fist, and they ran away, scaring the cat sleeping nearby.

She walked through the first floor of Santa Helena School for Young Ladies, past dramatic Romantic paintings and the enormous portrait of president Getúlio Vargas, past all classrooms, until she reached the last. Mondays had Portuguese, then Domestic Economy, French, and Literature, but at least she wouldn't suffer another round of Moral Education.

Basília entered the room.

There was someone occupying the desk that was always vacant by her side. Basília couldn't see her face, but she knew by her dark hair and small frame that she had never seen her before.

"Who the hell is that?" Basília barked the question in a low voice, stopping in front of another table.

Pérola raised her eyes, the large white bow on the top of her head bouncing with her. If there was anyone in the class who would know any fresh gossip, it would be her.

"Don't talk to me here," she whispered back, shoulders stiff, eyes on her open notebook. "I don't want the others to see."

Basília looked around. The class was not entirely full yet. She knelt beside Pérola, and pulled her by one of her ironed curls, forcing her to look at her face.

"Don't play dumb with me," warned Basília with a smile. She rubbed Pérola's light hair with her thumb. "You didn't complain the other day."

"The other day was the other day!" Pérola snapped, then looked around to see if someone had listened. "What's wrong with you?"

"*That*'s wrong with me." Basília pointed at the new girl with her chin. "Who is she and why no one told her to stay away from my place?"

Pérola frowned. "Why are you talking like that about Gilda, silly? You sleep in the same room as her for *years*."

It really was a prank. Someone was trying to get back at her, and the new girl must have been from another class. She decided it didn't matter; if they thought they could be bad, she could be ten times worse.

"So you were the one who left those shoes there," answered Basília. "Fine. We'll see, then."

Pérola asked questions in whispers—*Shoes? What are you talking about?*—but Brasília had already left. Other girls were taking their places: know-it-all Aurélia in the first row, Efigênia with her thigh-length braid, muttering a prayer, her sister Estefânia, bigger and meaner, Carlota and Lurdes talking loudly as they entered the class, both wearing ridiculously big bows on their hairdos.

Basília sat down, still ignoring the new girl.

"Go back to your class," she mouthed. "Before I drag you there myself."

Ms. Palmira arrived. Their Portuguese teacher was a feeble thing, whose voice was so low that the classroom was filled with giggles every time she tried to command any kind of attention.

"Good morning, miss Gilda," said Ms. Palmira with unlikely joy as she passed by their desks. "I'm eager to read your essay today."

Basília could have believed that some of the professors were part of the prank, but not weak Ms. Palmira, who couldn't even look at a student's face.

"Thank you, teacher."

The words came from the prettiest mouth Basília had ever seen. A well-drawn upper lip, a round lower one, half dark, half pink, corners upturned in a forever smile. Above was a delicate nose with wide nostrils, skin the same color of the mahogany walls, droopy eyes with a circle of green inside the brown. Her black hair fell in combed waves to her shoulders, and she had no bow, only the simple uniform of their school, with a white shirt under the sleeveless dress, and the same saddle shoes they were all wearing.

Gilda blinked at her with eyelashes as long as the legs of a spider, and smiled politely, her voice slow and pleasant like a purr:

"What happened, Basília? Don't you remember me?"

❖

No one else seemed to think there was something wrong with Gilda. The other teachers did not mention any transference, and all the other students insisted she had been there all along. *What are are you, stupid?* asked Estefânia, her hair pulled so tightly in a bun that her forehead was stretched back. *Did you hit your ugly head?* Her sister Efigênia didn't bother answering, running away as if the demon could possess her if she stood too close to Basília.

She intercepted Carlota and Lurdes before dinnertime, pulling them both by the collars toward an empty cabinet. *Why is everyone saying that Gilda has always been around?* Basília shook Lurdes by the shoulders, who shrieked like she was about to get hit. *Stop, you brute!* Carlota grabbed Basília's arm. *We know that you're crazy, but this is too much! You know Gilda for* years!

Even Pérola, who Basília sometimes met in the woods around the school, insisted that she was losing her wits. *Is this some kind of bad joke?* Pérola whimpered when Basília pressed her against a tree, the little hypocrite, looking like she would faint when her stockings got dirty with mud. *I always thought you were obsessed with her...*

Enraged by their similar responses, she decided to solve the issue by herself. Basília observed Gilda during dinner, where she did nothing but eat the pumpkin soup that had been served, and then in the dormitory, where she spent most of the time reading a book. Basília considered questioning her when the lights were turned off, but she fell asleep and only woke up with a muffled sound a few hours later.

Gilda pushed the covers aside, took something from the nightstand, and touched the floor with one small foot.

Tap.

The step was soft, almost impossible to hear. *Tap.* Gilda walked slowly in her nightgown, opened the door, and left.

Basília was not as silent as Gilda, who walked down the corridor with the grace of a ballerina, but the other girl didn't seem to notice there was anyone behind her. If they got caught, the principal, Ms. Zulmira, would punish them in any way she saw fit, as she had done many times. Once, when she was thirteen, Basília had been forced to kneel on raw corn for three hours, and the headmistress watched the whole ordeal with evident satisfaction. *You should remember this*, Ms. Zulmira had said when they had to take her to the doctor so he would remove the corns stuck to her skin one by one. *It's what a delinquent like you deserves.*

Gilda stopped in front of a large grandfather clock. The hands pointed eleven and fifty-nine, and she waited, her waves fluttering with the wind. Tick-tock. Tick-tock. Gilda unlocked the tower of the clock with an iron key hanging from her neck, and the door flung open, revealing a mirror inside. Basília frowned, and the chime melody reverberated through the entire school.

As the Westminster Quarters rang, Gilda bent down. She had a tangerine in her right hand, orange and perfect even in the darkness, and took it toward the reflection. Basília pinched herself to make sure she was awake, but there they were: Gilda, half of her arm inside the mirror, and herself, watching from behind one of the pillars.

When the melody ended, the mirror spat out the tangerine—rotten, dark, bitten, and covered in maggots.

Gilda smiled, closed the grandfather clock, and walked in swift steps back to the dormitory, so giddy she looked like she was dancing.

❖

EVERY NIGHT, GILDA would wait until all the lights had been turned off, and leave her bed to go back to the grandfather clock. When the windows were open, her nightgown inflated like a balloon as she walked, floating around her thin legs, then deflated, accompanying the breeze.

After the tangerine, it was a spoon. When it came back, its silver handle had been twisted several times until it formed a distorted spiral, and the head was rusty and full of holes. The following night, she threw a doll of one of the children inside, and the mirror spat out rags and ashes. Someone's blue dress came back in shreds, and a bowl of milk pudding turned into a viscous dark substance with flies glued to it.

The rotten tangerine was found by one of the maids, but they assumed it had fallen from a student's purse. The spoon was thrown in the trash. The ashes were found in the children's dormitory, and the teachers ruled it a cruel prank. A girl found her ruined dress, and the maids again cleaned what was left of the pudding.

On the fifth night, when Gilda hurried to the door, Basília was already back to her feet, a quiet shadow standing behind her. She grabbed Gilda by the wrist and turned her around, almost making her drop the parcel she was holding.

"Not so fast," said Basília, her other hand on the closed door. "Sneaking out at night again, are we?"

Gilda blinked, and looked at her frail wrist, engulfed by Basília's fingers.

"You really noticed," she said at last. "I'm surprised."

"Your nightly endeavors? You weren't too subtle."

Gilda considered her with her large eyes. The green hue around the brown looked like the clumps of moss that clung to dead trunks outside of Santa Helena School, a thin layer of slime that often caused students to fall on the mud. She unwrapped the parcel to reveal a fat slice of orange cake.

"Would you like to see it?" She opened a wide smile. "Come."

Gilda walked in quick steps, but soon she was sprinting toward the grandfather clock, carefree like a nymph. She guided Basília by the hand, small fingers intertwined to her long ones, smooth where Basília was dry and rough.

It was almost midnight when they arrived. Gilda dropped to her knees on the runner rug, leaving the parcel on her lap to unlock the tower and reveal the mirror.

The Westminster Quarters chime started again.

"Here, do it," urged Gilda. "Before it ends."

Basília took the cloth napkin from her hands, and before she could shove her arm inside the mirror, Gilda stopped her.

"You shouldn't put it all inside," she warned. "Unless you're not worried about what might come from it."

"Fine." Basília threw the parcel inside the distorted reflection, watching it disappear as if a large mouth had just swallowed it.

When the clock stopped, the mirror returned their offering: the embroidered napkin was damp, and the cake was covered in greenish black mold festered with worms.

Gilda's eyes sparkled even in the darkness. Now, the color was similar to the mold, rancid and decaying, contaminating the woody brown of her irises until the dark shade was completely gone.

"So I was right." Basília stood in front of what was left of the food. "You're not from here."

"I did sleep in that room for many years, but you're right—not here, no." Gilda touched the mirror. After midnight, it was just a rectangular piece of glass with a thin coating of silver. "Things are not quite like they are here where I come from. Are you curious? About the other side?"

Beyond the mirror, there's a topsy-turvy place, Gilda skipped happily toward the dormitory, the moonlight illuminating her soft features. *Everything here is so pretty, so delicate, so marvelously stiff... It makes me want to break all of it.*

Basília heard everything in silence, feeling, something change inside her. *Have you ever tried a living being?* Basília asked, and a different kind of smile appeared in Gilda's face. *No*, she admitted. *Good thing we have plenty of those around here, don't you think?*

❖

BASÍLIA ROLLED UNDER the blankets, wondering what could have happened if she, too, stepped into the mirror. At first, she imagined herself rotten, guts spilling out, flies buzzing in and out her hollow eyes. But no, that didn't seem right. Instead, another image came to her mind: a dainty and perfect Basília, straight black hair curled with pins, a white ribbon on top of her head, red mouth drawn with lipstick, face shaped like clay until it was pretty enough.

Yes, that's the effort I was talking about! Ms. Leocádia would praise with a big smile, and the other Basília would smile back.

She would excel at every class like Aurélia, pray in the chapel with Efigênia, reproach Estefânia whenever she was too rude, gossip with Carlota and Lurdes in the corridors. That Basília would dream of a husband, and would humor Pérola when she spoke of the most marriageable men in town.

Disgusting, she thought, opening her eyes. *Absolutely disgusting.*

But what about Gilda? Was she the only beautiful thing in a world that was upside down? Perhaps she had also changed when she crossed that mirror, her ugliness disappearing as soon as her new toes hit the ground. Basília liked that thought. It could be fun to force her back in to watch the prettiness disappear, just like it would be delightful to walk through the glass and find Gilda just as much as an outsider as she was.

"I'm content in my ugliness," Basília said as they marched toward the dining hall the following morning. She chose to ignore how Pérola exchanged whispers with the others, questioning what she was doing to poor Gilda. "I fear most being trapped by their ideas of perfection. Let me rot any day."

"Ugliness, you say... " Gilda sat across from her, spoon in hand hovering over hot porridge. Winters were rarely cold enough to warrant a porridge, but the staff liked to pretend they were in Europe. "That's not how I see it."

"And how do you see it?"

"Sometimes, things are out of place. Sometimes, places are inadequate for the things in them." Gilda stole a spoonful of porridge from Basília's bowl. "But I do like where I come from, and I have the feeling you might like it as well."

"I think you want to come back all shattered and spoiled." Basília smirked, taking the spoon from her hand to have a bite. "What, are you planning to use me as an experiment?"

Gilda smiled.

"Goodness, no! I want us to help each other, can't you see?"

If the place is inadequate for you, Gilda hugged Basília's arm as they walked toward the classroom. *Let's make it more adequate.* Together, they decided that their first real victim could not be human. A small animal, perhaps, or part of a larger being.

I have an idea, said Basília, eyeing Efigênia as she made the sign of the cross. Her long straight hair was the only one besides hers that was not curled, combed, ribboned or pulled in a meticulous style, and instead fell down her back until the back of her thighs. *It was a promise*, Efigênia had claimed, *a promise to the Lord.* Well, Basília had never cared about promises, but she did remember every time Efigênia went to the principal's office to denounce any perceived slight.

Basília didn't follow the rules, she would say, knowing very well that Basília would be punished for that. *Basília said a dirty word.* For years, she had been convinced that Efigênia truly believed she was doing the right thing. But one day she saw it: as Ms. Zulmira struck her palms with a rattan cane, making Basília count out loud the number of times, Efigênia was there, watching eagerly from the keyhole. *She likes it*, she realized then, switching eleven for twelve, a failure that added five strikes to her punishment. *Pig.*

When Basília exposed her plan, Gilda looked like she would burst with excitement. *I can do it for you.* She touched Basília's cropped hair, cut so roughly it had bald spots. *No, I would* love *to do it for you.*

After everyone went to sleep, and the school was silent except for the tick-tocking of the clock, Gilda rose from her bed.

Basília opened the door for her, and she walked quietly, cradling the scissors like a child. *Third room at your left,* whispered Basília, *but careful with the other one.* Gilda skipped to their dormitory, her shadow spinning and twirling, and her hand falling on the doorknob.

For a moment, Basília couldn't breathe. She expected to hear Efigênia screaming in horror at seeing a demon over her bed, and Estefânia would wake at once to protect her sister. Estefânia, who smiled triumphantly whenever Ms. Leocádia spoke of the wonders of femininity while looking directly into Basília's dark eyes, as if saying *you, yes, you, so different from the rest of us,* but smacked the girls who didn't obey her every whim...

Estefânia could overpower Gilda in no time, and Efigênia would do the rest: *oh, Ms. Zulmira, what did I ever do against her?*

No one screamed when Gilda walked past the door, closing it behind her back. She no longer had the scissors, only a long mouse-colored braid that she whirled between her fingers, glancing at Basília with a smile. *Come,* she seemed to say. *Come.*

Basília ran after her down the long rug that muffled the sounds of their feet. Gilda tittered, the braid whipping the air like a cat's tail, and she stopped in front of the grandfather clock.

The iron hands pointed at eleven fifty-seven.

"I wonder how long it will take her to notice." Gilda placed the braid around Basília's neck like rope.

"As soon as she wakes up, I hope."

"Maybe I should cut all their hair..." Gilda's finger brushed the hair sticking out of the braid. "And they would all be like you."

The Westminster Quarters began to chime, and the sound reverberated inside Basília's chest, her ears ringing and her fingers trembling with excitement.

"Together?" Gilda asked, and they threw the braid inside.

❖

A HIGH-PITCHED SCREAM woke them up. Basília jumped out of the bed and looked at Gilda, whose eyes grew as the sound echoed through the second floor. Her spidery eyelashes, long and black, fluttered, and her eyes looked fully green and mold-like.

The yelling continued, but now it wasn't only one voice. One, two, three, four voices shrieked, and hurried steps came from the stairs. Teachers knocked on every room, until they appeared on theirs.

"Explain yourself!" Ms. Leocádia said right away, grabbing Basília by the face. "What is the meaning of this?"

"Good morning to you too, miss."

"This might be the last straw, Basília," she warned, dark circles under her eyes and disheveled hair caught in several pink rollers. "But I believe in redemption. If you admit and apologize, maybe..."

"What happened, Ms. Leocádia?" asked Gilda in a sweet voice. "A robbery? Is anybody hurt?"

"Someone—It's very unsettling, in fact. Why did you cut the other girls' hairs, Basília? And the other thing... It's too much, even for you."

Basília blinked.

"Girls...?"

"Basília did nothing wrong!" Gilda clutched her own chest. It would be too obvious to anyone who knew her true face, but Ms. Leocádia seemed to believe her. "She was here the whole night. I would know, since I could barely sleep with her snoring."

Ms. Leocádia grimaced. "Are you absolutely sure, Gilda?"

"Yes, Ms. Leocádia." She wiped a tear from the corner of her eyes. "I did hear some noises, but I assumed it was just one of the girls going to the bathroom, and I didn't want to be indiscreet."

"Heavens, this is even worse than I thought..." murmured Leocádia to herself as she left the room.

Outside, Basília recognized at once the long shape in the middle, gurgling in a pool of dark blood: pig intestines, pinkish and raw, around twenty meters in length, moving with life of its own. When they had dragged it from the mirror, it was dry and soft, but as soon as they left it on the floor, something thick and viscous leaked, and the bowels pulsated since then.

Efigênia was on her knees, but she wasn't praying. She stared at the intestines, touching her own short hair, her golden cross sparkling. Tears trailed down her pale face, but the one who wept loudly was Estefânia, whose bun had also disappeared, leaving only fine strands that barely covered her scalp. The other girls had been affected too: Aurélia's hair was cropped like a man's, and Lurdes cried, touching her bald head.

"When... ?" Basília asked without moving her mouth.

Gilda hid a smile.

The only ones who had not been attacked were Gilda, whose beautiful black curls fell effortlessly on her shoulders, Carlota, who tried to comfort Lurdes while her cat sniffed the bowels, and Pérola, whose skin had blanched to an unnatural grayish white. Apparently, the scissors had been found under Efigênia's blanket, and there whispers in the dining room that she was the one who did it. *Both to herself and the others*, commented a thirteen-year-old, glancing at them. *Laughing like the devil, I heard...*

Instead of Moral Education, Ms. Leocádia and Ms. Palmira spent the entire period fixing their hairs. They brushed spiky strands, tied ribbons, and gave Lurdes a headscarf.

There, there, sweetheart, said Ms. Palmira, gentler than any student had ever been to her. *You're a beautiful girl, and hair grows back.* Ms. Leocádia wasn't as sweet, but she did her part in cheering them up: *Soon, you will be able to style your hair like Ingrid Bergman in her last movie.*

Still, they were all interrogated by the headmistress. Ms. Zulmira left her cane on the table, frowning behind her glasses as the students stumbled. Usually, Basília would have been the main suspect, but whatever Gilda said when it was her turn had changed Zulmira's focus to Pérola and Carlota, whose nurtured manes had not been damaged, and Efigênia herself, who had the scissors and an excessive concern regarding demonic possessions.

"I'm quite surprised you don't seem to be involved in this incident," admitted the principal. Behind her was another portrait of President Vargas, of whom she was a fervent admirer, and an ironed suit jacket that she bought from a collector, convinced that it had belonged to the man. "I'm most concerned about the pig bowels; I don't know what kind of delinquent we have in this school that would have managed such a feat... "

"It's too wicked even for me, headmistress." Basília walked toward the door. "But I will report back if I hear anything."

Gilda and Basília spent the rest of the day bursting into laughter whenever they thought of the pulsating organ that had to be removed from the corridor. It was good, the feeling that she could get back at them, all of them, that she could ruin that school like she had always dreamed.

They will never find out who did it, Gilda promised as they walked in the woods. Other students were playing domino or cards after cleaning their dormitories and helping in the kitchens. *But the others will know that someone's for their throats.*

"Have you heard anything, Pérola?" Carlota asked later in the common room. Her Persian cat meowed in her lap as she brushed her fluffy white fur. "You always know what happens in the school before everyone."

She glanced at Basília, who was smoking near the window.

"I haven't." Pérola, painting her almond-shaped nails with coral lacquer in a half-moon, made her best to pretend they were alone in the room, and that the strong smell of smoke was not giving her allergies. *It bothers my nose,* she would tell her friends, curling her mouth in disgust, but whenever they were alone, she would smell the collar of Basília's shirt, rubbing her face against her neck. "Who could possibly be so horrid... ?"

"If it had been me, I would have come for the two of you first," said Basília, blowing a smoke ring. Gilda had styled her hair that afternoon: she smoothed it with pomade, parted it on one side, and combed it over to create a wave. It wasn't perfect, for sure, but it was better than anything she had ever done on her own. "Chop chop."

"Why are you talking to us?" Pérola grabbed the skirt of her dress so tightly that her knuckles went white. "Are you trying to intimidate us?"

"Don't listen to her," Carlota whispered. "She might... "

"She might what? As far as I know, you two did it." Basília laughed and put out the cigarette against the window, ashes falling on the carpeted floor. "Wiping out the competition, who knows?"

"I don't understand you. We have been nothing but polite to you, but you keep disrespecting us." Pérola's voice broke at the last *us*. She seemed to be trying very hard to keep talking, which surprised Basília, as she had always found Pérola to be particularly cold. "I wish you nothing but the best, Basília, and yet... Why can't you grow up?"

A coy tear fell from her face, then another, and another. Pérola's cheeks were red, and she sniffled, covering her face. The cat jumped to the floor, and Carlota hurried to hug Pérola, caressing her hair and murmuring words of comfort. *She has no heart*, Carlota soon started to cry too, as if the tears were a contagious virus.

Basília was stunned. Carlota pulled Pérola by the arm, telling her they should go to Ms. Leocádia's office and report how cruelly Basília had behaved. *Before she hurts someone else*, they said.

❖

THEIR NEXT TARGET was the cat. Fifi, the white Persian purchased by Carlota's parents on her fifteen-year-old birthday, lived in Santa Helena School since then, and roamed the building at night while her owner slept. It was Gilda's idea; when Basília told her what happened, her eyes went from the color of a Brazil nut to the same shade of the fern hanging near the window of the classroom.

For a second, Basília had expected Gilda to lash out. She looked so furious that her teeth had sunk into her lower lip, and a scarlet drop sprouted from it when she smiled. *We need a living being, right?* Gilda smeared the blood with her thumb.

Let's see what happens now.

Their agreement was that Basília would wait near the grandfather clock while Gilda lured Fifi toward it with pieces of chicken from the galinhada leftovers. Fifi went after the trail of meat, eating piece by piece as she followed Gilda through the runner rug.

Come, kitty, she sang, looking at Basília from over her shoulder. Eleven and fifty-eight.

When they were close enough, Gilda took the cat in her arms.

"I wonder what will happen to her... " She petted Fifi's head, and threw the cat brusquely inside the mirror. "See you later, kitty."

The clock continued for a long minute. When the school turned silent again, a shadow jumped from the other side, trespassing the glass like it was liquid. Fifi was back, but she looked like she had been turned inside out: she no longer had fur, her gum and fangs were exposed, her muscles had a few patches of yellow fat, and her organs hung from her pouch as she walked, releasing a fetid smell.

A grotesque sight, Fifi was, but she meowed and moved like any other cat. There were tufts of white hair scattered around her body, and her legs had been bent until they were turned backwards.

Gilda looked at Basília, her crystalline giggle the only thing that could be heard in the night:

"She looks lovely now."

Fifi left behind little paw prints on the floor, as if her pink pads had been dipped in tar. The two ran after her, muffling their laughter with their hands, wondering what the headmistress would say. *She just woke up like this, Ms. Zulmira,* Basília pretended to talk like Carlota, adjusting an invisible bow. *I swear I had nothing to do with this, ma'am!*

Gilda pulled Basília to enter the room, breathing heavily when they stopped in front of each other. The closed door gave Basília the impression they were somewhere else: a place that could not be accessed by others, far away from what they had just done, no matter how close the other girls were.

"I want to go with you," she announced, eyes fixed on Gilda's. "Through the mirror."

The other girl smiled. Her chest went up and down under the nightgown, and Basília took the curls from her collarbone.

"Even if we don't know what might happen to you?" Gilda touched the front of Basília's pajamas.

"Does it matter? The cat is doing well." Basília mirrored her, playing with the straps of Gilda's nightgown like Gilda was playing with her buttons. One of the straps slipped to her arm, and the other followed. "Besides, I'm much more interested in knowing what will happen to your pretty face. I want to see how hideous you can get."

The nightgown fell on the floor, pooling itself around Gilda's feet like a white cloud. Basília admired her, considering that could be the last time she would see her like this, beautiful and perfect. Gilda threw her arms around her neck, bringing Basília closer to kiss her lips, and Basília hooked her waist.

Outside, the cat meowed, sounding more guttural than she should, like something else had come with her from the side beyond the mirror. When Carlota woke up and started to shout, neither Basília nor Gilda moved from bed.

❖

FRIDAY WOULD BE her last day at Santa Helena. Basília buttoned her shirt, wore the washed-out blue dress, and the pants she preferred to have underneath. She sat on the mattress while Gilda brushed her hair, styling it with pomade. If she stayed, she would never know how long she could still have this almost freedom allowed by the teachers. They complained, yes, but nothing had ever gotten out of hand. Her parents were oblivious, and Ms. Zulmira had parroted to them the same story Basília had told about her hair: *it was lice, miss, I swear it was lice.*

How long until their fine line of patience broke? The summer of her seventeen years? She was not ready to have her insides pulled and twisted like the mirror had done to the cat. Not in the way she feared, at least—the other side could deform her as much as it pleased.

"It's going to happen tonight," Gilda reminded her under her breath, with a discreet red spot appearing under her jaw. "I can't wait, can you?"

Carlota was absent during most of the classes, but came back for Moral Education at the last period with Fifi in her arms.

"The veterinarian assured me it's a skin disease," Carlota said as the other girls surrounded her. Lurdes covered her nose, disgusted by the smell, but Carlota kept petting Fifi's head. "But it's nothing serious. Her health is fine otherwise."

"Maybe it would be more compassionate if you ... " suggested Pérola, but Carlota brought the animal closer to her chest.

"No! It's Fifi, the same Fifi, she's just... " Carlota glanced at the cat. She smelled rotten, and started to boredly lick her paws. "No. I can take care of her."

Pérola glanced at Basília, the only one who was far from the circle. Even Gilda was there, cooing at Fifi and petting her exposed muscle.

The circle dissipated when Prof. Leocádia arrived, and their eyes turned to the blackboard. *No more of you*, Basília thought with a grin, *no more of any of you*. Every minute that passed, she felt closer to the mirror and further away from them. Away from the gossip, away from the frills and dresses, away from the passive-aggressiveness. Whenever their eyes met, Gilda smiled reassuringly, as if saying: *soon, soon.*

At night, Gilda appeared in the dormitory with something folded in her arms. The suit jacket from Ms. Zulmira's office, Basília realized.

"Here." She helped Basília wear the white shirt, the pants, and the jacket. "Looking all proper now."

Gilda was still in the nightgown, but she slipped inside the red shoes that glittered as she walked.

"Shall we?" asked Basília, taking her by the hand and opening the door.

The runner rug still had the black stains of Fifi's paw prints, and they walked on it until they reached the grandfather clock. The large windows showed dark trees outside, and the moon cast a soft glimmer.

Gilda knelt in front of the clock.

"Don't let go of my hand." The Westminster Quarters started, and she trespassed the mirror, swallowed by her own reflection. Only Gilda's hand remained on that side, still grasping hers.

Before Basília could follow, someone touched her shoulder.

Pérola stood behind her, trembling in her own nightgown. Her light brown hair fell limp on her shoulders, straight and brittle, and her nails looked transparent without the polish.

"I saw it," she murmured. "Everything. The braid, the cat, and everything before it."

Basília looked from Pérola to the mirror. The chiming continued.

"And?"

Tears fell down Pérola's face and dripped down her pointy chin. Her fingers still held Basília's suit, but not as strongly as Gilda's grasp.

"Of course, you're going to cry about it." Basília smirked, feeling like terrorizing one of them for the last time. "Why, Pérola, let me remind you that you don't have an audience today."

"Why did you only attack the others?" This time, it wasn't the delicate and dignified tears she had seen before, but a low, ugly sound, and Basília found herself shocked that Pérola might have meant it. "Am I that unimportant?"

The hands of the clock were almost reaching twelve and one.

"Oh, so you're jealous, that's what it is." Basília looked at Gilda's hand, still holding hers, and her smile grew. "Not enough to talk to me in public. Not enough to defend me. Just jealous. Well, if you want it so much, you can jump after me, but you would have to leave your tears and bobby pins behind."

Pérola didn't move.

Before she could hear an answer, Gilda pulled her, and Basília reached the other side.

Mulberry and Owl

Aliette de Bodard

*Year of the Âm Dragon, fifth year of the Peaceful Harmony Empress,
Great Mulberry Nebula*

THUỶ STOOD IN her cabin in *The Goby in the Well*, her bots
arrayed on her shoulders and clinging to her wrists,
and watched the heart of the nebula.

There was absolutely nothing remarkable about it: the
Great Mulberry Nebula was large, sparsely dotted with
nascent stars, and so remote that getting there, even via deep
spaces, had required a three month journey. On the overlay
in Thuỷ's cabin—a thin sliver like a screen, showing her the
merged data of all *The Goby in the Well*'s sensors—there was
very little to see, either: a darkness that seemed to spread
absolute from the centre of the overlay, and a corresponding
gravity spike for the trapping of the light.

"I'm not going any further, child," *Goby* said. The ship
projected her avatar into the cabin: a smaller version of
herself, the metal of her hull sheening with the characteristic
light of deep spaces.

Thuỷ sighed. "I know, elder aunt," she said. "That was
the bargain, wasn't it? Thank you for carrying me this far."
She fingered one of her bots, feeling the small, fist-sized body,
the fragile metal legs spread all around its crown of sensors.

It ought to have been comforting, but she was so far beyond comfort.

Getting there had required so much—not just the three months, but research, and stubbornness, and bribing a dozen officials all over the Empire, from the First Planet to the unnumbered stations and orbitals. Chasing a rumour so elusive it was almost a myth.

Thuỷ stared at her hand: faint traceries of light materialised the pass she'd bought from a drunk and demoted former Commissioner of Military Affairs. He'd said it would take her there, right into the heart of the gravitational gradients—and more importantly, get her back out.

"Do you—" *Goby* paused, for a while "—do you think it's the right place? Do you think *she*'s there?" *Goby* used "enforcer", a pronoun that carried both awe and fear.

"I don't know," Thuỷ said. "Do you want to find out?"

"You can always tell me afterwards." The ship's laughter was humourless and brief. "If you survive."

Darkness, in the centre. A pointless chase leading to another black hole or some other phenomenon—or exactly what she was looking for, what she needed. What Kim Lan desperately needed.

Rehabilitation. Forgiveness.

"If," Thuỷ said, very deliberately not thinking about it, and dismissed the overlay with a wave of her hands. "I'll go get ready now."

❖

Twenty years ago

IN THE REACHES beyond the numbered planets, rebellion against the Dragon Throne wasn't so much an unspeakable crime as utterly banal—an act of despair, self-preservation, or rage against the unavoidable losses to the empire's wars—a contagion like a match lighting up paper after paper, daughter following mother, sworn or gut-sibling following sibling.

Thuỷ fell into hers following Kim Lan, as she'd always done.

They were in the teahouse, having a drink and watching the poet in the centre moving through her performance—summoning ethereal overlays with every sweep of her sleeves, brief fragments of sight, sound and smells like other realities—ones in which war, food shortages, or network outages were utterly absent.

I need help, Thuỷ had said, when Kim Lan had asked how it was all going—and the thought of everything Thuỷ had been juggling—all the debts, the food shortages, her salary being worth less and less with every passing month—had all become too much, and she'd almost burst into tears.

Kim Lan had looked at her, thoughtfully. *Wait here*, she said, and came back with someone in tow.

"Here, lil'sis," Kim Lan said. "This is my friend Bảo Châu. She can help you with those back taxes."

Châu was an elderly, forbidding woman, like one of the aunties at the market who'd seen everything: a topknot with hairpins as sharp as daggers, bots the colour of rust and the darkness of space, almost invisible on the stark utilitarian robes she wore. "Thuỷ, is it? You trained for Master of Wind and Water, once."

Thuỷ flushed. "Yes," she said. "It was the year of the Dương Ox. When the schools burnt down." They'd never opened them again after that, merely slashed the number of available slots—and people like Thuỷ had left. Coming from the margins of the empire and with no means to pay the gifts of the void to officials to grease their way through the system, they'd never stood a chance.

"Yes," Châu said. She smiled, and it was grim. "I can sort things out with the Ministry of Revenue, but you'll owe us, in return."

Thuỷ would have asked who "us" was, but even at twenty-five she wasn't that naive. "What do you want?"

"Nothing you can't provide," Châu said. "Expertise. Ships that need to be fixed. Systems that need to be...coaxed." She said nothing: merely looked at Thuỷ, sipping her tea as if it were the greatest of delicacies in the imperial court on the First Planet.

Thuỷ looked at Kim Lan, who gazed levelly back at her. She raised her hand as if holding an invisible bowl of offerings—that same gesture they'd made in her mother's compartment, entwining their arms at the elbow and making a binding, peach-garden oath.

Though not born on the same day of the same month in the same year, we hope to die so...

Standing by each other, and they'd always done so— through the years that got leaner and leaner, and the failings of the empire—through the death of Kim Lan's mother, and Thuỷ's failed engagement—through feast and famine and days of the war.

The punishment for rebellion was not just the slow death for her, but for nine generations around her. But she was Kim Lan's oath-sister—and it was the fifth tax notification in as many months, food on the table was scarce, her aged parents getting visibly thinner, more and more of the compartment's systems and bots failing.

"I'll do it," she said, and Kim Lan smiled.

"Welcome, lil'sis."

◈

Thuỷ had forgotten what it was like, to go out.

She'd been in a shuttle at first, and then, as the gravity increased, she'd had to abandon even that, and put on a shadow-skin to go out in order to avoid damaging the shuttle and incurring one more debt to *Goby* she wouldn't be able to repay.

The shadow-skin's thin and supple fabric was soaked, sticking to her own skin, even before she exited into the void, hands clinging to the small glider that helped her manoeuvre. Around her, light fell in swathes, but ahead of her was only that growing darkness, and her sensor bots reminded her with regular alerts that the gravity was increasing steadily.

As she went deeper in, they plotted her course. Space started distorting—time, too, the sensors making the depths of the distortion, how much slower than *Goby* she was going and what rate of correction her comms needed to be sent with. The mark on her hand started glowing as she navigated between rock fragments—nothing she could see, but a corridor opened ahead and behind her, a gentle coaxing of the gravitational gradient into a path that wasn't an impasse.

The glider was impossibly heavy in her hands. The mark stung, and then faded: *here*, it seemed to say, without words.

Thuỷ hung in the darkness, in the void—weightless and with nothing but the sound of her own heartbeat in her chest and ears, her own breathing.

Here.

She'd been wrong: the darkness wasn't quite that absolute. Distant stars glinted behind her—and ahead, in the shadows, was something—a hulking shape that suddenly loomed far too close, far too large, on the verge of utterly swallowing her in its folds.

It was true. Oh ancestors, everything was true: the pass, the jail.

The prisoner.

The Owl with the Moon's Tongue. The enforcer of the Empress's will—the ship that had roamed the borders of the empire, assassinating and executing rebels one after the other—in compartments, in teahouses, in the middle of crowds, sowing the terror necessary to end the rebellion.

Thuỷ thought of Hải's face, of An's face, the way they'd stood still for a blink moment after *Owl's* scream had kicked in, the sheen trembling in the depths of their eyes, suddenly sweeping free and spreading in mottled patches over their entire skin, the patches sloughing off, bones melting and their entire bodies flopping like a coat suddenly emptied, the crowds on the concourse slowly backing away from the blood staining the metal floors, utter silence and on every face that blunt, inadmissible truth: how lucky they felt that they hadn't been *Owl's* target.

"A visitor. It's been far too long since I've had company." The voice was female, light and sarcastic; the pronoun used the one for "elder aunt": an age and status gap between them both, but not such a large one.

"Enforcer." Thuỷ used the same pronoun *Goby* had.

Laughter, echoing around her in the dark. "Enforcer? A title I've not had for a while. What brings you here, little one?" The pronoun she used wasn't even "child", but a subordinate one, of a subject before authority. "Why enter my orbit?"

"You have something I want."

"Do I?" *Something* lit up, then: one light, then two, then ten thousand, and abruptly she was hanging, small and weightless and utterly insignificant, in the orbit of a ship that was the size of an entire city. The light was so strong it was blinding: even with her suit immediately moving to darken its visor, she could only catch a glimpse—a mere moment of clarity, of seeing sharp protuberances and the hull bristling with weapons ports—before all she could see was bright, painful light.

Kim Lan, laughing at her after they robbed the Granaries, their vehicles full of rice seedlings and cheap alcohol. Kim Lan, raising her arm in that ghostly toast, a reminder of the oath they'd sworn—downing the tea after they got word that *Owl* had killed Diễm My, and Vy too— and then that last drink they'd had together, her face flushed as she spoke of the imperial amnesty, how desperate and wan she'd looked.

"I have a friend."

"Ah." *Owl's* voice was mocking. "Ah. A dead one, I imagine."

She thought of Hải and An and Châu, and of the years on the run—being picked out one by one, killed one by one. "You killed them," she said, her fists clenching. She used the plural pronoun.

"Oh, several friends, then. A little rebel, are you?"

"Once." A long time ago, in another lifetime. The Mother Abbess would say that Thuỷ needed to let go—to stand unmoored from the troubles of her former life. The Mother Abbess meant well, but she didn't understand. "It's not relevant anymore."

"Is it not?" Her laughter filled the space around Thuỷ.

"Irrelevance. How quaint. I killed your friends then, and I enjoyed it. Every moment of it, from the imperial decree to their deaths, to tracking them down—to finally finding them—that long slow rise of power in the targeting system until it could finally fire—until I could feel them, torn apart and boneless—until I saw them finally collapse and it was all over. Tell me: is that all irrelevant?"

There was a reason why *Owl* was there, and it wasn't just that the empire was at peace, it wasn't just that there was a new Empress, one who was trying to knit the torn fabric of their society back together, to make former rebels inhabit the same stations and planets as loyal officials. *Owl* was there because she was a monster. Because there might be a time and place for a ruthless enforcer, but one that delighted in slaughter and pain...that one was best put away—made harmless and imprisoned, at least until she was needed again.

"Stop," Thuỷ said.

"Pleading?"

No, because that was never going to make her stop, was it?

"Because that's not what I'm here for. You didn't kill my friend."

"Oh." A silence, but she could tell *Owl*'s curiosity was piqued.

"You're a witness."

"Am I?"

Thuỷ forced herself to breathe. "She took the amnesty. You have her statement."

"I was never much of a person for taking statements," *Owl* said. "Is *that* what you're here for? Go to the magistrate."

"The magistrate is dead." Incinerated in the same riots that had killed Kim Lan—but the archive she'd uploaded to *Owl* would still be in the ship's memory. "There are no records."

"And so you've come all the way here for mine?" Again, laughter, but it didn't quite have that same edge. "What is it that you want?"

Thuỷ swallowed, tasted bitterness on her tongue. What was it that she wanted? Forgiveness. Atonement. A dead woman's smile; a lie that everything would be all right again, a touch and a toast. Dead things, dead memories, dead feelings. "She died a rebel. Her entire family is still under an extermination order." They'd fled, of course—outside the reach of the Empire, into the uncertain places, the isolated stations and orbitals, the small asteroid mining centres where people didn't ask too many questions so long as you did the work. "I want it lifted."

A silence. The ship in front of Thuỷ—large, massive, blinding and uncompromising—didn't move. She didn't have to: she was slowly drawing Thuỷ to herself, towards an inexorable orbiting of each other, an endless embrace. "I assume you didn't come all the way here just to try and *talk* me into this."

Thuỷ swallowed. "No," she said.

"The keys to my freedom?" *Owl*'s voice was curious. "You won't have that, will you."

Thuỷ had a pass, and she had half-expected it not to work. It certainly would not let out the ship the prison had been built for. "No," she said.

"I'm not interested in money."

"I don't have that." Not anymore—not after coming back, bribing too many people, finding a mindship willing to bear her that far.

"And clearly you won't give me your life, as it won't help your friend if you're dead. Not that it's of much value, is it."

That *hurt*. It was that life Thuỷ had run away to save—putting it above everything else, even ties of sworn-sisterhood—and to have it so casually dismissed was as if *Owl* were slowly, casually pushing down on old wounds until they split open.

"What is it you have that you think I desperately want?"

Thuỷ swallowed. "I can repair your weapons system."

Owl's laughter tore Thuỷ apart—as if her weapons system were still operational, as if she could still scream and make Thuỷ collapse the way all the others had collapsed. "My weapons.

And leave me here? Why do you think I would even be interested in that?"

Thuỷ had had three months in deep spaces to think on it—and before that, in the monastery, when she'd first found out that *Owl* was still alive—that there might be a chance to clear Kim Lan's memory. "They called that your scream. The weapons systems."

Silence, from the ship.

"When they arrested you for the war crimes, they took it apart. It was too dangerous. Even in a jail. Even in the middle of nowhere."

"Are you done telling me things I already know?"

Thuỷ plunged on. There was little choice left. "But that's not what is it to you, is it? A scream is a voice. They took away part of your voice."

"And you think I could use that part for something else besides killing?" *Owl*'s voice was light and ironic.

"I think you want it back. Even if you're jailed. Even if it's of no practical use. I think you want it back because it was always part of you."

"Part of me." A silence, but that one was barbed. "You haven't answered my question, have you."

"No," Thuỷ said. "Does it matter? Who are you going to kill out there?"

The unspoken answer hung in the air: of course Thuỷ was the only living target. "I assume you'll want some assurances that you'll survive."

"No," Thuỷ said. She kept her voice light, inconsequential—but inwardly she saw An's face, Châu's face, heard the crumple of dead bodies on the floors. That was what everything that would happen to her, if *Owl* decided she wasn't worth sparing. And when had an imperial enforcer and mass murderer ever decided former rebels were worth sparing? "I want to see my friend's statement to make sure you do have it, but I don't need your assurances. I came with a mindship."

"I know. They're much too far away to save you."

Thuỷ smiled, beneath the shadow-skin. "You don't

understand. If I don't come back, they'll know you've killed me, and they'll take the evidence to the Numbered Planets. Your jailers will know I fixed your weapons. How long do you think you'll get to keep them?"

A silence. She could feel the gravity pulse around her, tightening—like a slow rising of anger. "Clever," *Owl* said, and it sounded like nothing so much as a threat. Something shimmered within Thuỷ's field of vision: not a file with its authentication, but a mere image of it. *I, Phạm Thị Kim Lan, accept that I have erred, and that the Peaceful Harmony Empress has chosen to extend her infinite mercy the way she extends her grace, like a cloth covering us all with all the stars in the sky...*

At the bottom, beneath the vermillion seal, was Kim Lan's familiar and forceful signature, authenticated by her personal seal.

The statement. It was real. *Owl* had it. Thuỷ could—she could finally make amends for what she'd done.

Something changed, in the mass of light in front of Thuỷ: a slight adjustment, but suddenly she could see the ship—the bulk of the hull, the sharp, sleek shape with bots scuttling over every surface, the thin, ribbed actuator fins near the ion drives at the back—the paintings on her hull, which she'd half-expected to be blood spatters but which were apricot flowers, and calligraphed poems, and a long wending river of stars in the shadow of mountains, a breathtakingly delicate and utterly unexpected work of art. Something moved: a ponderous shift of the bots, drawing Thuỷ's eyes towards a patch of darkness at the centre of the painting, between two mountains.

"Come in, then, clever child. Let's see what you can do."

❖

Fifteen years ago

ON THE NIGHT after they broke Châu and An's children out of imperial jail, they celebrated.

An and Khiêm were in the hideout—an empty compartment

on the Apricot Đỗ habitat they'd hastily hidden beneath an overlay of a busy teahouse. Nothing that would stand up to close imperial scrutiny—but in the empty, desolate spaces of a half-destroyed habitat most of the inhabitants had evacuated, it would serve.

Châu and An got drunk, and made elaborate overlays as they did: seas of stars, ghostly dragons, spaceships slowly growing to fill the space—and An's children laughed and danced and declaimed drunk poetry, their bots' legs clicking on the floor.

Thuỷ ought to have felt relief they'd succeeded, but as the night went on—as she thought of the skirmishes on the numbered planets, of the litany of lost ships—not theirs, their little organisation barely had enough to have a few shuttles, but there were other splinters of rebellion elsewhere—as she thought of the Imperial Fleet—the tightness in her chest grew and grew, until the compartment felt too small, too cramped, and she went out for air, cradling the cold porcelain of her teacup.

Outside, the corridor was deserted, and it was silent—not just the usual silence of the habitats, with only the faint background hiss of the air filters and sometimes, the clicking of a bot's legs on the floor as they scurried from one maintenance to another. This was a silence that sounded like a prelude to the end. The overlays were minimal: flickering displays of the vital statistics from oxygen to temperature, but no news, no vids of songs, no adornments from the other compartments: just fatigued metal that felt as bare as Thuỷ did.

"You look glum." Kim Lan effortlessly slid in the space between them. "Here." She had a basket of dumplings, which her bots handed to Thuỷ.

Thuỷ didn't speak for a while. "Did you hear? There's a rumour *The Owl with the Moon's Tongue* is coming our way."

"Mmm." Kim Lan sat down, nibbling on a steamed bun. Her hair rested against a broken duct—it creaked, and her bots gently pushed it out of the way. "She is."

"And you're not afraid?"

Now it was Kim Lan's turn to say nothing.

"We're losing, aren't we? We saved Châu and the children, but we're never going to win. We're never going to overthrow the empress." Or even change the empire— or if they did, it was change that would bring about their destruction, and the extermination of everyone onboard the habitats in the belt.

"You assume this was about winning," Kim Lan said.

"What was it about then?"

Kim Lan's face was hard. "Survival."

"How are we going to survive against *Owl*?" She'd heard the rumours. She'd watched the vids. She'd seen that it didn't matter where the victims where—so long as the weapons system locked on them, they would die, as if a long finger of death were pointing their way from *Owl*'s orbit.

Them. It would be them dying, taken apart as examples for anyone who dared to rebel.

"I don't know," Kim Lan said. She sighed. "Do you think you could have survived a sixth tax notification? Do you think your parents could have?"

She had food for them. Alcohol and stolen meals. And the tax collectors and the officials had fled the system in the wake of their activities. And whatever her other faults were, she'd never been less than honest with herself. "No," Thuỷ said.

"There you go."

"How do you think any of that is going to protect us against *Owl*? How?"

"You don't understand." Kim Lan's voice was soft. "The choices we made were we'd get there. One thing at a time." She reached out, held Thuỷ's hand for a bare moment. "I know you're scared. That's all right. I'm here. I'll always be here."

And for a moment they were both back in that kitchen compartment, flush with drink and youth, their paths now inextricably entwined by choice.

Thuỷ held her cup, staring at the exposed wires of the habitat. Bots scuttled, sad and lonely, as if ashamed of what it had come to. She heard the words of the oath of sworn sisterhood echoing in her thoughts. *Though not born on the same day of the same month in the same year, we hope to die so...* "We hope to die so." A peach-garden oath, now and forever. "Except the goal isn't to die."

Kim Lan smiled. "Exactly. We got this far. We'll get further, you'll see. There's always a way out. Now come back inside, will you? They're waiting for you before the next round of poetry holos."

❖

Year of the Âm Dragon, fifth year of the Peaceful Harmony Empress, Great Mulberry Nebula

THUY̓ HAD EXPECTED—actually, she didn't know what she'd expected when she'd enter *Owl*—some kind of fanciful lair of blood-encrusted corridors and bones stacked in coffins, which made no sense, because why would *Owl* have any of that onboard?

Instead, there was a corridor much like the one in the habitats—rundown, with too few bots, exposed bits of wiring and gaping holes where panels had fallen off, except the gravity wasn't strong enough for her to be upright. It felt a little bit like the mining asteroids: a very faint sensation of weight in her bones, but nothing that prevented her from floating. Thuy̓ held on to her glider as she moved through it.

As she did, the lights came on.

They were blue and red and gold, slowly cycling through the colours of some impossibly far away festival—weak and flickering, and the overlays in their wake were not opaque enough to mask the ruin beneath. But it had been beautiful once: those paintings of starscapes and temples on the First Planet, those holos of beautiful statues and teapots and jade figures, those faint, broken harmonics of a now unrecognizable music.

"This way," *Owl* said, a scuttling of bots guiding Thuy̓ onboard.

More corridors, more emptiness: gaping cabins with no adornments, looking like the looted compartments after the civil war—larger places that must have been like pavilions but now lay empty, with scuffed floors and floating debris.

And a door, opening like magic in a wall like any other, behind a translucent painting of a dragon amidst the stars.

Inside, darkness, and then in the centre of a gradually widening circle of light, something that looked like a tree with sharp branches—and draped over it, a large and pulsating mass of flesh and electronics.

The ship. The Mind that drove the body, connected to every sensor, every room, every overlay onboard.

"Your weapons system is in your heartroom?" The ship's most vulnerable place—like the brain to a human—and she'd just given Thuỷ casual access?

No, not that casual.

Because the bots—the ones missing all over the ship— were there. All there, a sea of gleaming metal between her and the Mind, legs bristling—a *sharpness*, a heaving multitude just waiting for a signal to swallow her whole. "Try anything," *Owl* said, lightly and conversationally, "And I'll choke you."

Thuỷ tried to breathe, failed—all she could see was the bots, the way they'd rise, the way they'd swarm over her, slithering into her suit and breaking her visor, leaving her wide open to the drowning vacuum.

For Kim Lan. She was doing this for Kim Lan. For what she'd failed to do in another lifetime. "I want the proof," she said. "The statement."

"Before you fix me? I think not."

"You'll give me nothing afterwards."

"Will I? Do you not trust me?"

"You're a murderer. No."

"I'm not the one who abandoned her friend." *Owl*'s voice was malicious. "What worth are your promises?"

Though not born on the same day of the same month in the same year, we hope to die so...

The words burnt her. "I did not," Thuỷ said, far too fast and far too painfully. "I did not!"

"As you say." *Owl*'s voice was mocking. "Nevertheless...I'm not giving you anything until you've fixed it."

And there was no way Thuỷ was going to fix it without

any guarantees. She weighed options—negotiating tactics—
and came up with little of interest. "Then I guess we're at an
impasse, because I'm not starting." There was a hole in a wall,
near the bots—and something glimmering within. When she
came closer, she saw what was in the overlay: an illusion of
what had once been there. Behind it, though...

Her intuition had been right: the jailers had been lazy. It
was the end of the war, and they were in a hurry to put *Owl*
where they didn't have to worry about her. They'd just torn
connectors and made a mess of control panels, but they hadn't
actually *destroyed* the system itself. They'd known they might
need it again, in less peaceful days. "It was there, wasn't it?"

Owl didn't speak, but she could feel the temperature in the
room shift. Approval.

Thuỷ let go of her glider, using its magnetised surface to
stick it to the wall, and turned out the proximity nudgers
on her suit. She flipped open the glider, opening its
storage space, revealing row after row of spare parts and
electronics—everything that had been on the schematics the
military commissioner had sold her. The commissioner had
thought it was only curiosity, secure in the knowledge Thuỷ
wouldn't dare do anything with these. The commissioner
had been wrong.

Another shift of temperature: interest, tension. She knelt,
peering at the inside. "It's going to take me six hours to fix.
Maybe eight."

Silence, from around her. The Mind pulsed on her throne.
The bots watched her, and she was at the centre of the attention
of an entire ship, feeling the weight of it on her like lead.

Thuỷ considered, for a while. *Owl* didn't really care about
Kim Lan's statement, one way or another: she just wanted to
be fixed. She wanted the weapons back as part of herself, of
her power. The main issue there wasn't unwillingness: it was
lack of trust, and *Owl*'s natural tendency to needle and inflict
pain on others.

"Tell you what," Thuỷ said, forcing herself to sound casual.
"We could create a safehold. A place to hold my friend's
statement—and it would only send it out if the system got fixed."

"I could stop that anytime, couldn't I?"

Thuỷ shook her head. "A safehold where we both withdraw our access privileges in an irrevocable fashion. I can't affect it, and neither can you. But it won't send until this comes back online, so you get the system taken care of, and I only get paid, so to speak, if I successfully finish."

"I've heard of such things," *Owl* said. More silence. She was tempted, Thuỷ knew.

"Let me show you," Thuỷ said, floating closer to the alcove and starting to put together the connections to create the safehold—and as the ship's whole attention turned her way, she knew she had her.

❖

Eight years ago

THUỶ JERKED AWAKE. Someone was knocking insistently on the door of the safe house.

The imperials. They'd found them. They'd take them away and make them face *Owl*—or arrest them and publicly execute them, giving them the slow death that had haunted Thuỷ's nightmares for the past few months on the run—the same death they'd given An's children, bots slicing off one piece of flesh at a time, the smell of blood and the screams broadcast to the entire habitats...

Calm down. She got up, her bots arranging themselves on her shoulders, their sensors struggling to come online. They hadn't been fixed in a long while.

The knocking had stopped. Thuỷ stepped over the others, who were sleeping huddled on the floor and barely starting to wake: Ánh Lệ was rubbing her eyes, Vy was struggling to rise, and it seemed as though nothing could really wake up Diễm My, who was merely mumbling and going back to sleep as if nothing had happened. The luck of youth.

"I've got it," Thuỷ said to Ánh Lệ and Vy—with far more confidence than she felt.

She took a deep breath, bracing herself, and opened the door.

It was Kim Lan, wan, her bots pressing a bloodied cloth to her side.

"Big'sis!"

"It's all right." Kim Lan made a gesture with her hands, but she was shaking. "No one followed me. Can I come in?"

"Of course." Thuỷ ushered her in, closing and bolting the door. The patches they'd made on the network and its surveillance cameras were still in place—she double- and triple-checked them as Kim Lan sat cross-legged in front of a low table, breathing hard. Her bots were peeling off the cloth; Thuỷ sent her own bots to fetch bandages from their meagre supplies.

"What happened?"

Kim Lan grimaced. "Had a skirmish with some of the militia a few days ago." Up close, her skin was a network of small, red pinpricks. Burst veins. She didn't look good. "They think me dead. I did have to plunge into space without a shadow-skin for a few blinks."

Kim Lan sat in silence, sipping her tea. Ánh Lệ and Vy had joined her, and even Diễm My was groaning as her bots poked her into wakefulness.

"How long do we have?" Thuỷ said. The empire would find them. They would end them as they had ended all the others.

"We can still go to another one of the other habitats," Vy said. Her voice was shaking. "Or leave the Belt, go into the Outside Territories or the Twin Streams."

Kim Lan said, finally, "I didn't come here to make you flee elsewhere. I came here because there's news."

"News?"

"You won't have heard. The Calm Strength Empress is dead. Her heir will ascend to the throne as soon as the ceremonies have been completed. She's offering an amnesty."

"An amnesty?" Thuỷ turned the words over and over again. They made no sense.

Vy said, "They hounded us. They killed us one by one. Why would they—"

"They can't keep fighting half their population," Kim Lan said. Her voice was gentle. "Civil war is tearing the empire apart. They could kill us all. It'd be a lot of work. Hence the amnesty."

"Never," Vy said.

Kim Lan set her cup on the table. "I've told this to Thuỷ already. We're not fighting to win. We're fighting to survive. The new empress says she wants to make reforms. Make the empire a better place."

"And you believe that?" After all this, after all the years they'd gone through...

"Maybe. Maybe not. I do know there's fewer and fewer of us. We're getting picked off one by one. I'd rather take the way out, before we all die. If we survive, we can always fight another day."

"You want to take the amnesty."

"Yes," Kim Lan said. "It's my choice. I won't be selling anyone out." Her eyes were hard. She was expecting a fight—but everyone around the table was tired, and scared, and drained—the light had gone out of them such a long time ago.

How could she—how could she believe them—how could she believe the people who'd starved them into rebellion, who had killed Châu and Hải and An and An's children as casual acts of intimidation?

"They'll kill us," Thuỷ said. "An amnesty is just a way of letting us come to them. *Owl* is still in the system. Why would you leave your enforcer there if you're going to let everyone live?"

Kim Lan said nothing.

"You can't trust them!"

But she'd made her decision, hadn't she. Thuỷ took a deep breath. "I need some space," she said—there was no space in the safe house, it was so small, but she did manage to put together a few privacy filters that gave her the illusion of being alone: the sound from the others' discussion muffled, and everything made to feel more distant visually.

How could she? How she could do this, how could she expect Thuỷ to follow, how could she–

"Lil'sis." It was Kim Lan, gently asking to be let in.

"No."

"You're scared. I know you are. It's all right to be scared."

"I'm not scared," Thuỷ said, dropping the privacy filters a fraction so Kim Lan could be included in them. They were having a semi-private conversation now, one that the others wouldn't be overhearing unless they made a concerted effort. "I think you're being thoughtless and imprudent."

"And endangering you all?"

No, that wasn't it. "I don't want to lose you," Thuỷ said, and it hurt to say it out loud.

"You asked me once if we were losing. We are." Kim Lan's voice was gentle. "I said it was about survival. And now it is. There is no survival in running from safe house to safe house, losing more people with every passing day."

"I—" Thuỷ tried to speak, and found only the truth. "I can't. I just can't do it. I can't follow you. I can't walk into the possibility of wholesale slaughter."

"You're scared."

"I'm rational!"

"And I'm not?"

"You—you keep setting the terms and expecting me to keep up."

"Because of the oath?" Kim Lan laughed, and it was sad. "I release you from the oath. You don't have to do anything you don't want to."

"It—it doesn't work like that!" Thuỷ had done things— so many things, raided so many places, gone so far against the will of the empire, and throughout it all, she'd had the comfort of knowing she wasn't alone. That Kim Lan was there. That they were here for each other. But now that had become shackles: a gravitational well that drew her in regardless of whether she wanted to, just because Kim Lan had gone ahead of her. "I can't just break that oath!"

"Of course you can." Kim Lan scratched her bandages between the swam of bots, and then got up. "As I said: you do what you want." But she sounded angry and disappointed.

Thuỷ sat down, trying to be kind. Trying to follow Kim Lan as she'd always meant to.

But everyone was dead, because the empire had killed them. *Owl* was prowling the habitats, waiting for a chance to find their signatures and target them; the militia was on the lookout, and the execution racks had been readied in every tribunal of the belt. The amnesty was never going to happen, and even if did, they'd get killed by some overzealous militia person before they ever got a chance to accept it.

She'd sworn an oath, with Kim Lan.

I'm here. I'll always be here.

We got this far. We'll get further, you'll see.

And Thuỷ knew, then—sitting small and scared and angry in that safe house that was no longer one—she knew that she couldn't go any further.

❖

Year of the Âm Dragon, fifth year of the Peaceful Harmony Empress, Great Mulberry Nebula

FIXING THE SYSTEMS was slow and painstaking: taking out connectors, finding new, compatible ones, taking care of the exposed wiring.

"You said I didn't kill your friend." *Owl*'s voice swam out of the morass of her thoughts. "How did she die?"

Thoughtlessly. Carelessly. "There was a skirmish in the Lotus Vũ habitat. One of the militia got scared and killed her." Thuỷ had learnt of this only afterwards—after she'd left in the dead of night, after she'd joined the monastery and severed all her familial ties, to make sure the Empire couldn't find her or hold her family responsible for her acts anymore. After she'd changed her name and laid low for years, and thinking Kim Lan's silence was due to anger— never realising she was dead and her family in hiding.

"Ah. The riots. The same ones that destroyed the tribunal. War is never kind." It sounded almost companionable.

Thuỷ slotted a cylindrical piece into place, her bots swarming over it to check the connections. "Did you lose anyone during the war?"

A silence. *Owl* laughed. "My freedom."

"You must have a family," Thuỷ said. It felt...wrong to

say that, as if to acknowledge that monsters were people was to grant them forgiveness.

The lights pulsed, softly, as Thuỷ added another connector to the rack in front of her. "I'm old enough to have lost them all. Not that it matters."

"It should," Thuỷ said.

Laughter, bitter and wounding. "Feeling pity?"

"I don't know if I would call it that," Thuỷ said. "It doesn't change what you are, or what you did. Or that you enjoyed all of it."

"Pity but not forgiveness, then." The lights flickered on in *Owl*'s heartroom, and those same sickly, diminutive overlays came on, but this time they were people: a sea of faces and bodies walking and talking and laughing. Thuỷ wasn't sure who they were at first, and then she saw An's face, Hải's face, Châu's face. All of the people *Owl* had killed. Some kind of mocking memorials, surely—except the overall impression was one of profound loss. "As I said: not that it matters."

"They keep you company," Thuỷ said, finally. She wasn't sure whether to feel anger or sadness.

"Alone in the dark and in the silence." *Owl* laughed, but her voice was tinged with old hurt. "I guess they do."

One last piece: not a connector but one Thuỷ had had made based on the schematics. It was long and sinuous, and it went from the capacitors to the targeting system—and once she'd put it in and checked the connections, it would be fixed, and *Owl* would be operational again, alone in the darkness. It felt both incredibly portentous and anticlimactic.

She put it in, checked the connections—breathing in, trying to steady her nerves. "Here," she said.

The lights came on. Not weak, not sickly, not translucent, but strong and unwavering. There were vibrations, like these of a motor accelerating—or a heartbeat—so strong that Thuỷ could feel them through the suit. The safehold released Kim Lan's statement, automatically transmitting it to Thuỷ, and from Thuỷ to *Goby*.

Big'sis.

It was done. She had all the evidence she needed to exonerate Kim Lan, to restore her name, her family's name. "Here," she said, again—and reached for the glider, to head back to *Goby* and the world that waited for her. "I'm done."

She felt light-headed, and limp, and the future was uncertain.

I'm done.

More than done, wasn't it? She'd set up the safehold, the transmission back to *Goby*. She'd made the arrangements for *Goby* to pass the statement on, to deal with the magistrate who would restore Kim Lan's name. She'd made herself unnecessary to the whole process.

The lights blinked, on the restored weapons system, and somehow she was not surprised when *Owl* laughed. "Yes, it's finished, isn't it?"

There was a low buzzing within the shadow-suit, an impossible whistling that ramped up in intensity—the same vibrations she'd felt before except these burrowed into her until the bones in her body vibrated in sympathy, a red-hot rhythm that caught hold of her and was playing itself on her ribs, on her pelvis, on her skin—louder and louder until everything hurt, and still it didn't stop...

The *Owl*'s scream. The punishment for rebels, for the disloyal to the empire. For those who had abandoned their friends.

Thuỷ had chased atonement all the way into that nebula, and on some level she'd known, she'd always known, that she didn't expect to come out after fixing *Owl*. "I am," she said. "Do you think it's worth it? They'll just dismantle it, after I'm dead."

"Oh, child. You're the one who saw so much, and so little. It's my voice. It's part of me. I'd rather scream once more in all my glory rather than leave it forever unused. It will be worth it. All of it."

You saw much, and so little.

But on some deep, primal level, she'd seen all of it already.

The pressure was building up and up within her. Her bots popped apart, one by one, like fireworks going off—there was nothing in her ears now but that never ending whistling, that vibration that kept going and going, her bones full to bursting, her eyes and nose and mouth ceaselessly hurting, leaking fluid—and her lungs were shaking too, and it was hard to breathe, and even the liquid that filled her mouth, the blood, salt-tinged one, felt like it was vibrating too—and all of it was as it should be—

Thuỷ laughed, bitterly. "I saw so little? I chose to come here. I *knew*."

"Ha. All your own choices, then. Always leading back here, to atonement and death." *Owl*'s voice was mocking. Thuỷ could barely see the heartroom or the Mind: everything was receding impossibly far away. She was curled up on herself, struggling to keep herself together—to not give in to the quivering, because the moment she did everything would fly apart and all her bones would pop like her bots had, one by one until nothing was left... "The final appeasement for your friend's soul. Justice." It was a word that seemed to tear through her.

All her own choices. All her own life.

And yet...

I release you from the oath.

You keep setting the terms and expecting me to keep up.

It had been Kim Lan's own choices, too.

You assume this is about winning. This is about survival.

She'd always followed Kim Lan, and yet it didn't have to go that way. It could have been different. Kim Lan could have *asked* before accepting the amnesty. They could have discussed; come to a joint agreement. They could have done anything that didn't involve Kim Lan's pulling at the oath-bond until Thuỷ couldn't take the consequences anymore. They had an oath of sisterhood, not obedience—and she wasn't the only one who had broken it.

"She could have *asked*," she whispered, through the red haze.

"You said something? Hush, child. It's almost over."

She could have *asked*.

Thuỷ had come here to atone for a death she'd caused, but the truth was—Kim Lan, too, carried the responsibility of what had happened. Of her own death.

The truth was—Thuỷ deserved to live, too.

"It is not over," she said, slowly—and when that elicited no response, "It is not over!" screaming it through wrung lungs and burst ribs.

The thing holding her—*Owl*'s scream—paused, for a bare fraction. Interest, again. "Why?"

She deserved to live, and there was only one way she would survive, if it worked at all.

"Because—" Thuỷ forced herself to breathe, swallowing up bile and blood, "That would be too easy."

A silence. She was held in that embrace of collapsing bones and organs, struggling to move—and said, "You enjoyed it. Killing them. Causing pain. Suffering."

"Always." *Owl*'s voice was malicious.

"Then tell me. Is my guilt or my death easier?"

Silence, again. The embrace flickered, but did not vanish.

"You want to release me, go ahead. Death is cheap."

"You wanted to die," *Owl* said, and she could feel the frustration. The pondering on how most to inflict hurt.

"I did. I do," Thuỷ said, and it wasn't quite a lie; just an uncertainty. She thought of the row of faces in the heartroom—not a memorial but an inadequate shield against loneliness. "You should know how much of a punishment solitude is." She said nothing more, waited.

The room distorted and buckled, and the pressure in Thuỷ's bones spiked, wringing a scream of pure pain out of her as everything felt about to shatter. Then it was all gone, and she was curled up in the vacuum, gasping and struggling to come together.

"The weight of guilt," *Owl* said. Her voice was vicious. "Go. Since you've been so good at making your life a living hell."

Thuỷ uncoiled, muscle after muscle—reached for her glider, shaking, the taste of blood and salt in her mouth— powered it in silence, going through the cloud of debris from her burst bots.

Go.

Death is cheap.

Go.

Thuỷ clung to her glider as she passed out of *Owl*, out of reach of all the faces of the dead in the heartroom—with Kim Lan's face in painful but fading memory—and headed towards *Goby* and the long trip home, to give meaning to the rest of her life.

The Lake, the Valley, the Border Between Water and Wood, and the End of Things

WATSON NEITH

S TANDING IN THEIR galley kitchen, Juniper sank her knife into a soft block of smoked goat cheese. She had left it out to soften for so long that the cheese practically parted before the knife touched it. She considered the other sliced and chopped hors d'oeuvres on the tray: cheeses, check; sliced cucumber and whole cherry tomatoes, check; olives stuffed with garlic, just needed straining; sliced baguette, check; blueberries from Laila's enspelled hothouse, check; seasoned almonds for Lydia and salami for herself, check. All foods she loved, but she was starting to get sick of snacking for all her meals. She was reaching for the wine when the pipe that ran from the kitchen down into the shop's back room peeped to indicate someone was talking.

"I'm about to run out of matchbook cases." Lydia's voice was an echo distilled and transmitted by the charms drawn onto the body of the pipe; their living space above the shop was otherwise too well insulated for voices to carry unless someone started shouting.

"I'm almost done." Juniper grabbed the corkscrew and cut the seal off the cork so she could start prying it out of the bottle. "Which ones do you need?"

A moment's pause. "All of them. But we're especially low on inner peace, uplift, and instant seagreen hair, style #3, all hair types."

She should have guessed. Everyone liked an instant hair transformation that left no bleach damage and looked exactly the same on any hair color or texture. She would make more matchbook cases for the other popular colors while she was at it: silver, style #2, which was currently streaking through Lydia's tight curls and therefore extremely popular; electric blue, all styles; bright violet, all styles. Juniper sighed. The matchbook charm packs were Lydia's idea. They were brilliant, easy to use, very popular, and right now, the absolute bane of her existence.

"Ok. I'll stamp some in a moment." Juniper gave the corkscrew a good yank and the cork popped out in her hand. She splashed wine into two glasses, grabbed them by the stems, and caught the tray in her other hand. "But I have to eat something first or I'll die."

She heard the pipe whisper, "You'll be fine," as she pushed the door open and trundled down the stairs.

When she reached the bottom step, she turned left past the wooden bookcase of practical craft books, past the natural history, environmental sciences, gardening and nature books, and edged past the table of fiber arts books and kits they had discounted for the visiting artist workshop this month. On the far wall was the always-open door where they kept their crafting space; built around it was a floor-to-ceiling brass and glass locked case that held their inventory of charms. Or would, except that they desperately needed to restock.

Thus: why they were eating cheese plates for every meal and busy drawing and assembling matchbook charm packs at nine at night. Juniper set the tray down and relinquished one of the glasses. Her wife glanced up, smiled at her, and kept putting the finishing stitch into a little matchbook of migraine relief charms. To activate the written charm, all the user needed to do was tear it from the pack.

"Are those for Marcel?" Juniper asked, a dim memory surfacing of him stepping in while she was counting inventory.

Lydia nodded. "Special order. The last session for his tattoo got bumped and it'll be two months before the artist can complete the spell."

"That's too bad." Juniper rolled up several slices of salami and stuck them in her mouth before going to the supply cabinet and bringing down a carousel of inks and the rubber stamps for the hair matchbooks. Then inner peace, uplift, and restful sleep, another popular one even though it required a prescription.

"He also wanted to know if we will have a matchbook for lactose intolerance soon."

"Um." There were still enough pre-cut matchbook cases on the table, each one printed with the logo for Matchbook Remedies & Sundries, that she didn't need to grab more. "Don't you think there are too many factors to offer a generic? We'd need metabolic labs... and better make sure that it's not really a milk allergy with accompanying intolerance..."

"That's what I said. I told him what tests he would need, but I think something over-the-counter would work as well as a bespoke charm."

"Well, it's nice that he keeps bringing us business." Juniper held up a stack of freshly stamped 'seagreen hair, style #3, all hair types.' "I will give this to you if you take five bites of anything on that tray. There's three types of cheese and the almonds are dusted in cocoa."

"And I appreciate it. I'll get to it."

Juniper set the stack aside, out of Lydia's reach, and picked the inner peace stamp. The wind rattled against the door. "Did you know," she said, pausing to take a sip of wine, "That some couples spend their evenings together doing things that aren't work?"

"I've heard that before," Lydia said, rethreading her needle, "But I don't really believe it. There's too much to do."

She looked up, picked up a wedge of brie, and popped it into her mouth.

"One bite down," Juniper said. "We should revisit hiring a shop assistant. Or maybe an apprentice; we might be eligible for a grant if you're worried about the cost."

"I don't think we have enough experience. We've had the shop less than five years."

"People drive hours to get here. I think we have the reputation to—"

The doorbell rang.

The sound rose and faded. Juniper glanced at Lydia. "You didn't schedule a night appointment, did you?"

The doorbell, again. Now Lydia glanced at Juniper. "It might be an emergency?"

Juniper closed the inkpad. "I'll check."

When she walked into the front of the shop, no one was visible through the picture window in the door. The doorbell still rang.

"Lydia," she called, "I think something is wr—"

A vortex of air shot the door open, sending the stack of paper bags beside the till flying. Books ruffled and fell from their tables; the tools on the wall behind the counter rattled; Juniper jumped as she heard a sharp crack and realized a pebble had struck the glass display case. Behind her, Lydia shouted a word of power to the security ward.

If it did anything, Juniper couldn't tell, but the wind died and the milling papers began their featherfall descent to the ground. Her pulse raced in her ears as she glanced around the shop for the culprit, seeing nothing—oh. There. A translucent being, coiling and uncoiling around the display tables. It grew in opacity as she focused her attention. Serpentine—no, vine-like—fronds unspooled and retracted among books and scattered knickknacks. Ephemeral water pooled across the floor. Small yellow flowers budded from the walls.

"You damaged our home. You should have asked permission to enter," Juniper said. Her mouth felt dry, but what she felt more than fear was bafflement; this wasn't some mischief sprite or a ghost. It was a great spirit of the earth. They had immense power, but they were sedentary things.

She knew the one anchored to the town's surroundings. What was this one *doing* here?

This is a place of business. You run an emergency clinic. The voice formed soundless, wordless, and physical, all at the same time, in her head.

"Only on Tuesdays," Lydia said, finally committing to the policy Juniper had insisted on three months ago. "The rest of the week there are two witches in residence at the Greenscale ER."

They are most proficient in flesh magic and that is not what I require. I must have assistance with a binding. It is urgent.

Juniper felt Lydia's eyes on her back. She sighed and unlocked the glass case so she could take their second to last matchbook full of energy blast charms out of inventory. She ripped away the first sheet and felt a sunbeam of vigor flood through her. "Why do you need a binding?"

I have been attacked. We are still fighting and it has been three days.

"You're projecting," Lydia said. "How far away?"

I am the lake the valley the border between water and wood.

In some ways, the great spirits were not good conversationalists. Juniper felt all of these things—land and water, treeline and shore—but she couldn't tell how far away or in what direction. "We have to prepare some things first," she said. "And you need to show us the way to go, or we won't be able to find you."

The tendrils flexed and grew across the walls, winding around chair and table legs. Then they weren't. A small, warmish orb rested in the palm of Juniper's hand, colors swirling in a way that reminded her of an oilslick.

It will show you the way. Come soon.

The store was left quieter, less vibrant, but no less of a mess. The door wavered on its hinges.

Lydia said, "I thought you were retired. It was too dangerous. Retail is safer."

Juniper turned around. As she did, she brushed one of the books on the fiber arts table and it thudded to the floor. "What would you rather we do?" she asked. "How is this any different than you taking housecalls at all hours? The spirit came to us because it needs us."

"Charms for migraines aren't dangerous."

Juniper went upstairs to get her kit, which she kept packed and stowed under their bed. Maxine, their geriatric calico, was slumbering there too, having apparently abandoned her favorite spot at the foot of the bed during the spirit's visit; Juniper ruffled her ears, then backtracked to open a new can and top off her water in the kitchen. Then she jotted off a text to her sister, asking her to check in on Maxine if she didn't hear from Juniper by tomorrow evening. Lydia was exaggerating the danger, but time could go strange around the great spirits.

When she got back downstairs, Lydia had put a note up on the door and was furiously ripping through their inventory, pulling charm packs and papers out of their supply cabinets.

"You're mad." Juniper stayed near the door.

"I'm not... mad." Lydia shuffled through the papers in her hands, made a small noise, and then tucked them away in the messenger bag she carried everywhere. "I'm... frustrated."

"Now you know how I feel. Have you taken an energy blast? You'll need it tonight."

Juniper touched her shoulder and went outside to work on the motorcycle. Where they were going, they couldn't necessarily expect a road, so she turned on her phone's flashlight app and checked the intactness of the flight and weightlessness engravings she had etched into the fender and the sidecar. They were fine, and so was the energy efficiency charm the company had branded the tank with. She dropped her supplies into the sidecar.

Lydia came out with their helmets and passed one over, saying, "Unless you plan on eating bugs?"

Juniper took the offered helmet and leaned over to kiss her. "Thanks. I'm glad you're coming."

"I couldn't leave you to do it alone." Lydia climbed up behind her and leaned into her back, watching over her shoulder as Juniper released the orb the spirit had given her.

It bobbed in the air before them and took off before she got the motorcycle aloft. A luminous streak shot over the tops of trees like it was drawn magnetically back home; miles passed below so quickly Juniper couldn't look down unless she wanted to make herself nauseous. Houses scattered and gave way to rolling hills blanketed with trees.

"What if we're late to open the shop tomorrow?" Lydia shouted.

"Tell me what you said when we land," Juniper shouted; it wasn't a conversation she wanted to have mid-air, even if the answer she wanted to give was "I plan on sleeping in and everyone can just deal with it for one day."

The air rushed around them. The skin on her slightly exposed wrists and neck ached with the chill. Lydia kept a firm grip on her waist. On the horizon, Juniper saw the lake, fringed by forest and distant ridges. She pointed and a blast of wind swept straight down the sleeve of her jacket.

The orb hovered stationary over a patch of ground. As they closed the distance, Juniper was relieved to see a gravel parking area, clear enough that they could land without worrying about striking branches on the way down. Nothing about the great spirit had made her think it could be thoughtful. As she turned off the bike's engine and grabbed their supplies, the orb wavered impatiently; then it shot down a beaten path so quickly they had to run after it. The path cut down along a bank and then veered up, turning into steps in a concrete embankment over a run-off drain that fed water into the lake.

It has retrenched itself. I trapped it here. Look.

Juniper glanced down, not certain what she was looking for. The spectral presence must be slight; she could not see it in the water.

There.

Oh. The run-off bubbled slightly darker than the rest of the water at night, as if reflected starlight and distant city light couldn't touch it. Or as if...

"It absorbs light," Juniper observed, very quietly. "Do you know what it's called?"

The great spirit shared a ripple of sensations: *spoilage entropy imbalanced the-end-of-things.* Scenes of their battle flickered into her mind.

Picking a bottle from the half dozen empties in her kit, Juniper swiped impressions of the entity's essence onto the bottle's surface with a paint pen. This didn't require precision, just intent: once the target was tethered to something, it would be considerably easier to bind or banish. She could recognize the phenotypes of dozens of mischievous spirits and hauntings by sight alone, and this was something different. That she didn't know it left her uneasy. But there was a time and place for dealing with those feelings, and it wasn't now.

I will rile it so you have access. Are you prepared?

Juniper nodded. She could see the great spirit in the water, or more accurately, of the water and the land surrounding it. Translucent waves jumped up into the drainage pipe, surged back and forth like the ocean at high tide. She might have to wade over there.

"Something is wrong," Lydia said.

"Where?" She didn't want to look away from the drainage pipe where her target foamed and bubbled against the energy of the lake, the valley, the border between water and wood. But her eyes followed when Lydia pointed to something floating in the moonlit distance. Then she spotted another object in the mud several yards away. In the dark, it was hard to make sense of the sight, but the smell guided her along the shore. With her flashlight app, Juniper stared down at browned grass and beached fish, their eyes silver and scales patchy and slimy. They seemed to crumble internally under her glance.

The great spirit was surrounded. Their opponent had used the naturalness of death and decay to circumvent its sense of what belonged in its territory and what had invaded. The thing hiding in the drainage pipe was a—"Trap!" Juniper yelled, and ran into the shallows.

The great spirit reacted just before the decay struck. Juniper was knocked off her feet in the spray of water as the spirit spun and lashed out. She caught her breath just before going under; submerged, all she could see was the rainbow energy of the spirit. She came up easily ten feet from where she'd been, in waist-deep water, her cell phone and the bottle somehow still in her hands.

The cell phone, she dropped into her jean pocket. It was probably doomed. The bottle she upturned so the captured water could escape.

"Get out of the water!" Lydia shouted from shore. She was on hands and knees, probably soaked from the wave.

She'd love nothing else. But if they couldn't capture part of the assailant, they couldn't banish it. Juniper forced her way through water that resisted like cement, focusing on the identity of the decay and trying to ignore the brilliance of the great spirit. Decay. What did it feel like? The frailty of cobwebbed leaves, skin sloughing and fungus blooming. Death and rot. She imagined it in the bottle, trapped and vulnerable.

The decay hiding in the drainage pipe shot toward the great spirit in a viscous arc. Juniper slipped in the roiling water and regained her footing a second later, and found her victory in her hands; her intent had diverted some decay into the bottle. She turned to face the great spirit.

Her hope died in her mouth. The decay wasn't fighting the great spirit. It was trying to *entangle* the great spirit. Its rainbow energy was struck through with spreading, brackish veins. Green, she'd almost call it, green like a muddy pond, but that was her mind trying to fit it into the world she knew. Moonlight touched the veins and vanished.

That was the plan, she realized. To possess the great spirit or force it from its territory. To leave a vacancy that could be filled.

Juniper stoppered the bottle and shoved it into the inner pocket of her jacket. If she didn't stop this, she didn't know what would happen next. All she knew was that it would be terrible.

From the banks, Lydia shouted indistinctly as Juniper waded deeper. The waves were too violent for sound to carry. She wanted to reassure her but there was no time. Honestly, she didn't think she could make it to shore if she tried; the undertow was too strong. There was just her intent and the rising water.

When the height reached her chest, she started swimming, all her thoughts on the essence of the great spirit. The lake, the valley, where water meets wood. If she could ignore the water that kept dashing into her mouth and nose, could envision it purely enough, she might be able to force a split between the two beings. The lake, the valley, where water meets wood. The scent of pine and cedar, squelching mud, dry sand and rocks on the waterline. Sunbaked earth and birdsong.

She thought about the shoreline in summer, and about it blanketed in snow and a thin crisp of ice in winter. Dragonflies on the water. The shifting, multi-colored aura of the spirit.

As a wave glugged over her head, she realized the decay had expected this, too. It found her like it had her name. For an instant she thought she was sinking, the water both bright and brackish, and then there was nothing. It wasn't darkness; it was nothing. She could not see anything, even the veins on the insides of her eyelids; she could not hear her pulse, much less the torrent; she couldn't tell if she was swallowing water or breathing dry air. Everything was gone.

Was she cold? She thought she should be cold.

The lake, Juniper thought. The valley. Where water meets wood.

Oh shit. Lydia.

No, she had to concentrate—the lake, the valley, where water meets wood. The lake, the valley, where water meets wood.

The lake.

She saw the rainbow radiance of the great spirit, and reached for it.

Juniper gasped for breath. She was on land. On her back. Her head hurt like she'd been punched. She turned and retched up water, and saw her name in green paint on a flat rock. To her left, further down the beach, another written rock, and the great spirit vast and semi-translucent, its myriad forms shifting beneath the moonlight. And further still, the end of all things, intact and vast, imploding on itself a hundred times over, flesh fading and bacteria blooming and vanishing—and between her and it, Lydia, her back partially turned and a matchbook in her hands.

Juniper shoved herself to her feet.

Something flashed like sheet lightning and she heard a popping sound. Then there was nothing on the beach except for the two of them and the radiant vines of the great spirit. Juniper ran anyway, grabbed Lydia by the shoulders and hugged her.

Lydia leaned into the embrace and then said, "We got lucky. I think we have a very big problem."

"I've never seen anything like that." She swallowed and stepped back to regard the great spirit in its full colors. She reached into her sodden jacket and found the bottle there, still capped. The wind ruffled through her layers and she shivered. "Thank you for getting my idiot self out of the water. I don't think I could have made it back to shore."

"I'm going to get the first aid kit," Lydia said.

As her wife walked up the incline to the parking lot, Juniper knelt by the great spirit's rock. With the same paint pen she'd used to write Juniper's name, Lydia had scribbled the valley and the line where the woods met the lake. One summoning and two bindings— the signs were quickly done and yet they had all still worked. She would never stop being astounded by Lydia's precision. "She had to separate you from the decay," she said, by way of explanation, "Or you might have both been banished."

She scratched through the sketch with one of her keys, breaking the link. "I think—"

That is what it wanted. If it could not subsume me, it wanted to leave a void here that could be filled.

"It seems like it." If the spirit was angry at Lydia, it wasn't showing it, which Juniper would count in their favor. "Do you know what it was?"

It could have destroyed everything. When a bobcat catches a hare, it feeds on the death. Scavengers consume the remains. Life grows in the hare's bones. When a fire passes through the woods, new growth springs up among the fallen. Death foreshadows new life, and new

*life foreshadows death. That...it would have broken the cycle.
Death would have offered more death, and nothing new would be
born.*

"What do we do?"

There must be a great convention.

Juniper held up the intact bottle. Inside it, nothing swirled,
but she felt it, knew it was there, as real as she was. Lydia's
matchbook spells had were directionally focused, and to
banish this shard of the end of things, they would have to
conduct another ritual. Unless... "What do you want to do
with this? I don't want to take this into my home."

It will be examined by the convention. The bottle vanished
from Juniper's outstretched hand as Lydia reappeared on the
banks, the first aid kit in her arms. She pulled out a blanket
and handed Juniper a warmth charm.

You saved us for now, the great spirit said to Lydia. *We will
speak further.*

It collapsed into the land around it.

"I want to go home," Lydia said.

Wrapped in the blanket like a cloak, Juniper walked up
the concrete steps to gather her scattered kit. "When," she
asked, "were you going to tell me you'd made matchstick
banishment charms?"

"When I knew they would work," Lydia said, sounding
hoarse. "I'd never used them until tonight."

"We're double lucky, I guess." She zipped up the kit and
swung it over her shoulder. "The banishment charms are
brilliant, Lydia. Game-changing."

"They need improvement."

So did the warmth charm; Juniper was still soaked,
but now the wetness was warm, and that was a different
unpleasant feeling. "Come on," she said. "We'll find out what
is coming next soon enough."

Of course, it wasn't that easy. First they checked
everything they wore for remnants of the end of things. Then
they combed through everything they'd brought through
them. Juniper convened a precautionary banishment on the
motorcycle.

After that came the cold flight back and, still later in the night, a steady search of the shop for anything the contaminated great spirit touched. They cast precautionary binding spells and reset the wards; Juniper roused and checked Maxine for signs of possession. The cat grumbled through the spell-casting and demanded new, fresh food in her bowl.

Sunlight made a red line on the horizon before she tossed her now-stiff clothing into the hamper, checked her phone— dry, but probably an expensive brick—and climbed into the shower. Her hair felt so greasy she shampooed twice before stepping out into the terry cloth bathrobe she almost never had a chance to lounge in.

Lydia had chamomile tea waiting for her before she even finished toweling off her hair. Juniper had heard her at the sink during her shower; she had scrubbed and changed and wrapped her hair in paisley silk.

"I'm not sure I'm awake enough to drink that."

"I put a new sign on the door of the shop. We're closed for the week."

Juniper nearly fumbled the mug. "The week?"

"I'll drop Marcel's migraine charms off this afternoon. And I've texted your sister."

"Thank you." Juniper took a sip of steaming chamomile and then set it on the bedside table so she could worm under the sheets. Maxine climbed up the little stairs they'd built for her and lay down on her feet after kneading the blanket and her skin into a suitable bed. "The week, though? Are you sure you won't explode?"

"I might explode." Lydia rolled over behind her to wrap an arm around her shoulders. If Juniper hadn't been so exhausted, she would have turned over and kissed her. Instead she melted into the sheets, enjoying the weight of Lydia's arm and the gentle presence of her breath on the back of her head. "But something's coming, and I realized I don't have the energy for it. We're stretched too thin at the shop. What we do is important for people but we still need time for ourselves or we'll burn out."

Juniper was warm, and comfortable, and her life was not in danger. She could barely keep her eyes open. "Can you bring me a pen and paper?" she asked. "I want to write that down so you can't walk it back when we wake up."

Lydia laughed and leaned in to kiss the back of her neck. "I don't think you'll let me. But I'm leaving the grant applications up to you."

Let all the
Children Boogie

SAM J. MILLER

RADIO WAS WHERE we met. Our bodies first occupied the same space on a Friday afternoon, but our minds had already connected Thursday night. Coming up on twelve o'clock, awake when we shouldn't be, both of us in our separate narrow beds, miles and miles apart, tuning in to Ms. Jackson's Graveyard Shift, spirits linked up in the gruff cigarette-damaged sound of her voice.

She'd played "The Passenger," by Iggy Pop. I'd never heard it before, and it changed my life.

Understand: there was no internet then. No way to look up the lyrics online. No way to snap my fingers and find the song on YouTube or iTunes. I was crying by the time it was over, knowing it might be months or years before I found it again. Maybe I never would. Strawberries, Hudson's only record store, almost certainly wouldn't have it. Those four guitar chords were seared indelibly into my mind, the lonesome sound of Iggy's voice certain to linger there for as long as I lived, but the song itself was already out of my reach as it faded down to nothing.

And then: a squall of distortion interrupted, stuttering into staticky words, saying what might have been *"Are you out there?"* before vanishing again.

Eerie, but no more eerie than the tingly feeling I still had from Iggy Pop's voice. And the sadness of losing the song forever.

But then, the next day, at the Salvation Army, thumbing through hundreds of dresses I hated, what did I hear but—

"I am the passenger...and I ride and I ride—"

Not from the shitty in-store speakers, which blasted Fly-92 pop drivel all the time. Someone was singing. Someone magnificent. Like pawn-shop royalty, in an indigo velvet blazer with three handkerchiefs tied around one forearm, and brown corduroy bell-bottoms.

"I see things from under glass—"

The singer must have sensed me staring, because they turned to look in my direction. Shorter than me, hair buzzed to the scalp except for a spiked stripe down the center.

"The Graveyard Shift," I said, trembling. "You were listening last night?"

"Yeah," they said, and their smile was summer, was weekends, was Ms. Jackson's raspy-sweet voice. The whole place smelled like mothballs, and the scent had never been so wonderful. "You too?"

My mind had no need for pronouns. Or words at all for that matter. This person filled me up from the very first moment.

I said: "What a great song, right? I never heard it before. Do you have it?"

"No," they said, "but I was gonna drive down to Woodstock this weekend to see if I could find it there. Wanna come?"

Just like that. *Wanna come?* Everything I did was a long and agonizing decision, and every human on the planet terrified me, and this person had invited me on a private day trip on a moment's impulse. What epic intimacy to offer a total stranger—hours in a car together, a journey to a strange and distant town. What if I was a psychopath, or a die-hard Christian evangelist bent on saving their soul? The only thing more surprising to me than this easy offer was how swiftly and happily my mouth made the words: *That sounds amazing.*

"Great! I'm Fell."

"Laurie," I said. We shook. Fell's hand was smaller than mine, and a thousand times stronger.

Only then did I realize: I didn't know what gender they were. And, just like that, with the silent effortless clarity of every life-changing epiphany, I saw that gender was just a set of clothes we put on when we went out into the world.

And even though I hated myself for it, I couldn't help but look around. To see if anybody else had seen. If word might spread, about me and this magnificently unsettling oddball.

Numbers were exchanged. Addresses. A pick-up time was set. Everything was so easy. Fell's smile held a whole world inside it, a way of life I never thought I could live. A world where I wasn't afraid.

I wanted to believe in it. I really did. But I didn't.

"What did you think that was?" Fell asked, in the parking lot, parting. "That weird voice, at the end of the song?"

I shrugged. I hadn't thought much about it.

"At first I thought it was part of the song," Fell said. "But then the DJ was freaked out."

"Figured it was just...interference, like from another station."

"It's a big deal," Fell said. "To interrupt a commercial radio broadcast like that. You need some crazy hardware."

"Must be the Russians," I said solemnly, and Fell laughed, and I felt the world lighten.

And that night, tuning in to Ms. Jackson, "This song goes out to Fell, my number one fan. Wouldn't be a weeknight if Fell didn't call asking for some Bowie. So here's 'Life on Mars?' which goes out to Laurie, the girl with the mousy hair."

More evidence of Fell's miraculous gift. A thousand times I'd wanted to call Ms. Jackson, and each time I'd been too intimidated to pick up the phone. What if she was mean to me? What if I had to speak to a station producer first, who decided I wasn't worthy of talking to their resident empress? And who was I to ask for a song?

Also, I loved "Life on Mars?" I wondered if Fell knew it, had read it on my face or smelled it on my clothes with another of their superhuman abilities, or if they had just been hoping.

I shut my eyes. I had never been so conscious of my body before. David Bowie's voice rippled through it, making me shiver, sounding like Fell's fingertips must feel.

I wondered how many times I'd been touched by Fell, listening late at night, trembling at the songs they requested.

I remembered Fell's smile, and stars bloomed in the darkness.

But before the song was over, a sound like something sizzling rose up in my headphones, and the music faded, and a kind of high distortion bubbled up, and then began to stutter—and then become words. Unintelligible at first, like they'd been sped up, and then:

"...mission is so unclear. I could warn about that plane crash, try to stop the spiderwebbing epidemic. But how much difference would those things make? I'm only here for a short—"

Then the mechanical voice was gone. David Bowie came back. And just as swiftly was switched out.

"Sorry about that, children," Ms. Jackson said, chuckling. An old sound. How long had she been doing this show? She always called her listeners children, like she was older than absolutely everyone in earshot. I heard a cigarette snuffed out in the background. "Getting some interference, sounds like. Maybe from the Air Force base. They're forever messing with my signals. Some lost pilot, maybe, circling up in the clouds. Looking for the light. Good time to cut to a commercial, I'd say."

Someone sang *Friendly Honda, we're not on Route Nine*, the inane omnipresent jingle that seemed to support every television and radio program in the Hudson Valley. I thought of Fell, somewhere in the dark. Our bodies separate. Our minds united.

"Welcome back to the Graveyard Shift," she said. "This is Ms. Jackson, playing music for freaks and oddballs, redheaded stepchildren and ugly ducklings—songs by us and for us, suicide queens and flaming fireflies—"

❖

FELL'S CAR SMELLED like apples. Like spilled cider, and cinnamon. Twine held one rear headlight in place. When we went past fifty miles an hour, it shook so hard my teeth chattered together. Tractor trailers screamed past like missiles. It was autumn, 1991. We were sixteen. We could die at any moment.

The way to Woodstock was long and complicated. Taking the thruway would have been faster, but that meant paying the toll, and Fell knew there had to be another way.

"No way in hell that was a lost pilot," Fell said. "That interruption last night. That was someone with some insane machinery."

"How do you know so much about radio signals?"

"I like machines," Fell said. "They make so much sense. Does your school have a computer? Mine doesn't. We're too poor." Fell went to Catskill High, across the river. "It sucks, because I really want to be learning how they work. They can do computations a million times faster than people can, and they're getting faster all the time. Can you imagine? How many problems we'll be able to solve? How quickly we'll get the right answer, once we can make a billion mistakes in an instant? All the things that seem impossible now, we'll figure out how to do eventually."

I lay there, basking in the warmth of Fell's excitement. After a while, I said: "I still think it was the Soviets. Planning an invasion."

"No Russian accent," Fell said. "And anyway I'm pretty sure the Cold War is over. Didn't that wall come down?"

I shrugged, and then said, "Thanks for the song, by the way."

Instead of answering, Fell held out one hand. I took it instantly, fearlessly, like a fraction of Fell's courage could already have rubbed off on me.

In that car I felt invincible. I could let Fell's lack of fear take me over.

But later, in Woodstock, a weird crooked little town that smelled like burning leaves and peppermint soap, Fell reached for my hand again, and I was too frightened to take it. What if someone saw? In my mind I could hear the whole town stopping with a sound like a record scratching. Everyone turning, pointing. Shouting. Pitchforks produced from nowhere. Torches. Nooses.

Space grew between us, without my wanting it to. Fell taking a tiny step away from me.

We went to Cutler's Record Shop. We found a battered old Iggy Pop cassette, which contained "The Passenger." Fell bought it. We went to Taco Juan's and then had ice cream. Rocky Road was both of our favorite.

Twilight when we left. Thin blue light filled the streets. I dreamed of grabbing Fell's hand and never letting go. I dreamed of being someone better than who I was.

As soon as the doors slammed, we switched on the radio.

"Responding to this morning's tragic crash of Continental Express Flight 2574, transport officials are stating that it's impossible to rule out an act of terrorism at this—"

"No *shit*," Fell said, switching it off.

"What?"

"The voice. They said *I could warn about the plane crash*."

I laughed. "What, you think the voice in the night is part of a terrorist cell?"

"No," Fell said. "I think they're from the future."

Just like Fell to make the impossible sound easy, obvious. I laughed some more. And then I stopped laughing.

"Could be a coincidence," I said.

Fell pushed the tape in, pressed play. After our third trip through "The Passenger," rewinding the tape yet again, they looked over and saw the tears streaming down my face.

"It's such a sad song," I said. "So lonesome."

"Sort of," Fell said. "But it's also about finding someone who shares your loneliness. Who negates it. Cancels it out. Listen: *Get into the car. We'll be the passenger.* Two people, one thing. Plural singular."

"Plural singular," I said.

I'm sorry, I started to say, a hundred times, and told myself I would, soon, in just a second, until Fell looked over and said: "Hey. Can I come over? I don't feel like mixing it up with my mother tonight."

And that was the first time I ever saw fear on Fell's face.

❖

MY PARENTS WERE almost certainly baffled by my new friend, but their inability to identify whether Fell was a boy or a girl meant they couldn't decide for sure if they were a sexual menace, so they couldn't object to Fell coming upstairs with me.

Three songs into the Graveyard Shift, Fell asked, "Can I spend the night?"

I laughed.

"I'm serious."

"Your mom wouldn't mind?"

"Probably she'd barely notice," Fell said. "And even if she did, it'd be like number nine on the list of things she'd want to scream at me about the next time she saw me."

"Fine by me," I said, and went downstairs to ask Mom and Dad.

Big smile. Confident posture. Think this through. "Cool if Fell spends the night here?" And then, without thinking about it, because if I'd spent a single nanosecond on it I would have known better, stopped myself, I added: "She already called her mom, and she said it was okay."

They smiled, relieved. They'd both been sitting there stewing, wondering whether what was happening upstairs needed to be policed. Whether a sex-crazed-menace male was upstairs seducing their daughter. But no. I'd said *she*. This was just some harmless, tomboyish girl.

"Yes of course," Mom said, but I couldn't hear her, just went by the smile, the nod, and I thanked her and turned to go, nausea making the room spin and the blood pound in my ears.

I felt sick. Somehow naming Fell like that was worse than a lie. Worse than an insult. It was a negation of who Fell was.

Cowardice. Betrayal. What was it, in me, that made me so afraid? That had stopped me from taking Fell's hand? That made me frightened of other people seeing what they were, what we were? Something so small that could somehow make me so miserable.

I was afraid that Fell might have heard, but Ms. Jackson was playing when I got back to my room, and Fell was on the floor beside the speaker, so that our hero's raspy voice drowned out every shred of weakness and horror that the world held in store for us.

We lay on the bare wooden floor like that for the next two hours. The window was open. Freezing wind made every song sweeter. Wood smoke seeped into our clothes. Our hands held tight.

Six minutes before midnight, approaching the end of the Graveyard Shift, it came again. The sizzle; the static; the chugging machine noise that slowly took the shape of a human voice. We caught it mid-sentence, like the intervening twenty-four hours hadn't happened, like it blinked and was now carrying on the same conversation.

"—out there. I don't know if this is the right...place. Time. If you're out there. If it's too late. If it's too early."

"Definitely definitely from the future," Fell whispered.

"You're so stupid," I said, giggling, so drunk on Fell that what they said no longer seemed so absurd.

"Or what you need to hear. What I should say. What I shouldn't."

The voice flanged on the final sentence, dropping several octaves, sounding demonic, mechanical. Slowing down. The *t* sound on the last word went on and on. The static in the background slowed down too, so that I could hear that it wasn't static at all, but rather many separate sounds resolving into sonic chaos. An endless line of melodic sequences playing simultaneously.

The voice flanged back, and said one word before subsiding into the ether again:

"—worthwhile—"

Control of the radio waves was relinquished. The final chords of "Blue Moon" resurfaced.

"There's our star man again," Ms. Jackson said with a chuckle. Evidently she'd had time to rethink her Air Force pilot theory. "Still lost, still lonely. I wonder—who do you think he's looking for? Call me with your wildest outer space invader theories."

"Want to call?" Fell whispered.

"No," I said, too fast, too frightened. "My parents are right across the hall. We'd wake them."

Fell shrugged. The gesture was such strange perfection. Their whole being was expressed in it. The confidence and the charm and the fearlessness and the power to roll with absolutely anything that came along.

I grabbed Fell's hand. Prayed that some of what they were would seep into me.

Fell touched my mousy hair. Sang softly: *"Is there life on Mars?"*

"We'll find out," I said. "Right? Machines will solve all our problems?"

❖

AT SCHOOL, TWO days later, during lunch, I marched myself to the library and enrolled in computer classes.

❖

"SHIT," FELL SAID, pointing out the window, driving us home through snowy blue twilight.

Massive green Air Force trucks lined a long stretch of Route 9. Flatbeds where giant satellite dishes stood. Racks of cylindrical transformers. Men pacing back and forth with machines in their hands. None of it had been there the day before.

"What the hell?" I said.

"They're hunting for the voice in the night too," Fell said.

"Because it's part of a terrorist cell and knew about a plane crash before it happened."

"Or because it's using bafflingly complex technology that could only have come from the future," Fell said.

Then they switched on the radio, shrieked at what they found there. Sang-screamed: *"Maybe I'm just like my mother, she's never satisfied."*

"Why do we scream at each other?" I said, and then we launched into the chorus with one wobbly crooked magnificent voice.

My first view of Fell's house was also my first view of Fell's mother. She sat on the front porch wearing several scarves, smoking.

"Fuck," Fell said. "Fuck me, times ten thousand. I thought for sure she'd still be at work."

"We can go," I said. I'd been excited to see the house, for that insight into who Fell was and what had helped make them, but now panic was pulling hard at my hair. Fell's fear of the woman was contagious.

"No," Fell said. "If I act like she can't hurt me, sooner or later she really won't be able to."

She laughed when she saw me. "Of course it's a girl."

"Mrs. Tanzillo, I'm Laurie," I said, holding out my hand. "I'm pleased to meet you."

My good manners threw her off. She shook my hand with a raised eyebrow, like she was waiting to see what kind of trick I was trying to pull. I smelled alcohol. Old, baked-in alcohol, the kind that seeps from the pores of aging drunks. Which I guess she was.

"Don't you two turn my home into a den of obscenity," she called after us, as we headed in.

Fell let the door slam, and then exhaled: "God, she is such an asshole."

The house was sadder than I'd been expecting. Smaller; smellier; heaped with strange piles. Newspapers, flattened plastic bags, ancient water-stained unopened envelopes. A litter box, badly in need of emptying, and then probably burning. My parents were poor, but not poor like this.

"You're shaking," I said, and pulled Fell into a hug.

They stiffened. Wriggled free. "Not here."

"Of course," I said. "Sorry."

The TV was on. Squabbling among the former Soviet

states. A bad divorce, except with sixteen partners instead of two, and with thermonuclear warheads instead of children. I watched it, because looking around the room—or looking at Fell looking at me—made me nauseous. A talking head grinned, said: *"It's naïve to think our children will get to grow up without the threat of nuclear war. There's no putting this genie back in the bottle."*

Fell talked fast, the shaking audible in every word. "This was a terrible idea. I felt good about us, like, it wouldn't matter what this place looked like or what you thought of it, because you know I'm not this, it's just the place where I am until I can be somewhere else, but now, I'm not so sure, I think I should probably take you home."

So Fell wasn't fearless. Wasn't superhuman.

So it was in Fell too. Whatever was in me. Something so small, that could chain down someone so magnificent.

Of course I should have put up more of a fight. Said how it didn't matter. But I hated seeing Fell like this. If Fell was afraid, what hope was there for me? Fell, who welcomed every awful thing the world had to show us. Fell was my only hope, but not this Fell. So I shrugged and said, "whatever you want," feeling awful about it already, and we turned around and went right back outside, and Mrs. Tanzillo thought that was the funniest thing she'd ever seen, and we didn't talk the whole ride home.

❖

"THAT *IS* WHAT it sounds like when doves cry," Ms. Jackson said, as the spiraling keyboard riff faded out, as the drum machine loop wound down.

I'd called the song in. I wondered if Fell was listening, if they knew what it meant. How hard it had been for me to dial that number. How bare the floor beside me was. How cold. How much my chest hurt.

"This extended block of uninterrupted songs is brought to you by Friendly Honda," she said. "They're not on Route Nine. Let's stick with Prince, shall we? Dig a little deeper. A B-side.

'Erotic City.'" Her laugh here was raw and throaty, barely a laugh at all, closer to a grumble of remembered pleasure. Some erotic city she'd taken someone to, ages ago.

The song started. A keyboard and a bass doing dirty, dirty things together. Strutting, strolling. Becoming one thing, one lewd gorgeous sound that made me shiver.

I imagined Fell listening. Our minds entwined inside the song. An intimacy unencumbered by flawed bodies, troubled minds, or the fear of what could go wrong when we put them together. Small voices inside our heads that made us miserable.

What a magnificent thing we would be. If Fell ever spoke to me again. If we could make whatever our weird thing was work.

Just when things were getting good, as Prince was shifting to the chorus, the static sizzle:

"There are a million ways I could have done this. But anything else, something more straightforward, well, I thought it might just blow your minds. Cause panic. Do the opposite thing, from what I wanted to accomplish."

Prince and the star man struggled for dominance, dirty talk giving way to flanged static only to steal back center stage. I only heard one more intelligible phrase before the intruder cut out altogether, even though I stayed up until three in the morning to see if they'd return:

"—know it's all worthwhile—"

❖

"I WANT TO find her," Fell said, the next day, when I walked out the front door and there they were, sitting on my front steps.

I hid my shock, my happiness. My shame. My guilt. "Find who?"

"The voice in the night. The one Ms. Jackson keeps calling the star man."

I sat down. "You think it's a she?"

Fell shrugged. I had been imagining the voice belonged to a male, but now that I thought about it I heard how sexless it was, how mechanical. Could be anything, in the ear of the beholder.

Cold wind swung tree branches against the side of my house, sounding like someone awful knocking at the door. I could not unhunch my shoulders. The magnitude of my awfulness was such that I didn't know where to start. What to apologize for first.

"How would we even begin to do something like that?" I asked instead.

Fell picked up something I hadn't seen before. The size of three record album sleeves laid out in a row. Four horizontal lines of thin metal, with a single vertical line down the middle.

"A directional antenna," they said. "It picks up radio signals, but it's sensitive to the direction of the origin signal. Point it directly at the source and you get a strong signal; point it away and you'll get a faint one. Plug it into this receiver"—Fell held up a hefty army-green box—"and we can take measurements in multiple directions until we find the right one."

They talked like everything was fine, but their face was so tight that I knew nothing was.

"Where did you get that?" I asked, making my voice laugh. "And how do you know how to use it?"

"I told you, machines are kind of my thing."

"So, wait, we just turn it around until we find the signal, and then go in that direction?"

"Not necessarily," Fell said. "It tells direction, but not distance. So the signal could be three miles away, or three thousand, depending on how strong it is. With just one measurement, we could be driving into the wilderness for days." Fell produced a map from the inner workings of the complex blazer they wore. "So the best way to do it is to take a measurement from one place, draw a line on the map that corresponds precisely to the signal, and then go to another location and take another measurement, and draw another precise line on the map—"

"And the point where they meet is the probable location!" I said, excited.

"It's called triangulation," Fell said.

"Amazing. But for real. How do you know all this?"

"My uncle, he learned this from my grandfather, who did it in the war. Transmitter hunting is kind of a nerd game, for amateur radio operators. They call it foxtailing."

"Your uncle as in your mother's brother?"

Fell nodded. And there it was, the subject I'd been trying to avoid.

"He was the closest thing to a dad that I had," Fell said. "We used to have so much fun together. Didn't give a shit about sports or any of that standard dude shit. He was into weird shit like directional antennas and science fiction. Then he met this girl, and moved to Omaha with her. Fucking *Omaha*. I'm sorry about the other day, at my mom's. I acted like an idiot."

"*You* acted like an idiot? Don't be dumb, Fell—that was all me. I'm the one who should be apologizing. I didn't know how to react when I saw how upset you were. I should have stayed. I wanted to stay."

Fell grabbed my hand. I had so much more to say, and I imagine so did Fell, but we did not need a word of it.

Mom might be watching out the window, I thought, but did not let go of Fell's hand.

"What if the source of the signal is moving?"

Fell nodded. "I thought about that. I don't have a good solution. We just have to hope that's not the case, or we'll be triangulating bullshit."

"It's not the end of the world, if we end up standing in some empty field together."

❖

WE DROVE TO the top of Mount Merino, to take our first measurement. And then we waited. Kept the car running, blasting the Graveyard Shift from shitty speakers. Across the street was a guardrail, and then a sheer drop to the river beneath us. The train tracks alongside it. We lay on the hood and looked at stars.

"You won't run out of gas like this?"

"The average car can idle for ninety-two hours—that's just under four days—on a full tank of gas, which is what we have," Fell said. "The battery will die long before we run out of gas."

I marveled at the intricacies of Fell's mechanical knowledge, but I had some knowledge of my own to share. I told Fell about my computer classes, and how, yeah, computers were incredible, they could do anything. Fell was as impressed as I'd hoped they'd be, but they kept asking me questions about the hardware that I couldn't answer. All I knew was software. Fell looked at programming the way I looked at machines: probably fascinating, but way over my head.

Fell told me about transistors, and how processing power was increasing exponentially; had been for decades. How eventually computers would be able to store as much information and process as many simultaneous operations as swiftly as a human brain. Then Fell showed me how to work the antenna, read the receiver, detect signal strength. We practiced on other radio stations, penciled lines on the map.

Then three hours passed. We were way past my curfew, and the star man hadn't shown.

"Fuck it," Fell said, at the end of Ms. Jackson's program. "Star person stood us up. We should go for a long drive. Charge the battery backup."

"Okay," I said, just assuming Fell was right and that was how those worked.

"Your parents won't mind?"

"Nah," I said, although they absolutely would, if they caught me sneaking back in, and there was a very good chance that they would because I am extremely clumsy, but that was the future and I didn't care about that, I only cared about the here and the now with Fell in Fell's car on this freezing night on this weird planet in this mediocre galaxy.

The radio show after Graveyard Shift was significantly less awesome, but we had to stick with it. Who knew whether star person would stumble onto any other stations. I had my portable radio and my headphones, so that I could periodically coast back and forth across the radio dial in search of our elusive visitor, but somehow I knew that this would be fruitless. For whatever reason, the signal was pegged to this specific station.

The new DJ talked too much between songs, and he had the voice of a gym teacher. The opening notes of "Where Is My Mind" came on and we both started screaming, but this asshole kept rambling on about a concert in Albany coming up next weekend, and he only stopped when the singer started singing.

"Goddamn him," Fell said, and then—static—then—

"—that's why I'm doing this, I guess. To tell you the future can be more magnificent, and more terrifying, than what you have in your head right now. And the one you embrace will be the one you end up with."

As soon as the voice began, Fell raised the antenna, held it out like a pistol. Turned slowly. We watched the receiver respond to the signal's varying strength, and hastily drew a bold thick line on the map when we found it. Cheered. Watched our breath billow.

"Told you he or she was a time traveler!" Fell said.

"That's *not* what that means."

"What does it mean, then?"

"We're picking up lines of dialogue from a movie, maybe. Or love letters from a lunatic. We should keep driving, wait for another one."

"It's late," Fell said. "My mom's not doing so well, lately."

The temperature dropped twenty degrees. The final notes of "Where Is My Mind" faded away.

"You can talk to me about it," I said, gulping down air as the ground opened up beneath me. "Whatever you're going through, I have your back. You know I love you, right?"

"I love you too, Laurie," but I could hear the unspoken rest of the sentence—like our minds had linked up already— like Fell knew, in a way I never would, how little love mattered.

"We'll go hunting tomorrow night," I said.

Fell nodded.

❖

AT SCHOOL THE next day, alone with the computer, I saw why Fell loved machines so much. Not because they were simple, but because the rules were clear. And when something went wrong, there was a way to fix it.

❖

AND THE NEXT night, hands clasped on the hood of Fell's car again, listening to Ms. Jackson with the directional antenna balanced across our thighs, I thought—if only *we* were machines. The sturdiness of hardware; the clarity of software. Not these awful meat puppets, in this awful world. Heads full of awful voices holding us back.

"I feel so good, when it's just us," Fell said, tapping into my thoughts with that eerie precision. "Our minds linked up inside the music. I want to stay there, forever."

"Maybe someday," I said, nonsensically, and Fell had the kindness not to point out that it was nonsense. We were what we were. Damaged minds alone in dying bodies.

Ms. Jackson exhaled smoke. "This one goes out to our friend the star man. Hope you get where you're going, buddy."

I groaned at the opening chords. "Starman," by David Bowie. "This song always makes me cry," I whispered, the lump already emerging in my throat.

Fell said, "I knew you were a Bowie girl."

We listened. The chorus hurt.

Fell heard me sniffle. "Hear the way his voice rises, between 'star' and 'man'?" they asked. "That's the same octave jump as in the chorus of 'Somewhere Over the Rainbow.' You hear it? Star-*man;* Some-*where*?"

Fell was right. I'd listened to the song a million times before, and never noticed. And now for as long as I lived I'd never hear it without noticing. And now I was crying. Because the song was so beautiful; because Fell was so incredible; because the world was too awful for love like ours to last.

The final chorus wound down:
Let the children lose it
Let the children use it
Let all the children boogie

And the guitar cranked up, and the background singers crooned, and we were doomed, Fell and me, I felt it as heavy as the skin on my bones, how impossible we were, how soon we'd be shattered, and then—there the voice was again:

"The future is written, you might say. What will be will be. What's the point of this? But so many futures are written. An infinite number, in fact. A billion trillion ways your story could end. I want to make sure you end up with the right future."

Fill raised the antenna. Turned slowly, searching for the signal. Found it. We drew a line on the map. We circled the spot where our two lines met.

Both of us were crying, but Fell's tears were happy ones.

❖

FELL DIDN'T CALL me the next day, the way they say they would. Nor did they come by the house. And there was no answering machine at the Tanzillo household, and no one picked up, no matter how many times I called.

I told myself this was something sacred, something practically supernatural, to go to the spot on the map where our lines crossed, where the star person's signal came from. So of course Fell was scared.

I told myself that's all it was.

I told myself that, the whole long bike ride to Fell's front door, where I knocked three times. The pounding echoed. How had I found the courage to come at all? What was I becoming?

"Quit calling my house," said Fell's mom when she opened the door. I'd only seen her sitting down before. She was taller than I'd imagined. Her long loose gray hair would have been glamorous on anyone else. "Christ, I feel like I spend half my time watching the phone ring, waiting for you to give the hell up."

"You could pick it up, actually talk to me."

She shrugged. The gesture was the same as Fell's, heavier on the left shoulder than the right, but this version oozed with cynicism and inertia instead of energy and exuberance. The news was on in the background, turned up too loud, more talking heads talking nuclear annihilation. On the way in, I'd passed more military trucks. Trailers getting set up along the Hudson River. Satellite dishes blooming like steel flowers.

"Where's Fell?"

"Not here."

"Do you know where?"

"Sometimes they go to sleep at their grandpa's place." Except Mrs. Tanzillo used the wrong gender pronouns, and clearly took great pleasure in doing so. "Old trailer, been abandoned since the man died ten years ago. Full of raccoon shit, and wasps in summer. I'll tell Fell you dropped by though." Her sweet smile made it clear she'd do no such thing, and then she shut the door in my face.

I got on my bike.

This pain, it was Fell's. It wasn't mine, and I couldn't do anything to diminish it. I could ride away and never feel it again.

I said that, but I didn't believe it. I remembered what the star person had said. About how we could have a future that was magnificent or one that was terrifying, depending on which one we embraced.

I got off the bike.

Fell couldn't see it, what a sad little creature their mother was. How absurd it was, that someone as magnificent as Fell could be made miserable by someone so weak.

Someone so small.

I knocked again.

She said nothing when she opened the door. Just smiled, like, *come on, little girl, hit me with your best shot.* And I had nothing. No practiced witty wise one-liners. Fell would have, for anyone but her.

"You're only hurting yourself, you know."

Her eyebrows rose. Her smile deepened.

"You might have the power to hurt Fell now, but that power won't last long. As soon as Fell realizes what a useless angry pitiful person you are, you'll lose that power." I wanted my words to be better. But I was done letting wishing I was better stop me from being what I was. "And Fell will leave you here, drowning in cat shit and bills, while they go conquer the world."

She said something. I didn't hear what it was.

❖

THAT NIGHT I heard the star man again. Somehow I knew it was just me this time. Like our minds were already beginning to overlap, and I could see Fell lying in silence in that dirty trailer, shivering under a blanket, no radio, listening to pine trees shush overhead, while I heard the star man whisper:

"...Two soldiers trapped behind enemy lines..."

❖

I STAYED LATE after school, in the computer lab. In the library. Reading the science and the science fiction Fell had rhapsodized about. All the impossible things that could save us from ourselves. Solar power; a post-petroleum future; superfoods. Cold fusion. Brain uploading. Digital immortality. Transcending the limits of the human.

Each time I shut a book, it was the pain of waking up from blissful dream to wretched reality.

But then, blissful dream: Fell was on my front steps when I got home. Alone in the deep black-blue of late twilight. Snow fell in half-hearted flurries.

"Sorry," they said when I ran straight at them. My hug took all the air out of them.

"Never disappear again," I whispered.

Fell nodded. A crumpled map in one raised fist. "Are we gonna do this?"

"We are."

A cassette blasted when Fell started up the car. David Bowie. We drove, heading for where our lines crossed. The gulf between us was still so wide. Maybe I believed, now—that we could work, that what we added up to could survive in this world—but Fell did not. Fell still believed what Mrs. Tanzillo believed: that Fell was hell-bound, disgusting, deserving of nothing good. The miles inched past my window, closing in on the X on the map, and I had no words, no weapons to breach the wall between us.

And then: Fell did.

"Whatever you said to my mom? It really pissed her the fuck off."

"I am so sorry," I said. "It was selfish. I didn't think it through. What it might mean for you."

"No," Fell said, and turned onto Route 9. "I never saw her like that before. I went home and she didn't say a word to me. Like, at all. Except to say you stopped by. That never, ever happens. I don't know how, but what you said messed her up really bad."

"She—"

"No fucking way," Fell said, turning off the main road. "This can't be it."

We'd reached the spot on the map. We were stopped outside the Salvation Army. Where we'd met, a mere two weeks before.

"Nobody's broadcasting from here," they said.

We rolled down our windows. Snow fell harder now. Science fiction scenarios blurred in my brain. Time travel. Brain uploading.

"They'd need so much equipment," Fell said. "If we heard it on the other side of the river? They'd need a massive antenna, but there's nothing. And—"

Fell trailed off.

I looked up at the sky. Snow tap-tap-tapped at my forehead. I remembered what the star man said, the night before, to me and me alone. *Two soldiers trapped behind enemy lines.*

It was talking to me and Fell.

"The equipment's not here," I said. "Or, it's *here*, but it's not *now*."

Fell got out of the car. I turned up the radio and got out after them.

"I get it," I said, laughing, crying, comprehending. One wobbly crooked magnificent voice. "You were right, Fell. It's coming from the future."

We stood. Snow slowly outlined us.

"It's us," I said. Fell had finally infected me. The audacious, the impossible, was not only easy—it was our only way forward. "That machine voice? That's...you and me. Our two voices together, somehow. A consciousness made up of both of our minds."

Fell turned their head, hard, like they weren't listening, or were listening and not understanding, or understanding and not believing.

"Plural singular," I said. "We are the passenger."

"Plural singular," Fell said, snow falling into their perfect face, while David Bowie told us *let all the children boogie.*

They still didn't see, but that was okay. There would be time to tell Fell all of it. To say that there was so much to be afraid of—nuclear winter, ecological devastation, the death spasms of patriarchy. That the next fifty years would see unspeakable suffering. But we could survive it. Overcome it. Surmount the limits of our flesh and our mortality and our separateness. Combine into some new kind of thing, some wobbly magnificent machine who could crack the very fabric of time and space. We could send a signal back, into the past, a lonely sad staticky voice in the night, to tell the beautiful damaged kids we had been that the future would be as good as they had the courage to be.

The Hidden Language of Flowers

Laurel Beckley

"I SN'T THAT *PRETTY*?"

Edith turned, glowering at both the youth and the bouquet shoved against her register, a step away from the trash bin. Her green-stained hands continued working her pestle, churning rosemary, thyme, pink rose petals, cilantro, and a single droplet of belladonna with half a dash of water into a slushy, chunky goo.

"It doesn't look like one of yours, though," Katherine continued, oblivious to Edith's irritation. "Too...spiky? But so elegant. Very haute couture." She beamed at her pronunciation, face illuminating with a new realization. "Why, Miss Edith, do you have a *beau*?"

Edith's lips pinched together as she strained the solution through a stained square of cheese cloth. Liquid dripped sullenly into a glass bottle. One drop. Two drops. Three. All the way to seven. There. That would do. She twisted the cap on and placed it on the counter between them, eyebrow raised.

"Do you want your tincture or not?" There would be no speculation on her private life in her shop, not now, not ever.

The girl colored, and slid two crumpled dollars across the counter, parting with a week's pay slinging ice cream at Dutch Girl's for three months of assurance against pregnancy. Edith handed over the bottle with the instructions to consume a drop with her morning drink every day of the week of the coming waning moon.

Edith sighed as the youth left, shop door tinkling behind her. A cold, deep fury burned within Edith's chest as she took in the bouquet for the thousandth time that afternoon.

Rosemary sprigs showed *she* remembered. Accents of purple fountain grass spiked at random intervals, indicating this was the initial salvo. Purple columbine, out of season, displayed double resolution in this fight. And a purple focal point of autumn crocus signified nothing more than a spark of memory. When Edith tentatively touched one of the violet petals, she had been transported to a hazy farewell in a field of flowers that ended in a kiss and continued into decades-lasting silence and heartbreak.

Do you have a beau, Miss Edith?

The innocent question echoed throughout the half-empty shelves lining Bisbee's flower shop. It ricocheted across the remnants of the V-J victory bouquets—still fresh thanks to a little magic and water—and bounced into the near-empty register. It seemed to hover over the bouquet, directing Edith's attention and ire. Delicate petals wilted from the force of her glare, revealing the note—plain, cream paper fresh from Seattle and neatly folded in half—tucked between two sprigs of rosemary.

Two words were scrawled in precise cursive, hidden until seen by the intended recipient.

I'm back.

There was no accompanying signature save the lingering tingles of the reveal charm.

Alice LaVelle née Dolores Hartley remembered the last Friday of August.

Edith's fists clenched.

It wasn't enough for *her* to return to Cottage Grove after all these years of *nothing*, with a new name, a rich dead husband, fancy city manners, and big ideas. It wasn't enough for her to set up a rival flower shop practically overnight across the street from Edith's family-run store, in a town still recovering from the after-effects of the Depression and four long years of war rations and belt-tightening. It wasn't enough to peddle fantastical mutations of plants from Hawaii and New York City, to bring a sense of much-needed glamour and sophistication and freedom.

No. Dolores-turned-Alice opened her store on the last Friday of August, sent her assistant to Bisbee's armed with a loaded floral arrangement, and declared war.

Edith shoved the bouquet—purple vase and all—into the trash bin and locked the register. She didn't bother counting the till. Katherine's purchase had been the only one over the past week. The work day was effectively over, with all potential shoppers saving their money and attention for the new florist in town instead of Bisbee's. No one wanted the same flowers they'd seen throughout the war. Adding insult to injury, Edith had overheard a rumor at the grocer's that Mrs. LaVelle sold tinctures even more potent than hers.

The comment bit deeply.

Her *solutions* had resolved a lot of potential problems over the years. She was the best earth witch in Lane County, better even than her grandmother. Despite her rough manners and sharp tongue, she was discreet. She kept their secrets and only asked for discretion in return.

And how it was repaid.

The sky was overcast as she walked to her car, grey clouds hiding the brilliant blue of summer that was the Willamette Valley's greatest secret. She fumbled with her keys as the sky opened up, the first sprinkles hitting the top of her head and dampening her curls. Curse her for forgetting her hat today of all days.

It *always* rained the last Friday of August in Cottage Grove. Had ever since *that* last Friday, over twenty years ago. Damn reporter from the *Oregonian* had been in town just yesterday to write a piece on the meteorological phenomena.

"Edith?"

Edith's shoulders tensed. She knew that voice anywhere. The heel of Edith's sensible T-strap sandals crunched along the sidewalk as she turned to face her enemy.

Alice LaVelle stood just outside The Flower Shoppe,

hanging on the door like a circus monkey. "It *is* you! Did you get my bouquet? Oh, it has been *ages*."

It *hurt* looking at her, the bone-deep ache of a half-healed wound scraped anew. A white apron covered her linen purple suit dress and an amethyst ring sparkled on a silver chain about her neck. An autumn crocus and rosemary arrangement was shoved artfully into her lapel, mimicking that spiteful bouquet. She wore a ridiculous purple curvette and black half-veil that hit mid-cheekbone, revealing perfectly applied red lipstick.

The juxtaposition between Seattle high-fashion and Edith's faded floral rayon dress and limp hair was stark. Even the fresh coat of mint green paint on The Flower Shoppe's storefront poised the contrast next to Bisbee's faded brick facade. They represented new versus old—the triumphant reinvention and the worn-out workhorse.

Edith's teeth ground. "I got it."

"And?" Alice's eyes glinted through the veil.

"Message received." Edith opened the door to her car and threw herself inside. Her knuckles whitened as she flung the car into a wide turn, nearly t-boning Mr. Jefferson as he pulled out from the hardware store.

She didn't release her death grip on the wheel until she was well on the way to Hebron. Her tension eased further when she passed the last house of the tiny town and entered the tree line and the wards surrounding her house. Her driveway was empty, the dry packed dust growing dark brown speckles as the rain picked up, as if the cloud was her own personal rainstorm.

Her latest visitors had left that morning, scurrying into their car at the first light of dawn on their migration south to Los Angeles and a new beginning. They always arrived late in the night, bodies tensed and scared and aching with exhaustion. She gave them discretion and a safe harbor in a country filled with sundown laws and hatred, knowing it wasn't enough. It was never enough.

Edith leaned her head against the steering wheel, trying to find some sense of equilibrium, not wanting to bring her foul mood into her home. The engine of her Studebaker ticked in time to the rain pattering against the metal roof of the car. The rain turned from drizzle to downpour, droplets tinking harder, and the tan driveway transformed into mud.

It was time to go inside.

Edith scrounged about the passenger side for an old newspaper to cover her head as she scrambled the several steps across the dirt driveway and onto her porch.

There was a new sign shoved into the doorjamb; the paper crinkled as though it knew it was not welcome. It fluttered to the ground when she opened the door, joining a sad pile of wrinkled notices, all stamped with officious seals ranging from the Army Corps of Engineers to Lane County government to the mayor of Cottage Grove.

She took a deep breath. She would deal with *that* mess later. Tomorrow. Maybe the day after. Within a week, certainly. The eviction notices were a minor insult twirling within the greater swarm of anger brewing in her chest.

Another deep breath and she was through the tiny house, kicking off her shoes as she entered her true domain—her garden.

Tension melted, but resolve remained, along with bittersweet memories of two girls kissing on a field of purple flowers. A secret promise transformed into permanent silence and rejection.

Until now.

So Dolores-turned-Alice wanted a war, did she?

Edith's lips curved as she gathered her supplies, half-chuckling under her breath. Never enter a flower war with an earth witch, especially not when pride was on the line.

She'd send her own declaration of war.

There was only room for one witch in town, and that witch was *her*.

❖

ALICE SENT HER reply a month later, on September twenty-third.

The blue box sat at Bisbee's front step, and Edith would have stepped on it save she'd been watching her storefront for hexes for the past month. The box was decorated with purple and pink ribbons. Inside, wrapped in pink tissue paper, lay a corsage.

Edith retrieved her faded copy of *Interpreting Flowers* from its hiding place under the loose floorboard below the front counter.

Pink carnations. *I'll never forget.* Clearly, Alice remembered Edith's boldness so many years ago and wasn't going to let her forget it either.

A lavender rose. *Capriciousness.* There was no need to interpret that one. Pulsing intent roiled off that magically imbued flower, so thick Edith practically tasted it.

Blue hibiscus, grown out of season. *I agree.* Alice had accepted Edith's challenge and would go to extremes to win.

The message was all twisted into a corsage to wear the curse at the wrist and sent on a Sunday for extra insult.

Edith returned fire October eighth with a boutonniere hex of orange and yellow carnations for disdain, garnished with reversed red chrysanthemums for hatred, the stems wrapped with aloe to showcase her deep bitterness of Alice's long-past silent rejection. Pink ribbons dangled in pretty twists, because Edith might be engaged in a battle for the fate of her business and her life, but she wasn't a monster.

On October eleventh, Alice stepped out into a town hall meeting discussing the upcoming Christmas Bazaar wearing Edith's boutonniere on her lapel and bright red lipstick underneath her black veil. Subtly embroidered flowers matching the colors of the boutonniere lined the brim of her black pillbox. Her amethyst ring was nowhere in sight.

"Where'd you get those gorgeous flowers, Mrs. LaVelle?" was the question of the night, asked over and over as Alice smugly patted the flowers on her chest and invited everyone to a soiree at the Cottage Grove Hotel after the meeting. She'd arranged a private room, no doubt to further bind the gullible townspeople into doing whatever it was she had planned. Already the tendrils of a spell stretched and wove about them. A thin green vine reached toward Edith, and she slapped it away, garnering looks and whispers as the people she'd supported murmured over *poor, odd Edith.*

"Oh, just somewhere." Alice's glaze flicked to Edith as she continued to stroke those damn flowers like she had *won* something. And she had—she'd effectively stolen all business away from Bisbee's with her hocus pocus and scientifically mutated flowers and fancy citified self. She wore Edith's hex like it was a victory banner.

Edith could no longer take the insult lying down. "This town is not big enough for two florists, Dolores." Her voice echoed across the room, rebounding and bounding.

The mayor stopped preening over Alice's boutonniere. "What did you call our dear Mrs. LaVelle, Miss Bisbee?"

Mrs. Smith, the baker's wife, put a hand to her mouth at Edith's rudeness. Two other women—old classmates, but *who wasn't*—tittered in delight at a possible scandal. A couple soldiers wearing Army Engineer insignia paused mid-drink by the punchbowl, and honestly who had even invited them to a town hall meeting?

"Dolores," Edith repeated. Two spots of red burned on her cheeks. "That's her name. Not *Alice LaVelle*. You should remember her, Billy. She went to elementary school with us and moved the summer before sixth grade."

Eyes swiveled between Alice and Edith, trying to reconcile fashionable Alice LaVelle with vague memories of a skinned-kneed girl child who flitted like a ghost along the riverbank near her grandmother's house, catching frogs and playing in the mud instead of acting a lady. The girl Edith remembered, because she had been in the mud beside her.

Dolores laughed. "You misremember."

"I do not."

Unspoken between them, the accusation of foul spellcraft. Because it had to be a casting. Surely everyone remembered Dolores Hartley, even if they'd forgotten her long-deceased grandmother.

"So this town isn't big enough for the both of us?" There was something in Dolores' eyes, something in her expression

Edith couldn't decipher beyond a fierce hunger.

Edith's chin lifted. She would not back down. "You heard me."

The entire town—and the entire green-clad complement of 2-162's headquarters and headquarters company—seemed to have packed into the high school gymnasium for this meeting, and they were now silent, hanging on each word. The vines of Alice's spell continued to stretch and bind, weave and coax.

Whispers rose between the tendrils of magic as the two women faced off.

Whispers Edith had heard her entire life but ignored because that's what it took to survive in this town—just as her mother and her grandmother and her great-grandmother had endured, stretching all the way back to the first white settlers in this small pocket of the Willamette Valley. Her hands clenched into fists.

"Well, we'll have no bickering among hens here," the mayor said. He eyed Edith up and down, warning her into silence. "This is a triumphant autumn. A return to normalcy and a chance to let our town grow. A time to welcome our heroes back from the war!"

"I don't know what normalcy we want to fall back to," Dolores murmured. Somehow, they'd drifted until they were an arms-length apart. The cloying scent of Tabu by Dana tickled Edith's nose with top notes of orange and coriander, while the middle notes of ylang-ylang and jasmine reminded her of the dangers of getting close to Dolores Hartley turned Alice LaVelle.

"The one where you *stay* gone," Edith snapped.

"Now, now, ladies." The mayor waved his hands to lower their antagonism. "How about a contest to settle this little spat?"

"What kind of contest?" Edith locked eyes with Alice, daring her to mention their *other* history, to reveal her deepest, darkest secret.

"Why, a friendly flower contest." The mayor flushed, clearly warming to the idea. "It'll be held during our Christmas Bazaar—see our talented florists and celebrate the birth of Christ and American might. We won the war, and we'll beat that rival Christmas celebration in Eugene. Exercise your creativity, ladies."

Dolores pursed her lips. "All contests have stakes."

Just like the one she'd shoved into Edith's heart, and now, her livelihood. The woman could not stop hurting her.

"I win, you leave town." Edith crossed her arms.

"Now, Edith, I'm sure Mrs. LaVelle didn't come to our fair town to push you out of it," the mayor said. "There's room for two."

Dolores ignored the mayor, her focus on her enemy. "And if I win?"

Edith grit out, "Then I leave."

"Ladies, this is just a friendly competition," the mayor said. "No one actually has to go anywhere. Edith, I'm sure people still love your little bouquets."

Something glittered in Dolores' eyes. Her smile faltered and she batted her lashes quickly before turning toward the mayor, her smile set once again in demure pleasantry. "It's a deal. I win, she leaves. She wins, I leave."

"Perfect." Edith spun on her heel and stormed out of the hall. Townspeople, folks she'd grown up with, gone to school with, sweated through the Depression and the War and made sacrifices alongside, healed and birthed and laid to rest and everything in between, stepped out of her way, their noses upturned in disgust.

She didn't need them.

She had never needed them.

But they had always needed her, even if they hated to admit it—even if they could never admit it bound as they were by the vines of Dolores' spell.

"Edith..." The word wafted after her, whispered from Dolores' lips and swallowed by the clouds breaking over Edith's shoulders.

❖

EDITH WOULD SHOW them just how much she was a part of this town, how deep her roots grew.

Dolores left them all and came back with her big city ideas and fashionable notions and pretty dresses and exotic flowers and a new name, just like her wild great-aunt Opal. She'd traveled the world and returned to town with a score to settle.

Edith *was* the town.

She was Oregon and Cottage Grove and Lane County. Her family had been there from the beginning of the pioneers colonizing the land of the Winefelly peoples. Her family had spoken Chinook jargon, married magics among the Douglas Firs, sung for gold in the Cascades, battled the rising winter floods along the Coast Fork, healed where they could even as the peoples native to this land were driven from it—hidden folk caught in the middle of a sundown county at dusk.

Her mother and her mother before and her mother before that and on and on had sunk their lives into this part of the Willamette Valley, had stood strong despite the rumors and the side-eyed glances at the long line of unmarried women of sin who refused to step into a church on Sunday. They had survived flood and famine and sickness and ignorance and heartbreak.

She would not be the one who ended that legacy.

But as the leaves on the deciduous trees changed color and fell, leaving the great firs standing tall and green and alone against a gray sky, business shifted almost entirely to The Flower Shoppe. Townsfolk gasped over tropical ice blue calathea, tittered over the scandalous orchids resembling women's secrets, and oohed over the marvelous widow's tragically fashionable self. Dolores ate up the attention, wearing a rotating display of black suits nipped in at the waist and black veils to mourn the husband lost at Iwo Jima.

After two weeks of no sales and no visitors, Edith rotated Bisbee's sign to closed—not for the first time in recent years—with a note of her grand reopening on New Year's Day, and focused on her plan.

She gathered cow parsnip and cat tail from the Row River.

She snuck into the Army Corps of Engineer's construction site under a full moon and stole mud from the base of Cottage Drove Dam.

In the middle of November, she received a simple pot of white, blue, and pink flowering cacti from her enemy. The thorns were prominent. One pricked her, sending three droplets of blood into the sandy soil.

She sent back a tin of chamomile to show her patience in the face of adversity.

She found trilliums blooming months ahead of season by following a deer trail to a hidden grove deep among the Douglas Firs along the Coast Fork.

She stole warped boards from Dr. Pierce's Pleasant Pellets barn.

She drove south, along the Umpqua River in rain so heavy she could hardly see out the windshield, walked through miles of old growth and wet ferns, and scrambled down boulders and over fallen logs to gather water from the base of Toketee.

A single poppy on her doorstep marked December first.

Edith did not respond.

She continued her trek, driving along winding switchbacks until she arrived at the vast blue of Crater Lake. She dug through the accumulating snow two miles from the lodge and collected five orange-red rocks. In between two boulders facing Wizard Island, she found a lone white skyrocket. She left it there. It was just the one, after all.

She went north, collecting moss from an old-growth forest in the foothills of the Coastal Range near Lorane, ferns from the old Bohemian Mining site, and lichen from the Oregon white oak behind the elementary school playground.

By the Christmas Bazaar, she had assembled her creation and bartered her prized blackberry pies for the use of her neighbor Henry's truck to transport it through the drizzling rain into the Armory, newly converted into a winter wonderland by eager high schoolers and young soldiers fresh from Europe.

Two seniors in varsity sweaters helped maneuver her triumph into place. They stayed, curious, as she gently peeled away the protective covering. Their jaws dropped, and she smiled. She dared Dolores try to beat this.

The mayor had opened up the contest to whoever wanted to participate, but only one other booth in this corner of the gym was occupied, its offering covered with a battered military canvas, a single cream card tucked into its folds.

Slowly, the gym filled with revelers. Edith waited behind her booth, fingers tapping. The judging would end at seven, the prize a ten-dollar check donated by the grocery store.

She ignored the townsfolk oohing and aahing, their appreciative nods.

Edith wanted their respect, but she hadn't made this for *them*.

She had poured her heart and soul, her anger and bitterness, her love and everything else she possessed, into her floral arrangement. Her flowers and findings woven into her most powerful hex of binding and warding and banishing all twisted into the shape of a covered bridge—just like the many dotting the landscape of her town.

Her finger tapping increased to leg bouncing as the night drew on, as the clock on the wall ticked toward seven and the official judgment of the contest.

Dolores didn't show.

Her booth remained bare, with just that canvas covered lump and that blank card crying for attention. Edith knew it meant her spell had worked, but dammit the woman was a witch and the spell didn't go into effect until moonrise anyways.

At 6:55 p.m. Edith could take it no longer.

She pushed past the admirers, strode over to Dolores' booth and whipped away the canvas.

A simple heart formed from blue roses lay on the wooden surface.

Soft gasps of disappointment came from the crowd, who obviously thought the impossible petals had been dyed instead of perfected over time, crafted with science and magic and patience. At a distance it was so simple compared to the complex masterpiece of Edith's perfectly created covered bridge pulled from natural elements. But up close, the edges of the petals darkened to a brilliant purple.

Edith stared, shaking her head. Before the heart lay a parchment-covered square bound in twine. Her name was written in the upper left corner. She unwrapped the twine and removed the parchment, revealing a book titled, *The Language of Flowers*. Many of the pages were folded over.

There was no accompanying note.

Edith's jaw worked. *What could it mean?*

Outside of her daze, the mayor announced Edith's win and wondered aloud where Mrs. LaVelle was. Edith ignored him, scrambling about for the note that had fluttered to the floor when she'd removed the canvas.

There had to be *something*. There had to be an answer, a key, *something*.

She found the note, fallen into a corner and half hidden. Her hands shook as she unfolded the card.

You win.

No. Not like this.

She needed a battle, a dramatic showdown, a great *triumph* to show Dolores that *she* belonged here, that she was in the right, that she should never have been abandoned like that, not after revealing her most secret self to the person she loved over all others and continued to love even with her heart broken into a million lost promises.

She flipped through the book, searching for answers, and turned to the first dog-eared page.

Rosemary: a sign of memory and remembrance. Can be used for tinctures and potions to pull away the memory of pain and induce healing. In floral arrangements, indicates remembrance of happier times.

Handwritten in the margins, next to the accompanying illustration of the herb: *You might not remember the field of crocuses where we kissed before I left for Seattle that summer, but I did. I never forgot you.*

Edith shook her head. She flipped to the next folded corner.

Purple Columbine: resolution of intent.

"No, no, no," she whispered, heart sinking as she scanned the note.

I came back to show you all I had learned. That I was worthy of you, my beloved witchling. My resolve is so strong I grew these out of season. They bloomed from yearning.

Her world was ending.

All preconceptions shattered.

History was overwritten.

The next page was a blank buffer separating chapters and covered in handwritten annotations. Unlike the other three pages, this one had been written long before, the pen strokes faded. Alice's notes to herself as she planned the second arrangement, the corsage sent on September twenty-third.

Carnations—because they're pretty, and even though they are standard they have set meaning. Pink to show that I will never forget her. Roses are the signs of love, with lavender petals because this is the love that was my first, despite lavender roses being the most fickle to develop and first love being so difficult to continue or overcome. Blue hibiscus for delicate beauty, and out of season as we had to hide our feelings for so long. But no longer. It needs to be something dramatic, something to show her I am no longer scared and will no longer hide. Something to wear, perhaps? To let the world know? A corsage, to wear my feelings on her sleeve. Perfect.

"No."

She had had it all wrong.

All wrong.

So, so wrong.

A tear hit the page, smearing the last word.

Perfect vanished into nothing but the suggestion of ink on paper. The wound that had festered so long inside Edith bled anew, for the loss of what had been before her this entire time. What she could not see was now gone, banished due to her own arrogance.

She clutched the book to her chest.

"Edith, are you—"

She pushed the person away and fled toward the door, ignoring the well-wishers, the mayor, and everyone else who had held her apart for so long.

Rain cascaded as she burst into the parking lot, changing from a drizzle into a torrential downpour that soaked through and chilled her to the bone. She tucked the book underneath her sweater to protect it and ran. She had to know. She had to find Alice.

The streets were deserted, everyone at the Armory, as she raced through Main Street toward the river and their stores.

The Flower Shoppe was dark.

She still ran to the door, tugging and pulling at the handle. It didn't budge. Everything closed so early in December, and today all shops had locked their doors to prepare for the Bazaar. She slapped her hand against the pane, trying to get someone's, *anyone's*, attention.

"Dolores!"

Edith pressed her face to the glass, struggling to see inside. The shop was empty.

Not the emptiness of a closed store, but barren, stripped of everything that had made it a flower shop in the first place.

"Dolores, answer me! I know you're in there. You have to be in there."

Magic tingled at Edith's fingertips, the tinges of the spell she had cast in her covered bridge creation. The biggest mistake she had ever made.

"Alice..." The grief she had crammed down over the years took over. Her knees buckled and she fell to the ground, pressing herself against the door as if she could melt into the shop, could find her in the bare floorboards, capture her essence in the lingering scent of lavender and lemon.

The rain fell forever into the night, swelling the river with her heartbreak. She curled her knees up to her chest and rested her head, back pressed against the empty shop, rear growing cold and wet from the sidewalk.

"I must say, this is a new low for you."

Sniffling, Edith looked up.

Dolores stood several steps away, an umbrella clutched in both hands. She was dry and beautiful and *there*, impossibly there.

Edith blinked.

"Well, are you going to just sit there wallowing in misery?" In the dimness of the streetlights, a corner of Dolores's red-painted mouth quirked up. "You won."

Edith rose to her feet, shaky and bewildered. "But I banished you."

Dolores snorted. "Please. You never were any good at hexes."

Edith rushed forward and wrapped her arms around Dolores.

"I see you got my note. I had a feeling some things were lost in translation with the flowers." Dolores pressed her forehead against Edith's, sobering. "I'm sorry," she whispered, cupping Edith's cheek with a bare hand, "it took me so long to come back."

They stared at each other as the rain pattered down on the umbrella, lost in a cocoon of warmth and shelter. The hurt of the years, the completely misinterpreted declaration of war and the battle of the flowers, the different language of flowers books, the contest, everything was just too much and too miniscule.

"I'm so, so sorry. I didn't—"

"Just kiss me. I've been waiting long enough. We can work out everything else afterwards."

She did.

And they did.

The Art and Mystery of Thea Wells

ALEXANDRA SEIDEL

T HE INTEREST IN Thea Wells even outside of the circle
of art lovers and connoisseurs remains strong, and
conclusions about her work range from the normal,
technical approach of art critics to the downright strange
explanations of the ardent believers in the paranormal. To
give a brief overview of her art, it does not do to linger too
much on either end of this spectrum. Instead, a few key
paintings of Wells may be seen as markers of her arc as
an artist, of where she started, of where she ended. These
paintings also show the overlap between the mundane and
those who seek the supernatural in Wells's work. Other
pieces, such as *Watercolor of an Ash Tree* or *Sketch of a Cityscape
from the Ledge* may have sold for five figures, but they never
wove that aura of mystery around themselves.

The evolution of Thea Wells's skill does not just lie in the
brushstrokes and her increased mastery of light and shadow,
but also in how she approaches her subject. Most art critics
agree on this, and they will point to *Shadows of Winged Insects
Before a Flame* or *Breath, from the Inside*. Her skill is best savored
through select prints of her work, viewed in chronological
order. The prints, while they allow paintings scattered in
museums and hidden away in private collections all over

the world to be seen next to one another, do not convey the vibrancy of the originals and the enchanting quality that makes people stand in front of a Wells and examine it, sometimes for hours.

❖

Féli in Nightgown

This is the earliest painting that shows Wells's lover Félicity M in the classic odalisque pose. Even to this day, no one was able to find out what this elusive muse's real last name was, where she came from, how she and Wells met. She would usually introduce herself without giving any further details about herself, brushing off curiosities in a polite and joking manner.

In the painting, Féli looks away. She reclines on a lavender colored ottoman, and looks at the observer with her green eyes half closed. Her phone is on a cushion on the floor, her left hand just hovering over the screen.

The door to a balcony is open in the background, and light spills in on a gust of wind that stirs the curtains.

Wells took great care to let us know what we can't see under the nightgown. Féli's breasts are delicately outlined against the thin, silky fabric, and the strands of dark hair that run over them reveal more than they cover. Her waist lets the nightgown flow like cream, and the long legs, though they are covered, are tensed as if in pleasure.

Notably, this painting was Wells's breakthrough. Ever since it went on display it has been targeted by thieves— though thankfully none have succeeded.

❖

The Masque

The Masque was painted perhaps a year after *Féli in Nightgown* at a time when Wells had made it big in the art world, when her paintings were fetching five or six figures (though only the works painted after *Féli in Nightgown*. Her paintings prior to this are a completely different style, and they lack the later works' pull.)

The Masque not surprisingly shows a masquerade, but Féli is the only guest, repeated nine times in nine different costumes.

She is an emerald-feathered bird with beak mask, a golden shimmering queen, a harlequin in chequered dress that shows her smooth skin generously.

As a ballerina, her legs are elongated by pointe shoes, she captivates with khol-lined eyes as a mystic with a custard pale snake draped over her shoulders and scales held in on hand, and enchants as a fairy princess with a necklace of black beads coiled around her neck.

Dressed in a robe of stars, she is the night, and with a milky sunrise costume that begins to let Wells's light and dark mastery show, she is the day.

The ninth costume is unusual. It is hidden in the back, near a curtain and the darkness at the edges of the painted room. Féli is wrapped in a dark robe, a dark hood, and a white mask covers her entire face. She holds a book in the crook of her left arm, and we cannot see much of the volume, except that it appears heavy and old. The mask seems to follow the onlooker. It is a haunting shape, and it could be someone else entirely watching the scene unfold and the observer alike but for the pale hand that reaches up as if to pull back the black hood. It is a woman's hand, and it looks like that of Féli hovering over her phone in *Féli in Nightgown*.

The Masque was first owned by a museum, but not for long. A private collector acquired it, and some sources have come forward over the years to claim the museum sold the piece because the people handling it, the people working in the museum and walking past it every day, suffered nightmares in which a hooded shape wearing a white mask featured prominently. The veracity of these claims is doubtful, even if Internet forums are full of stories of people who say they saw *The Masque* on display and also had the dreams.

❖

Sunbathing

This is a captivating piece that attracts crowds, so much so that museum authorities decided to keep the painting in its own room and allow visitors in only in groups, each group being allowed just thirty minutes with the painting.

Sunbathing is, at first glance, quaint. It was painted probably less than a month after the completion of *The Masque*. Féli is the very center of this painting. She sits, cross-legged, on a green and white beach towel, sand and beach grasses around her, the ocean a distant haze of blues in the background. She smiles. It is a very subdued smile and has been likened more than once to that of da Vinci's *Mona Lisa*. Féli is wearing a black bathing suit. The color is harsh against the pastels of the towel and the beach, but her green eyes are sharper still as they look outward, to the observer.

A bag by Féli's left knee spills over with things people do not normally take to the beach. There are old-fashioned metal scales, beads bound on a string, a mechanical music box. The strangest thing entirely about this painting, however, is the tome that lies open on Féli's lap, big and old, its pages possibly parchment, bound in leather. It pulls one back immediately to the book the dark figure cradles in her arm in *The Masque*. Experts have studied the open page. It is covered in the same script that has baffled scholars in the Voynich Manuscript for decades, and just like that enigma, what can be seen of Féli's book remains untranslated and not understood. The book was not among Wells's possessions, and it might be entirely a figment of the painter's imagination.

❖

The Diners

This painting is seen as the first sign in Wells's art that her relationship with Féli was coming undone. It is dated to almost two years after *The Masque* and *Sunbathing*, and experts have long speculated that there must have been other paintings of Féli between these two. Whether they remain in private collections, tucked away from the eyes of the world, or whether Wells herself destroyed them is uncertain but a matter of great debate.

In *The Diners*, Féli is seen having dinner with a stranger. The table is elaborately set, there are glasses one behind the other, and they twist and reflect the room, the table, the food; more than one enthusiast has found hidden symbolism here, like messages glimpsed in a crystal ball.

Red flowers spill their petals on the white tablecloth and the pinkish bloody meat served on a silver platter. Féli's guest is a man of supreme beauty. He outshines Féli entirely. His hair is dark like hers, as are his eyes, but his lips are flushed with color. Between the two, on the white tablecloth and hidden behind the glasses and the wilting flowers, there is the book again, now closed, and Féli's guest has his palm flat on the cover, fingers splayed. Neither Féli nor he spare the book any more attention than that; they are focused on each other.

They are leaning in close, caught in conversation. Underneath the table, Féli's hand is resting high on the stranger's thigh, and his free hand vanishes under her dress. There is much speculation as to whether this really happened, or whether it was some sort of vengeance, whether Wells put this scene on canvas for all eternity to see Féli as unfaithful. No one knows who the stranger is, and the painting was sold to an unknown buyer at an auction ten years ago.

❖

THE CHEF

THIS SHOWS WELLS's mastery of light and dark. Féli has her back turned and stands in Wells's kitchen over pots and pans bubbling on the stove. She is wearing a figure-hugging dress, long and black, and her shadow can be seen on the floor, stretching beyond where the canvas ends.

The light in the kitchen appears ephemeral, there is no source for it, no lamp, and no window. On Féli's left, ingredients wait to be tossed into the pots, onions and carrots peeled and chopped, chunks of glistening, bloody meat in a dish, the legs and head of a rooster.

Féli has a dark teal vial in her left hand. It could be an oil or spice. She is about to pour it into a pot.

Her hair is coiled and piled on top of her head, and strands spill out like Medusa's serpents.

After *The Chef*, Wells's erstwhile prolific nature changed; she became even more of a recluse and produced only two paintings to sell, though it is speculated these were older works from her private collection. Several dozen unfinished paintings begun after *The Chef* all show Féli, though they fail to move beyond a mere sketch.

The Chef was loaned to a gala opening at one point, for a single evening. There are reliable sources saying that all the meat dishes served at that opening were spoilt and inedible. Yet, the food had been freshly prepared on that very day. While meat going bad can be more likely attributed to other factors such as temperature and improper handling, some blame the painting for it.

❖

THE FINALE

THE FINALE IS the title given to this painting by curators. Some call it *The Last* or even *The Omega*. Wells herself never gave it a name.

This painting was discovered in Wells's atelier along with her corpse, though the date of its completion is uncertain. The painting is large, ten by seven feet, and it seems to be a riddle inside a riddle inside a riddle.

It shows a circus ring, and many things are happening there at once.

One of the first things that we see is the book, the big tome Wells so often added when she painted Féli. It is once again being held by a figure in black, robed and hooded, wearing a white mask. This time, the hooded figure reminds us of *The Masque*, but appears decidedly male and is looking toward the center of the ring. In his arms, the book is open. He holds up one finger as if he were reading from it and commanding the listener's attention. We also see Féli opposite the robed figure. She is dressed like a belly dancer. Most of her skin is visible. Snakes wreathe and slither around her body, her waist, her breasts and ankles, and the expression on her face is one of boundless joy and ecstasy.

A white tablecloth catches the light in the background. It is set on the ground almost as if for a picnic, though plates and silverware and glasses indicate something more elaborate. There is wine in one of the glasses and a pinkish shimmer on one of the plates. The teal vial from *The Chef* sits on the tablecloth, unstoppered, though whether it is full or empty, we cannot see. Apart from that, there is no food.

Seemingly random items are scattered on the ground. Black beads are spilled like breadcrumbs, and paper has been torn and strewn alongside them, old paper with traces of writing on it that has, unsurprisingly, prompted unsuccessful efforts to reassemble the torn pieces seen in the painting and decipher their meaning. Other things we are shown are the tools of Wells's trade: brushes, paints, all strewn haphazardly, including one canvas that has fallen face down so that we cannot say what painting it is. Another item that has caused speculation is an envelope. On it there is once more the indecipherable writing from the Voynich Manuscript, and we are left to wonder what message it contains.

In the center of the ring, drawn in shadows, is Wells herself, dressed in red and gold as the ringmaster. She is facedown, and her pale brown hair scatters in the puddle of blood under her. All of the fingers in her right hand stand at odd angles, broken. Her costume bears traces of paint, and it is torn in places. The violence is tangible.

An urban legend surrounds this painting, which is now housed in the Thea Wells Museum after it spent long years in police evidence. The legend says, when you focus your gaze on the figure in black who is reading from the book, you will dream and the dream will have no color at all. You will find yourself in perfect blackness, and there will be music around you as if heard from a distance, carnival music that echoes strangely distant and metallic, as if it echoed from an old music box.

❖

THAT LAST, UNTITLED painting is disturbing. It becomes even more so when viewed side by side with the photographs taken by the police of the scene they found in Wells's atelier, or at least those that were leaked following her death. While those crime scene photos say nothing about Wells as a painter, they bear mentioning because they seem to echo *The Finale*. Wells can be seen facedown in her own blood. In reality, Wells wore a simple red shirt and no costume, but the tears in the fabric, as far as visible in the photographs, match up with the tears we see on the ringmaster's costume in the painting. Wells's blood has dried to a dull maroon, not the scarlet seen on the canvas. She was cut and bruised, her right hand— the hand she painted with—revealed to have been broken extensively.

Wells had been attacked. In the police report, leaked shortly after the photographs, one officer said they had only ever seen wounds like that in the mountains, when a bear found a hiker and took them down with claws and teeth. No wild animals were reported in the area of Wells's residence, and no other signs of them were found in Wells's atelier.

One thing that is different in reality is the negative of a shape in the dried puddle of Wells's blood. It appears as if something large and rectangular was there when Wells bled out. When she was found, it had been removed. Some claim it was the tome, that leatherbound strangeness, that kept the floor clean where it lay because it drank all the blood that touched it.

Thea Wells's murder remains unsolved.

Féli has never been seen again, not even at Wells's funeral. However, if you look closely at all the photographs taken of that event, you will see a figure among the celebrities and pedigreed royals who have come to say farewell to a genius artist who defined a generation. The figure is in only one or two photos, and they seem to be wearing a long, dark robe. While their face is shadow-wrapped, it appears pale, smooth, mask-like. It could just be one of the mourners, seen from an odd angle with unfavorable lighting. Or not.

The question of the dark man, Féli's alleged lover, also remains. When *The Diners* first sold—minutes after it was hung in the gallery—people asked Wells about him. Wells refused to say anything about the painting or its subjects, having become eccentric and like a modern-day hermit by that time already.

To this day, Wells's paintings attract not just art-lovers and historians but also believers in the supernatural. The police are regularly called to Wells's grave to break up séances held by self-proclaimed mediums and their congregations.

Féli remains a mystery as well. Yet, one art historian has told this author, in confidence and on the condition that their name not appear in this article, that they have seen Féli, her face, her dark hair and green eyes, her uncannily pale skin and distinctive features. The historian found her on another canvas, which cannot be clearly attributed to an artist. Yet, that canvas was confidently dated to more than 300 years ago. It is the portrait of a seated woman who looks exactly like Wells's Féli. Far in the background, one can just make out the sinking bulges of a circus tent, a harlequin in their chequered dress walking inside through the flap. This painting's basis in reality, just like its creator, is not clear. How it managed to capture the woman that appears in Wells's paintings 300 years later, is unknown.

To Rest and to Create

L.A. Knight

F YOU DON'T disclose, you can't ask for accommodation...

We understand things are difficult, but these accommodations just aren't reasonable...

We're sorry, you're just not the right fit for this company...

There are so many ways to say the same thing. So many ways to lie so very sweetly and tell me that of course the company doesn't mind hiring a disabled autistic person, *of course* they encourage a diverse work environment, *of course* they're accessible.

If I close my eyes, the rain slides cool caresses down my neck like streaks of ultramarine chill and kisses my nose with little fizzes of celestine blue. I want to let it cover me in cobalt and forget the list of potential employers on my phone's Notes app. I want to pretend I'm not stuck in this hell-world of mundane misery and not even a shred of magic.

But I missed the magic window, or rather the magic Door. I'm in my thirties. Chosen Ones are chosen a lot younger than that to go through the Doors, the magical portals that take a good chunk of the population to places unknown. There have been studies. Some speculate that as many as one in three people end up going through a Door, most of them before they're even twenty. They go on to be saviors of worlds beyond this mundane one, or tyrants, or ordinary citizens but in places so far beyond the scope of our birthplace that it's just as extraordinary as being the hero or the despot.

Sometimes they come back. Sometimes they're kicked out. Sometimes they stay.

Sometimes they die.

But I missed the window, so instead of popping off through a portal to go save the magical world of my heart, I flinch from the shriek of car horns slamming down the street, the cacophony of water crashing on fiberglass rooftops.

The scream of the city bus's brakes chases me away from the bus stop. I hunch and walk. I can't walk long. My breath hitches, shallow and sharp in my throat. My pulse trips over itself like a clumsy dog, the disease stealing the oxygen right out of my blood.

But I don't know what else to do but walk until my temples press tight as a patch of sunburn and my toes tingle with the faintest edges of numbness. *Not enough air.* The warning whimpers through my spasming solar plexus. I have to sit down soon, stop before I kiss pavement and taste blood I can't afford to lose. Walk away from the advice, the lies, the two-faced backstabbing bullshit because I'm *unreasonable*.

In job interviews, they notice the eye contact first, always. I don't stim beyond a lick of my tongue over back molars to help me remember the taste and feel of pastel crystal beads on strings of transparent plastic lace sparkling with glitter, the click of them against my teeth. That, allistics don't pay attention to. They don't understand the tightness around my mouth when I try not to wince every time a phone shrills. They don't see the agony behind my gritted smile because the fluorescents sting like saltwater, like lemon juice, like acid.

No, it's my eyes the interviewers notice as soon as I sit down on the other side of their shiny desk. My refusal to offer them unearned intimacy, the lack of consent for their invasion, my attempt to avoid another blowtorch melting one of my metaphorical spoons to slag. And it's always downhill from there.

It doesn't help that everything about me screams *threat*! to them: the dark curling clouds of my hair, looser than my sister's but tighter than my brother's, the way my fake smile shows teeth like bleached ivory against the golden brown of my skin, the broadness of my nose.

They don't care about the way Mommy used to take hours to pick through my curls every wash day so she didn't snag because I was so tenderheaded, or the money Dad paid out of railroad retirement and his military pension to give me nice teeth after oral stimming gave me an open bite, or how my friends love the way I scrunch up my nose like Samantha from *Bewitched* when I'm thinking out nefarious schemes for pizza. The people behind the desks just see nappy hair, dark skin, big nose. They see the blood-red checkmark squatting next to *Are you disabled?* and the words "autistic" and "chronically ill" carved into the line demanding I explain what the hell is wrong with me, why aren't I normal.

And no, apparently they can't let me cashier from a chair to avoid passing out and no, of course they can't let me record team meetings on my voice-to-text recorder so I can keep accurate notes and what am I, some kind of baby snowflake Millennial? Of course I can't wear ear protectors; this is a place of business, not a construction zone or a Nightwish concert.

Always *no, no, no. No you can't have this. No you can't do this. No I won't explain this to you, you little freak. Use actual words. Stop taking so long, just spit it out. No you can't write it down, no you can't use an app, just talk. Why are you getting so angry, anyway? Geez, you people. That explains why you couldn't hack the Choosing.*

Like they can just tell, by looking at me, every second of every day of my life until now and it's a short, shitty write-up.

It's a pandemic. I'm immunocompromised. I'm chronically ill. The world is trying to kill us all but it's trying to kill me extra fast because I'm just special and lucky, I guess. And if I don't get another fucking job, there won't be anything in my stomach to hurl when I push my body too far. Going hungry will be the least of my problems. Where will I live? What about my cats?

Sickly green and purple sparkles dance along the edges of my vision and I trip over air and numb feet. Crap. Too far, too hard. Sit down. Have to sit down. I do, but my brain says, *No, not enough.* Have to lie down. Can't sit. Not enough to stop pain, weakness, nausea. Find a flat place. Here. Sidewalk. No trash. Bag on the ground, under my shoulders. Chin tipped up, head back. My heart higher than my brain.

My body is made of television static. Can't feel my hands, my feet, my face. Everything is dove-gray with bursts of aurora borealis. Tingles and gasping. Just breathe and it'll pass. Huge gulping breaths. Breathe, pass. Breathe, pass.

Breathe. Breathe. Breathe.

Gray. This will be over pretty soon and then I'll get up and go home and cuddle my cats and see if my landlord hates me enough to refuse a few more days' extension.

I close my eyes.

◈

THE WORLD IS white.

It shouldn't be, though. I was outside, in the rain, on the sidewalk, getting wet, trying not to faint. Everything should be stormy mistral-gray velvet overhead, and rain-slick slate-blue underneath, and the glowy pumpkin orange-gold of streetlights, and the yellow-green of the palo verde trees that line most of the major streets and vomit their gorgeous acid-yellow pollen everywhere.

I sit up on a soft white couch. Do a quick mental check: clothes on, glasses on, no pain, no numbness, and I don't feel like my stomach wants to claw its way up my throat and spill on the floor. But my feet are cold; no shoes. Where are my shoes? Where's my stuff?

Oh shit, oh shit, oh shit.

My bag slumps on the floor in front of the couch by my black Vans. Instant relief. I know Vans are shit for arch support but I've had this pair for seven years, and I'll wear them until they're shreds. I'm glad to see them sitting scuffed and shedding threads where the canvas has scraped open. I don't even try to stand before I snatch my shoes up and stuff them on my feet, double-knot my laces. The cold, cramping my toes through my socks, starts to fade as reassuring pressure squeezes around my feet. Some of the sensory panic eases. Now I can look around without needing to yank my hair or rock until I fall off the edge of the velvety couch.

The main carpet is voidling-black but the rug by the couch is bright, childlike blue. My wobbly legs drop me onto it when I try to stand up, and I just lie there for a long time, rubbing my cheek against it.

Fur? Velvet? Cookie Monster pelt? Who the hell cares? I can't get up yet; still too weak from almost fainting. For now my choices are blacking out or the rug.

Everything quiets as the blue smooths over my cheek and I fall into it. My eyes flutter shut and I'm in a world of towering trees as thick as skyscrapers, bark the color of ocean on a night with only stars and St. Elmo's fire, broad leaves as bright as lapis lazuli and furred with silver. Dried golden leaves underfoot shush so softly it doesn't even hurt to hear it when I take a step. The light is cool and dusky violet and the air is sweet as winter melon and this place is beautiful, nothing hurts here, I want it, I want it—

My eyes snap open as a voice murmurs with impossible gentleness, "Very good. You found the second world without even having to search. You're exactly what we've been looking for."

Xe stands there, watching me without trying to catch my eye. Locs down xyr back like ropes of burnished copper sway gently when xe turns, making sure I know xe isn't trying to get me to make eye contact. It's a relief strong enough to gut-punch. I look at xyr mouth, wide and full as mine but dark as plum wine. Xe smiles, and it's as gentle as xyr voice. Somehow, just by looking at the dangling silver chains tipped in crystallized stars glittering from xyr ears and the opal-and-void-shard labret through xyr lower lip, just by admiring the long swish of xyr silver gauchos and the generous curves of xyr belly and breasts and shoulders and arms, hugged by a shimmering midnight rainbow of silk from a world I've never seen, I know what xe is. Who xe is.

"Holy shit, this is a House of Choosing."

A House of Choosing. The places between worlds where Chosen Ones go to find the Doors that lead them to the worlds where they belong. I'm supposed to be too old, too worn out, too tired for this. I am tired. *Always* tired. I was tired back when I was still young enough to be Chosen, too tired to cry or scream or do anything but curl up like a snail in my blanket-tent at home, and try not to shake apart after all my teachers refused to write me recommendation letters so I could take the first set of Choosing Tests. Before my blood got sick and before my brain learned words like *depression* and *PTSD*. Even before all that, I hadn't been allowed to even try to get here and go through the full set of Tests.

But I'm here now.

Xe grins, a flash of teeth just a little too sharp and suddenly I can't breathe. It's not my oxygen-starved blood trying to choke me out again, not the screaming agony of a meltdown barreling down on my brain like a homicidal freight train.

It's hope.

A pure, impossible pearl of it hanging in front of me like the pomegranate in front of a desperate Persephone, trying to escape every mundane crap thing about her old life. I've wanted to escape my birth world most of my life. The shrieking noise and agonizing smears of color and everything too bright and loud and painful. The repetition of *not enough, loser, freak*. I've wanted to just get *away* as long as I can remember and now I can, I can *escape*.

But...

But wanting to get *away* from somewhere is not the same as wanting to go somewhere else. When I was a kid, I didn't think about that. I just wanted to get away, somewhere I could be accepted and happy. Now, though...

"I don't want to Choose a world," I blurt out.

Because I don't. I don't know what would happen, if I can be enough for another world. If my story would be tragic and terrible or deadly and delicious or happy and humble. There are too many variables and I'm not a computer, dammit. I hate not knowing what will happen and I don't want to have to worry about things. I'm so tired of having to worry all the damn *time* about all the things that I don't know, an entire *world* of *things*.

Maybe this is why people aren't usually Chosen past twenty or so. We're all too exhausted and anxiety-riddled? Too afraid of the other shoe readying to drop? Too terrified of everything going to absolute shit right when we start to feel secure?

But I need a job. If I can't get work, I can't pay rent. If I Choose another world, maybe I won't have to pay rent.

Maybe I will have to pay rent because the world I go to is basically just as shit as this one. Or maybe I don't have to pay rent, but in exchange I'm sacrificed to a Dark Lord and die a painful bloody death and then my cats starve.

Oh crap, my cats.

"My cats—"

"Don't worry about your cats," xe says. "They're here. This is a House of Choosing, after all. They've been placed in your rooms, which await your approval. But we're not looking for another world-walker. We're looking for a *world-maker.*"

Um.

"A who-da-what, now?"

Xe sinks gracefully to the floor in a smooth tangle of pillowy brown limbs and billowing sleeves and pant-legs. Then xe does something nobody has ever done with me before—xe lies down on xyr back so that we're on the same level. Xe folds xyr long-fingered hands together and rests them on the cushion of xyr stomach.

"We need someone who can *make* the Doors. Who can find the seeds of different worlds and bring them blooming to life, then carve the Door that leads there. You can do it. You felt a world just now, when you touched the rug."

I study xem; xe isn't looking at me, thank everything holy, but the arched ivory ceiling overhead. Xyr eyes have impossibly long fringes of black lashes like onyx lace that curl lightly against xyr brown cheek, and swirls of color like fire and twilight glow across xyr eyelids. I can almost see a place there, with a huge dusty-indigo sun perpetually tethered just at the horizon, and a colossal ringed planet the vivid orange-purple of nectarines hanging in a sky that gradates between the color of red clay and the soft gold of pollen, and strange obsidian butterflies the size of hawks and their wings —glinting with flecks of amethyst, and lilies sparking with celadon light against golden earth—

"That's Hesperide," xe says without looking at me. I blink and lose the ghost-images of the butterflies. "The world you just saw in my makeup. That's my medium—makeup, thread, fabric. Fashion and everything it entails. Yours is something else, though, I think."

"I don't..." I have to say this carefully, but wording is hard. "I don't know what you mean. My medium. Seeing worlds." I don't want to screw this up, but what would be worse is saying I know what I'm doing and then dying in a fiery explosion when I fuck up and bomb.

"You know about Doors, of course."

I shrug. Everyone knows about Doors, so why ask me? Is this a trick? Another test? I study xem, all shadow and silk and twilight embers.

"I tried to take the initial Choosing tests in elementary school." I don't like saying it. The words crunch in my teeth like broken glass.

Only the initial tests cost money—a lot of money. Anyone can take them at any liminal location: libraries, gas stations, schools, military recruitment centers, beaches, art studios, cemetery gates, but payment is required if a kid doesn't feel like waiting for a House of Choosing to just snatch them off the street and wants to try testing instead. The government will jam its sticky fingers in anything and everything just to make a buck and screw with people.

Passing the tests is a different matter. Only the Chosen can pass the tests that bring someone to a House of Choosing, and nobody but people who dwell in the Houses knows how all that works.

"And?"

I narrow my eyes. "My teachers wouldn't write me the recommendation letters, and we couldn't afford the fees without them."

That was before the very recent reforms of the last few years, which are trying to make being Chosen easier on anyone who isn't upper-middle class, white, and abled. Not because Congress actually gives a shit about the marginalized, but because conservatives realized they don't actually *want* their little darlings gallivanting off to play hero in other dimensions. If Junior's busy slaying dragons and winning princexes and learning who they really are without Mother and Father glaring over their shoulder and stuffing them into tiny boxes, who'll take over the family megacorp? Think of the stock market.

Xe nods and says, "Ah. I thought so. Well, where do you think the worlds come from? Someone makes them, just as someone made our world, our universe, once."

"And people just *make* worlds?" I'd never heard of that, but the worlds had to come from *somewhere*...

"Well," xe says, "you'll have to *learn* how, of course. How to make and finish the making. Most world-makers have a talent, but don't know how to harness it fully. Monet didn't just slap his hand in a bucket of finger-paint and invent impressionism."

I think of the cool slime of finger-painting, the thick pressure of it under my fingernails like dirt and the itch of it drying as rust-brown as old blood in the creases of my fingers, and have to swallow twice to keep from throwing up. If I have to *stick my bare hand* into pools of paint, there's no way in hell I can do this.

"Your medium probably isn't paint, though," xe continues, "judging from the look on your face. What do you like to do?"

I stare at xem. Xe still doesn't look at me, which is the only reason I can swallow enough to ask, "Why do you care?"

"This is a job interview."

Oh. *Oh.*

Holy shit.

"Since I'm the one interviewing you, I need to figure out what, uh...department you'd be best in. What accommodations you need. You're autistic, aren't you?" When I nod, xe adds, "Sensory input is an entirely different world to you, isn't it? A thousand worlds. Sometimes they're paradise, and other times they're Hell. Aren't they?"

I nod, surprised. Most allistic people don't understand this. Belatedly, I remember to push my eyebrows up to *show* my surprise where xe can see it.

"Here's the job: you find your medium, and you find your worlds, and you create the Doors you want to make. Just because you find a world doesn't mean you have to open the way to it. And you create wonders and hope and stories for the world-walkers."

Make what I want to make, the way I want to make it...for other people.

"What if I end up finding a world I want to go to? What if I decide I want to be a world-walker?" Can I even do that? If I'm cracking open all these worlds, I could absolutely find one that doesn't scrape sensory claws across my gray matter or trigger panic-spiders in my skull, so...

Xe shrugs. "Then we fill out the paperwork and you do that. If there's a world that's perfect for you, or a dozen worlds you want to visit, you can. You can even continue to make Doors from your new world if you want. That would be HR's problem, though."

Huh. "How do I get paid?"

"If you choose to live outside of the House and need currency, we'll provide a living wage that allows you to exist comfortably, whatever that is depending on what place on what world you decide to settle. It's small enough thanks for an invaluable service.

"If you choose to live in the House, we provide room, board, work materials, and a stipend for any fun things you might want. We also barter information and skills for goods between ourselves if there's something one of us wants. For example, Ms. Alice and Ms. Gertrude are excellent bakers and Mr. W in the penthouse suite makes wonderful clothing.

You might want to see if they have anything you'd like to try ...should you take the job."

I turn my face more fully into the rug. The plush blueness caresses my cheek, a sapphire embrace that pushes away some of the biting confusion and lets me think. Wages, a place to live, my cats, food, even clothes.

"What about insurance?" I mumble.

"You mean medical, dental, that sort of thing?" Xe asks. I nod, then remember xe isn't looking at me, but before I have to figure out how to verbalize something, xe says, "We provide insurance. When something is needed, we simply open a Door to a world with standardized universal healthcare and a charming lack of bigotry. They do exist, though they're rare."

Huh.

"What if I want to leave?"

"You mean quit? You'd have to put it in writing and give us a month's notice, like any decent place. Similarly, we have to give you a month's notice before termination."

"Do I have to talk to people?" I can talk to people on good days, usually. But bad days, when I'm overstimmed and feel like every word is a chunk of granite bashing against my skull, I can't handle conversation, or words, or noises.

Xe shrugs. "Only if you want to. We do need status updates every two weeks on worlds discovered and approximate number of Doors made, but you can submit those in writing or via recording or whatever way works best for you. We try to keep track of the different worlds, their names, what they're like. Mx. Kathryn and Ms. Susanna in the Archives are in charge of that, you would answer to them. They have a very efficient catalogue system, and they believe in giving fair value for a job well-done."

Makes sense. But...

I stroke the silky carpet fibers and chew my lower lip. My toes curl in my shoes, scrunching and unscrunching against the comforting press of worn canvas as I fight to swallow noises. I didn't even know Doors *got* made, much less made by regular people. I didn't know someone who isn't destined to swing a sword through an Army of Evil Undead or fall down a Rabbit Hole could come to a House of Choosing. I didn't know people could get plucked off the street and brought to a House at my age.

There's a metric crap-ton I didn't know before this...job interview, and a metric crap-ton I still don't know. Like how to even do what xe is asking me to do. There's a reason I don't draw or whittle or embroider anymore, besides being broke; I've got jacked up hands that shake at all the worst times. How am I supposed to make an interdimensional portal?

But...everything has been so impossibly good, so accommodating in a way I'd never have imagined before this. So maybe...

If you don't disclose, you can't ask for accommodation...

My knuckles pop like Rice Krispy cereal in milk when I dig my fingers hard into the plush sapphire under me and I manage to gasp out, all in a rush, "What if I can't figure out how to make a Door?"

Xe smiles. "I'm glad you asked. We offer paid training, and there are a thousand and one ways to make a Door. Would you like to try now, to see if you can figure out a way that works best for you?"

I shove my face into the thick fur of the rug to help soothe the sudden spike of my panic, the echoes of *can't do it, can't do it, can't do it.*

"Okay." It's muffled, but xe understands.

"Look up at the ceiling."

I turn my head enough that if I roll my eyes, I can see the white vault overhead. It's blank, an empty expanse. It feels like it shouldn't be, but I'm not sure why. It's just annoying to me. Like a piece of grit stuck to the bottom of my sock.

"Now, try to find the place you saw before. The place you felt in the rug you're lying on. Worlds are found in the smallest sensory details. The crack of ice in water, the flicker of silver-painted lashes, the waving tendrils of an anemone. Try to remember what you were feeling before."

What I was feeling before? It's not hard. I can still feel the rug under me. It's still stroking cobalt fronds over my skin in tickling whispers. When I close my eyes I can see the silver-furred leaves and the giant skyscraper trunks, the dusky light as thick as syrup and the malachite sky spangled by aquamarine and indigo stars. The air tastes sweet and crisp and cool, I want to drink it, and the world is so quiet. There's only the soft sigh of the wind, hollow and fluting and distant.

"Cast it onto the canvas."

I shouldn't know what that means. It doesn't make sense, there is no canvas. But since I'm focusing on the way the leaves feel against my cheek, the glass-slick smoothness of the bark under my fingertips, I don't even think about it, I just *do* it so xe will stop talking and let me focus on the perfume of the golden buds just beginning to crack open on one of the boughs. I flick out my hand like I'm tossing something into the garbage.

"Do it again."

I lean against the smooth tree and feel the faint, fuzzy crackle like television static against my skin, like snuggling a balloon. I used to do that, I remember vaguely. When I was little, before my parents made me stop. I wanted to enjoy the light popping fuzz of it. I flick a hand again, but I'm focused on that velvety buzz and tingle.

"A good beginning, especially for a first attempt," xe says.

My eyes snap open. The forest is gone. I'm back in the white room with the black floor and the blue rug and I can see, hovering a few inches off the ground against the alabaster backdrop of the ceiling, a ghostly image of a Door. Dark, glossy wood like the ocean on a moonless night, bound and chased in silver, carved with towering trees and many-petaled flowers. What in the absolute hell...?

"It'll need to be firmed up before it can be opened, but I was right. You're a world-maker. The sheer force behind your enjoyment of the world you find or create, your need to experience parts of it, allows you to make the Door."

I don't say anything. I just stare at the phantom Door. In it, I can see the trees, smell those golden flowers just beginning to open, taste the evening air. It's beautiful, and...

And *I* did that. I *made* that. Me. And it didn't even hurt.

"For me, it's when I do makeup. Once I start painting my own face, I find a place in the colors, beyond the edges of the world," xe says. "And I want to see more of it, touch all of it. So I do. And while I paint it on my face in swirls of powder and cream, I paint the Door, too."

I smooth my fingers over the silky tufts of blue. The seed of an entire, brand new world, and *I* opened the way to it.

"For some of us, it's color. For some, it's food, or perfumes, or flowers, or music. We see the world in a grain of sand, a tuft of swan's down, a blade of grass. I think for you...I think it can be anything you want, as long as it thrills your senses."

I've gotten lost in sensation before. For minutes, even hours sometimes. I've lost hours just watching a fire dance, or feeling hot water rolling in glorious spills down my back in the shower, or listening to rain tinkling like silver chimes against the windows, or flapping my hands through mountains of snow-white sweet-scented foaming soap, or pressing my nose into the velvet petals of a rose in full scarlet bloom. I've found worlds in there before, places of safety and beauty and rest.

Places of *rest*. I am so tired all the time, and so sick of having to worry. I want to escape, to sink into a place of safety and beauty and rest. I want to give that to other people and help them escape, too.

I want to rest, and to create, and to be happy.

I look at xem.

"When can I start?"

A Technical Term, Like Privilege

Bogi Takács

GET HOME and the rental needs to drink my blood. Again, always, the fourth time this week and it's only Wednesday. I strip off my top, undershirt. I'm not going to take off my pants, I don't care what the rental thinks. Does it think?

I think it only feels, feels a deep resentment of humans living inside its caverns, its air bubbles. Housebeasts have sensory nerve endings on the inside, feel us tickling them as we live our petty lives, squeeze us for blood.

The life of flesh is in the blood, the preachers say. The housebeast doesn't need my blood, type O, good for transfusions. It needs the magic. But most people, their magic is sparse, less heavily invested in their body. The housebeast needs the blood, to squeeze out every drip of sustenance— not from the blood itself but from what it carries.

While tentacles slither around on my skin, while the wall glues itself to me, I wonder for the fifth time what I can do to get out of this. I feel my bone marrow straining to produce more red blood cells. I need a break. The wall grabs a lock of hair, and I know it's a total loss—I'll have to cut that one off too. Should've just worn a cap, should've cut it all short— should, should. I need to call the rental office.

Twelve apartments in this beast, or was it fourteen? The third beast on the block, a student neighborhood. It was all right before the semester started. I don't know what the new students are doing, but the beast needs so much more magic now. Are people puking in the disposal-holes? Trying to squeeze out broadband from the beast-nerves?

The worst part of it is, it feels good while the beast drinks. It needs me, yes, but I can feel that it loves me. It wants to keep me close.

I stagger away from the wall, rubbing my bruised skin, crashing onto the sofa, staining the cover. Too tired to take a shower, but at least we'll have enough water pressure now. My hand is searching for the receiver, and it helpfully pops out, shakes drips—of what, synovial fluid?—off of itself. I groan into the receiver, ask for the rental office.

"Yes, I understand it needs the magic. Yes, I understand these were the terms when I signed. I was"—I take a heavy breath—"just wondering if it needs to be so... direct. I mean, I can give it magic without the blood. I can do that."

I scratch the side of the receiver with a stubby fingernail. It squirms. I'm too faint to understand the explanation from the chirpy person on the other end of the line in an office somewhere nearer the head. But it's a no—it's always a no. "The contracts aren't written with someone like you in mind, you have to understand," but heck, they need me if they want to keep the beast going. Maybe they should recruit from the Department of Applied Magic and not from, I don't know, engineering students.

Then again, I didn't go into magic either. That shit is for the highborn.

I fall asleep, wake a few hours later. I am late with my homework in Entirely Useless Studies, but I can't muster the enthusiasm. A graduate degree, yes. Your fellowship will pay your tuition, yes. But all the money I get from teaching on the side goes into renting this room that I couldn't even call a cavern. And the food, the iron supplements lately, those cheap industrial hotdogs pushed out by a factorybeast. I hear some of the highborn mages are vegetarian, and I wonder how they swing it. I need to get another twelve-pack of eggs, low-cost protein. I wonder if I could raise chickens without the rental office noticing. Is chicken feed cheaper than eggs? Chickens smell though. I wonder how long I'd last before I roasted them on a spit—live for today, don't mind tomorrow.

By the heavens, I'm hungry. I rub my face, but that doesn't summon food. I find my last hotdog in the cooling pouch. I eat it cold, can't wait out the minute to warm it up. I need to shower. I need to go. I saw this flyer on campus, and maybe it can be just the thing.

❖

I RUN MY fingers along the words. I feel scrubbed. The hot water was great in the shower—never mind it took my blood and sweat to boil it.

ONWARD TO ARMS! FOR THE REVOLUTION!

The Communards of Szederkei County invite YOU to our Campus Meetings...

The address is off campus but close by. Some university official probably ousted them. No one wants to deal with a bunch of rabble-rousers, well, except the rabble-rousers like me. I crunch the leaflet back into the pocket of my robe.

Two tall, pale dudes are by the door, and I feel acutely scrawny. Possibly also insufficiently cis. But that's not what they complain about. At least, I *think* it's not that, though one never knows really.

One of them fingers my pendant, and I flinch from the touch. I had too much touch today already, even if not the human kind.

They say something about no mages—and I can't quite make it out, I'm worse off than I'd thought—and I get into a debate with them. One of them just keeps on repeating that mages are a privileged class. As if that was some technical term, and for all I know, it is.

"You can do something other people can't. That's a privilege."

I can't even muster a glare. I feel like I can't do anything because I'd been sucked dry of every last drop of blood.

And I can't argue well either because what, I mean, he's technically right. I can do things other people can't.

I walk away wordless, but a debate rages in my head. All the highborn mages, that's privilege. But why can't I. I mean I can. Maybe it's just that I'm a failure. I wanted to pick myself up by my bootstraps, get a fellowship, study Useless Studies—I mean mathematics. (I actually love it. When I can keep my eyes straight to stare at a page.) Get into fights with engineering students, grow up, get into grad school, stop getting into fights. Moan about engineering students and how they vomit into every available receptacle after a night of drinking and more fights. All while I need to make sure the housebeast has enough energy to digest all that crap. I'm sure I did the same as a first-year, but that was before the rental hikes, before grad students got pushed out of on-campus housing.

I was better at fights, to be honest. Still not late for a career as a cage fighter maybe, but I value my brain cells, and I can't afford the protective enchantments.

❖

Rika stares at me over their bagged lunch: a sandwich of what, bread and cheese probably. They're looking tired today, colorful hair hidden in a hastily wrapped scarf, their skin patchy pink. "Stop thinking about witty repartee," they say.

I shake my head. I've been thinking of so many rejoinders. I could've yelled at those people that I was trans, but if they didn't guess, wasn't that also *privilege*? What if they did guess? It wasn't like I could quiz them. "How did you know?" I ask Rika.

"It's all over your face," they chuckle, their voice dry. "Staircase wit, it's called. You come up with it when you're already walking down the stairs."

"Well yeah, other buildings have staircases. Mine has an esophagus."

"You could unionize." They just toss that out there as if that was so easy.

"What, a renters' union?" I'm laughing.

"Exactly that." They're frustrated with me, I can feel. Their mind vibrates. They put down the sandwich and lean forward. "I'm not studying sociology because it's so good. I'm studying it because I want to beat them at their game."

A blanket *them* that can cover everyone. From greedy landlords to Revolutionary Communards.

I shake my head. "I couldn't even get into a proper resistance meeting."

"Eat something. You'll feel better." They tilt their head. "Want one of my sandwiches?"

"What's inside?"

"Um, bread and cheese?"

I take it.

❖

AT HOME AGAIN, my turn to squeeze broadband out of the nerves. I read and read, and all I conclude is that everyone has their own jargon, subversives included. I feel resentment toward *the apparatus of revolution*. I'm not the right kind of comrade, and I feel I can't even complain.

Even if I could find a new place mid-semester, which I couldn't knowing my luck, who's to say it won't go exactly the same? I used to live on Butchers Row in the inorganic housing before it got demolished, and at one point, the floor cracked open, and I found myself knee-deep in my downstairs neighbor's ceiling just like that. Another housebeast, and that'll probably go the same. Every place that has an opening this time of the year will probably be salivating for magic. The beast or the owners, I wonder.

Am I the only one in this situation? I don't know, but I guess everyone else who might be is probably likewise flattened out from all the blood loss.

I glare at the dark-purple walls, the rugged, ribbed interior of the housebeast. Why does it need me? I can't even hate it. I feel bad for it. It's trapped same as I am. It needs my cheap blood filled with magic and whatever power comes out of a hotdog after it's digested. I'm surprised my terrible diet hasn't poisoned it already.

Well, that would certainly be a way to take revenge on the rental office. Or just to make the argument again that I could be doing this without the blood. Maybe that would convince them.

I half cough, half guffaw. Instead of pamphlets, I could be reading about the biochemistry of housebeasts.

❖

IT TAKES EFFORT to find out which substances can accumulate in my blood with less harmful effect to me than to the housebeast. Everything takes effort when I'm so woozy, lying on the sofa, scratching my still-churning belly. Exhaustion can look a lot like laziness, and I only hope an idle rental clerk isn't looking in on me via the beast's internal photosensor cells. It can be done.

I hope I'm not interesting enough.

It takes even more effort to find a substance I can easily add to my diet. I've never stolen food, and maybe it's not the best to begin when I'm keeling over from anemia and a distinct lack of magic. I budget and rebudget. The numbers don't add up. Maybe Rika has a thunderfruit tree in their back yard. Maybe I can find a restaurant that gets rid of a few pounds of a very specific mushroom every day. Maybe, maybe. I could use my magic for this if I had any left over after feeding the beast. As if.

I feel like dirt for even contemplating harming a living creature, but I can't keep up this feeding schedule. It's not about hurting an animal for fun. It's about bare survival. Would I slaughter a cow to eat it? Oh yes, I would. I'm an inveterate city dweller, but I'd give it an honest try if the need was pressing. Is this so different?

I scribble numbers on my slate. I look at an Intro to Pharmacokinetics text. I make guesses about my metabolism. Fuck if I know how magic affects all this.

Two full measures of thunderfruit a day while minimizing other liquid intake. That shouldn't be so hard. In just a few days, this will cause striking cutanous symptoms on both interior and exterior membranes. Of the housebeast, not of me. Worst case, I might get a mild rash. Diarrhea from all the thunderfruit.

If I time it well, skin will slough from the ceiling straight into people's breakfasts. I wonder if I can adjust it so that it happens in the offices near the head first, where the rental company is safely cocooned.

❖

PUBLIC DATABASES ARE a close second to magic. Here are all the public trees on city plots. All the fruit-bearing trees. All the thunderfruit trees. Here, watch me draw a path connecting them all. If I take one from each, I'll have two full measures per day easy, and no one will notice. You're not supposed to harvest them, but you can take for personal use.

My personal use is just a little more demanding is all.

Here is the path. Only three Imperial miles on foot. Per day. While my bone marrow cries in agony as it grinds away at producing new blood cells.

All my limbs hurt. By the second day, I know I'll have to involve somebody.

❖

I EXPLAIN MY plan to Rika, sitting in the park at a chessboard, pretending to play. I connect imaginary dots.

"Once they realize my blood is useless for the beast, they'll surely allow me to give my magic without giving blood. I just have trouble getting enough thunderfruit."

They shake their head. "What's to say they won't just boot you from the rental?"

A sudden pounding ache in my stomach. I can feel my magic going askew. I must *believe* in my plan, but Rika... Rika is so sensible. They're probably right.

"Believe me," I say, but I can't believe myself anymore.

❖

I'LL JUST HAVE to stop talking to Rika. Stop talking to anyone. *I will be my own internal revolution,* I think to myself as I mash the thunderfruit together in a bowl, shovel it into my mouth. It is gooey sweet and just vaguely medicinal, that kind of pharmacy aftertaste.

Two measures of thunderfruit a day is an awful lot. Bodybuilders do this with rice and what, chicken? I'll think of this as my spiritual discipline. I should believe in the kindly powers, but the kindly powers had never so much glanced at me; they stranded me with enough magic to be sucked dry but not enough standing to become a mage. Not the right family, not the right gender, not the right anything. What is the right gender even.

The housebeast skips a day with its requests, and another. Is it suspecting something?

My blood stews. Then my guts churn. I didn't think about this—will my excrement poison the beast even faster? I considered everything so carefully. How did I miss this? I should've gone into Useful Studies, like medicine.

I drag myself to the academy and lock myself into one of the restrooms there, near the Department of Complex Systems where no one ever goes anyway. I think wistfully of my research projects, now abandoned. I am my own project.

There is a sticker in the toilet stall, telling me where to look for help with domestic violence. There is no sticker about being eaten alive by your rental. I still wonder about reaching out. Does this count? Surely there has to be a limit to how much blood can be extracted from a person on a regular basis. My contract only specified something vague based on "needs and capabilities." It's just my luck that I'm probably the most magical person in this particular housebeast. It's like not having enough bandwidth because there is only one outgoing nerve bundle for the whole floor.

I stumble against the door when I try to exit the stall. I'm not one for religion, but even I think about invoking the kindly powers.

❖

RIKA HAS LEFT a message while I was gone, and I ignore it. I can't risk being discouraged.

As I topple on the sofa, I feel a pang that's something new, not my upset stomach or my head foggy from blood loss. I feel a need, and I'm not sure if it's the beast's or mine. It feels good, being fed on, after all. And for three days, I've gone without.

I laugh bitterly. The housebeast beckons.

This is the time. Breakfasts and convoluted schedules are irrelevant. Now is the time.

May the kindly powers help me. Help us all.

I peel off my shirt, tearing a strap in the process. I fumble with my undershirt, sprain a finger that I hooked under it just wrong. I laugh-cry. I lean against the wall, and the wall leans against me, tentacles reaching out. Even my own smell feels different. Has the change in my metabolism been so drastic already?

The housebeast drinks deeply and pauses for a moment—

It retches the blood out in a spasming stream onto my floor and my half-full, half-empty backpack.

I sit on the floor, a familiar numb shock, and time passes and passes and passes until someone from the rental office comes by to draw my blood, test it. I offer my arm without words.

"You have a week to make sure your numbers are within range and your blood passes the filter," the clerk says chirpily, her hair arcing straight around her face as she tosses her head to the side. "Otherwise, your contract will be terminated at the end of the week."

My mouth moves finally, slowly. "How am I supposed to find a place mid-semester?"

Filters. I didn't think the beast would have filters. What do they filter out?

The clerk says something that's not even apologetic.

"Can I give. My magic. Without the blood. I can do it. Just look at my results," I croak and beg.

I don't understand the answer beyond the *no*.

"Can I please. I promise I can do it." I raise my voice.

"You need to stop threatening me," the clerk says.

I'm small and half-covered in my own blood and feeling like I'm about to die. *I'm not* threatening *you,* I think—but I don't say anything. She's read me as male, I know. As someone potentially threatening. I don't want to give the company yet another reason to boot me from the rental.

She is going on about how they're going to make sure it'll all go on my record. Something about the police. Something about one last chance to get my act together and stop drinking that filth that passes for alcohol in the alleys near the academy. One week. Or she'll make sure—*you have to understand it's not about your person*—that my "violent behavior" gets reported.

That wouldn't put an end to finding a room. It'd put an end to my studies, to everything I've scraped together all this miserable life.

❖

I WANT TO pace the room, but I can't. Mopping up the blood has used up all the energy I had left. I lie on the floor, convinced there's still a puddle underneath me, but I can't.

Why do they need my blood?

"The kindly powers have saved you from me," I tell the housebeast and chuckle. "They've saved you, not me." My abdominal muscles spasm from my attempt to laugh. Speaking is hard. I can just think at the beast—we are connected well enough at this point.

I don't want to hurt you, I think. *But I can't keep this up.*

The beast is so hungry.

You're in a bad situation too, huh? I turn to my side, fetal position. Even my thoughts are hard to sustain. *In a reasonable world, the rental company would just hire some mages to deal with the shortfall.*

What is it that my blood does that my magic can't?

❖

RIKA FINDS ME on the floor, and I'm muttering the same question to them.

They always take me seriously. They answer, talking to me while they're sponging me down, feeding me with something refreshingly solid. Rice cakes?

"Giving your blood ensures you don't have enough energy left to rebel," they say. "You have more than enough magic to cause a mess."

That's certainly possible. I nod.

"And also..." They fall silent, bite their lower lip. "Divide and conquer. If you can be kept away from other people fighting for equality, so much the better for the people in power."

I blink at them.

"Don't tell me you bought into this bullshit take on class struggle." They glare at me. "I'll be blunt with you. Magic doesn't make you into an aristocrat."

"I still pass as male," I say weakly.

"Look, take this from one trans person to another, all right? You don't pass anywhere near consistently, I'm sorry. And do you even want to? I mean, you're not a man exactly."

I groan. "My gender is a mess."

They wave at me. "Your gender is just fine. You just need some stability in your life. Look, you're trying to convince me how privileged you are just as you are in the process of being slowly eaten alive. Can you have some compassion for yourself?"

I will not cry. Am I crying? "I tried to hurt the housebeast."

"That's the same thing. You think of the housebeast as your opponent, not as your comrade."

"It is trying to eat me...?"

"It's hungry because it's been deprived of resources. That's my best sociological analysis really."

I stand up, immediately dizzy, and sit back down. Rika is right. Terribly, terribly right. "Why are you helping me?" That's not what I want to say.

"You helped me out back in first year, and now I'm helping you out." They pause. "But to be honest, I'm just telling you this so that you can feel satisfied. I know that for you it's all give and take. But sometimes I just want to help out my friends. I can't stand to see you all alone, working yourself into a small desperate corner."

I try to protest, but Rika is still right. They don't have much magic, but their thoughts move along such orderly lines that they pull my own thoughts along.

❖

AFTER RIKA LEAVES, I lay down to sleep, but it's as if some kind of barrier had tumbled down inside me, and instead of dreams, I join—join the housebeast.

The housebeast is hungry and sad and disappointed and frustrated and hungry and disappointed. Heck, now *I'm* hungry.

The housebeast has an immediate response to run away, to fly—

Hold on, I think at the housebeast, at myself, *running away would solve precisely nothing. Where would we go? What about your other inhabitants?*

I am treated to a plan of all the inhabitants' movements, a time-lapse, points of minimal and maximal activity—

You've thought about this, have you?

Was *I* keeping the housebeast from running away? I was a prime source of sustenance. But I could send magic remotely if with some additional difficulty...

That's why it had to be blood. If people were allowed to feed housebeasts with pure magic without a carrying substrate, anyone could go anywhere. Housebeasts could go anywhere. Broke grad students could go anywhere. Societal control would be loosened.

I'm starting to think like Rika.

I can feed you without the blood, I think at the housebeast, *if that works for you.* My magic replenishes faster than my red blood cells at least. *We won't have to tell anyone. We'll just pretend.*

The housebeast doesn't quite understand *pretend* and is hungry, so hungry.

We can sort it out. I shrug, my shoulders shot through with pain at the motion, my awareness abruptly recentered on my body. I have just eaten— my last hotdogs if memory serves. I can do this. I tell the housebeast, *You can feed.*

Do I sleep, or do I just blink off, I don't even.

❧

I KNOW WHEN I wake that something is askew. I drag myself to my feet, and the floor tilts. I fall. My left ankle cracks. The startle blanks out the pain. I don't have a window—windows are only on higher levels—where's the door? I'm in some random shirt and underwear and naked legs, and it shows how bad the situation has gotten. I can't be bothered about the legs. I half walk, half topple out the door, and it opens with the usual smacking sound, but there are some weird harmonics in it that I can't quite tease out.

I crash into the rental clerk with the fancy hair. We all have our ways of trying to hold on to something that makes us feel human, I suppose. I understand her all too well for a moment, and I wonder if I have too much magic left, if that can even be a thing.

"The anchors have detached," she says. "All shards have failed." And this has to be a technical term too, like *privilege*.

I feel ridiculous. What did Rika say, something about revolution being structural change that cannot be achieved by any one individual's heroic actions, something something? This is bad. Is the housebeast flying? The housebeast's flying after taking enough power from me to tear off the anchors and rise to the skies. So now we'll probably get shot down with anti-air cannons for all I know. My one-person rebellion—how privileged. How pointless.

"I've let it loose," I mutter. "Sorry, I didn't mean to." But truly, did I?

The clerk stares at me, and no, I can't make out her thoughts. The floor wobbles and I feel a pull, a pull at my guts, or at least something somewhere inside me—

❖

"YOU FAINTED," THE rental clerk says. Am I on the floor? I must be. She's somewhere out of arm's reach. It makes sense. She doesn't dare to be closer to me.

"No one's thinking about anything," I tell her, and in my head, this makes sense too. The beast didn't think this through—a characteristic of beasts of all sorts. I didn't think this through.

Even without the blood, the beast will fly and drain me and drain and...

"Almost everyone is out at this hour," she says. "So I figured it had to be you. Of course."

"Structural change," I say with brutal effort, fighting my mouth gone rubbery numb. "We need to descend. Do you know how to steer?"

"Steer what? They are supposed to be anchored—"

Rika would surely have an amazing idea. There is no plan, nothing, just my need to get away from it all that the housebeast has clearly internalized. A big, giant cursing that fills the skies. The kind of pointless anger that makes the rental clerk flinch away from me as I stagger to my feet. I still don't know her name, but I can't move and speak at the same time, and something's got to go.

The beast didn't digest the poison, but something made it through the filters after all. Something that's grimy and base as only emotion can get.

I'll hate myself in the afterlife, surrounded by the kindly powers gently but insistently telling me off.

❖

I ONLY KNOW this, am only driven by this—I need to at least see for myself what's happening before we all pancake on the ground.

The front gate is so far. It opens, opens, and I'm stunned. I expect the rushing air, but there's some kind of giant flap that had extruded out of the wall, and it's keeping the worst of the impact off me.

Also, we are close to the ground. Uncomfortably close. Tears the snot out of my nose close.

Are we right above Rika's housebeast?

I brace for impact. The clerk at my right loudly prays.

Down just below, I see the other housebeast's front gate open, and I cuss.

Rika looks up at me, our eyes lock across the distance like they shouldn't, and Rika's incredulity makes it across whatever connection we have built, mind to mind.

Their beast wobbles. Moorings detaching? Rika ducks back inside. Are they whooping? They must be. I'm not sure how I can tell through the noise, must be the magic. Their beast is eager to join mine. Something draws them together. Pheromones or possibility? Magic, physics, wait maybe that newfound social context—so hilarious as to feel plausible. Wrenching really. The beast breaks loose from the ground with a crack I feel in my teeth.

"This structural enough for you?" I scream at the top of my lungs, and I laugh, laugh as my housebeast swings low and up again on a neat parabola as Rika's housebeast gains speed and altitude as all around us the masses of cheap rentals detach from the ground, take to the air.

Every jug of water has that one last drop before it overflows, I find myself thinking. The conditions were here: the hungry beasts, the grip of control loosening its hold. I'm just one person, and the heroic deeds are for another, but out of the mess, this emerged, and maybe others can make sense of it.

The ocean's near, so near, and all I can hope for is that when I pass out, we'll be above water and maybe, just maybe, free once and for all.

Root Rot

Fargo Tbakhi

B Y THE TIME I hear that my brother is looking for me, and has somehow scraped together enough credit to get on a commercial flight to New Tel Aviv, and that he's also brought his three-year-old daughter on her first interplanet trip, my insides are already rotten. Can't get to the doctor without citizen papers, but I know. I can feel it. Lungs, liver, stomach, whatever—they're done for. Most days I wake up, bleed, drink, bleed, and pass out. I am fucked beyond any reasonable doubt.

When the two OSPs are finished beating the shit out of me outside Farah's (only place in the Arab Quarter with a liquor license which means what's happening currently, a beating that is, happens less frequently than if I was drinking somewhere else) one of them checks for warrants. I'm swaying like something in the breeze though the provisional government never fixed the generators so there isn't any breeze this part of planet. Sometimes I blow in my own face just to remember what wind felt like.

"Hey, you got a brother?"

Word drops into me. Shakes me up bad to hear it and for a second I almost don't process what it means. Then I do and want to die. I spit out some blood and nod.

"Posted a bulletin. Yesterday, looks like. Asks if anyone's seen you. Want me to forward your location?"

I try to think and then try not to think, and for a second I am really still, and then that second is one of the worst things I've felt in years, so I stay quiet and make a gesture like I'm going to hit the OSPs and they start in again and, later, when they've gone and I get feeling back in my body and start to register the pain, I go back inside and then I pray and then I don't look at anybody and then I drink until I pass out.

❖

WHEN I START wishing I was dead I know it's morning. I spend a few minutes trying to work out where I am. Still at Farah's maybe. In prison maybe. In the street probably. As long I'm not at the house. Take a few minutes and press at my body. Feet. Stomach. Throat. Eyeballs. Thighs. Feel like crying but don't.

My fingers are crusted with blood, and I think one might be broken. For a second, I think the blood might be dirt, that red Mars soil, and I get confused and think maybe I've still got a job, maybe it's years ago and I've just been dreaming all of this pain, and maybe I'm still handsome and unbroken, maybe Farah and I are still in love and I can still make something grow, I can still get my fingers in the dirt and hear it, and then I shift slightly and get a bomb's worth of pain from my ribs and my vision blurs blue and when it clears I know the soil is blood. I know where I am and who and why.

I turn over and make myself puke, and it's that familiar yellow color with the little bit of blood threading through it like embroidery. Try and see my face in it but can't. I'm sure if I could I'd look worse than dead. Skin pale and covered in bruises, my hair falling out, a few teeth gone in the back and I swear I'm getting shorter too. Maybe if I just lay here for a while nothing will happen and then I can start drinking again.

"Get up."

Maybe not. Guess I'm at Farah's. He kicks me in the ribs and cusses me out until I sit up.

"Hi," I say. Voice sounds like a bad engine and I know my breath is probably toxic. I'm struck by the hugeness of how unwantable I am. Farah used to think I was pretty when I was clean. I used to think so too. Well nothing's inevitable but change and skyscrapers as they say.

Farah's just standing there and his arms are folded across his chest. I want to lick it like some wounded animal, him or me I don't know but there's some combination of animal and wound. "Hi," I say again.

"You can't come back in here."

When Farah and I were together we used to draw on each other's chests little maps. Plots of land we wanted to live on, spots on Mars we'd go and build our freedom. He would laugh and then when things got bad he wouldn't laugh so much. But the ones I drew on his chest were so real to me. I never laughed.

"I'm okay, I just need to rest today. I'll be okay. I won't come back tonight, I'll go somewhere else and cool off and come back tomorrow."

"You can't come back in here, ever."

Really detailed mine were with all the land sectioned off into what types of plants I was going to have and then I'd get so excited to tell him how I'd figured what they needed from Mars soil and sun and air and he would listen and smile or listen and look so sad when things changed and I did too.

"Okay."

"You haven't paid your tab in months. And when you get in fights outside it's bad for business. Offworld Settlement Palmach fuckers are over here constantly for you and no one wants to deal with that."

Farah was the one who was waiting for me outside Ansar VI when I got out but I didn't know what to say and neither did he so we didn't. And he took me back to the bar and poured when I asked and that's it and that's where we've been since.

"It's bad for business. And it's bad for me. They'll take the liquor license and maybe my papers too. And I don't want to ever look at you again."

I sit there like a puddle and try not to think. If I keep my eyes focused on the puke I won't let what's happening in. It'll stay out so I can move and breathe some. I stare at the little thread of blood in the bile and in the corner of my eye I see Farah start to go and the desperation in me rears up.

"Fathi's here," I say.

He stops and I can see he's being really careful with what's on his face. Blank like a stone wall.

"He's looking for me. OSPs told me last night. Please don't do this."

"Maybe you should see him."

"Don't want to see him. Please. I love you."

"Fuck you."

"Okay."

"You owe me too much for that. Just too much."

"Okay."

We both shut up and I know that we might not ever stop shutting up now. That we might be shut and closed forever and no openness ever coming back. Every day there are moments like this when whatever might have been waiting for me in the future just goes away, I can feel it just burning up. I wish I could stop drinking. No I don't. I wish I'd never come to this planet. No I don't.

"I'm going to code the bar's door against your breath until you settle the tab. Maybe Fathi can help you. I don't know. I don't think I can anymore. If I ever could. I'm sorry."

Yes I do.

"Please. I can't pay. I don't have anything left."

Farah and I touching the dirt before this was New Tel Aviv, when it was still new. Holding seeds. Playing with gravity and dreaming of freedom. Kissing. The way I could make him laugh like the sun was out and we could photosynthesize.

"You could always sell it. You know somebody in the city will pay good money."

It. Flash of red. Memory. Dirt. Petals. Whatever.

"Don't have it. Confiscated. All gone," I lie.

Farah shakes his head, really tired-seeming. Looks like

he's going to say something, maybe argue, push me to do what I should, but he doesn't. I think I'm glad about that but I'm not really sure. It's a long time before he talks again.

"Either pay your debts or don't come in here again."

"Okay," I say. He reaches out and puts his fingers on my knee and I remember how much he used to like touching it, how he liked to feel where it'd been broken and reset. We hold still like that for too long so I say "Can I have one more drink, just to get me going, for today?"

For a second his face looks like it's got something like pity on it, and for that I'm grateful. It's all I ever want.

I get out and sun hits me like a missile, and if anyone outside is looking at me with any kind of anything on their face I don't know it, I can't see anything at all.

❖

GETTING TO THE other side of the Arab Quarter means going through the New Tel Aviv settlement civic center but I really don't have a choice if I want to get some cash and keep drinking. If I had better papers and hadn't been in prison I could drink somewhere anonymous and illegal and maybe fade away but oh well. Walking to the delineation gate I stop by the dried out water tanker (left over from when we were still trying to fully terraform the Quarter, when any of us thought this could be home) to visit the cat. She came up on the second or third rocket from somebody's alleyway in Khalil and when things were good she was adored and we joked about making her mayor. Then we all got fucked and she did too. Once the settlements got on the Mars train and surrounded what we had we were all panicking and trying to stay free and in the panic nobody took her with them. Now she's forgotten like me. Like all of us I guess, but me especially I like to think. I check on her when I'm sober enough to remember.

I crouch, eye the underside of the tanker. She's there looking like I feel. We look at each other for a while and eventually I reach out my hand to try and pet her. Too far

back and I'm stretching to just get a scratch, something to let
her know I'm here. No luck. Oh well. Yank my hand back
out and go to look at her again but she's gone. I stay down
there for a moment because it's cool and my head hurts. The
space where she was, where my hand couldn't reach.

Closer to the delineation gate I find some kid selling flasks.
I manage to convince her to take some synth watermelon
seeds I found in my pockets for a flask of arak which is all I
can afford since nobody drinks it anymore. It does the trick
and soon I'm numb again. The thing about drinking a lot
is that there's nothing meaningful about it. Just fucks you
up and you're not in the world anymore and there's no past
or future really just one foot in front of the other if you can
manage that. And sometimes you can still kind of experience
what's around you only it's not as intense on a personal level.
Like now, when the arak's fuzzed me up, the settlement
drones flashing hasbara holograms aren't so annoying.
They're kind of like insects that aren't biting. Just something
to look at with corpse eyes.

At the gate the guard asks where I'm going and checks
my papers, which are shit, obviously. I say I'm just going
across to the other side of the Quarter and I'm sticking out
my arm before he's even finished looking. Window opens
and the little mechanical arm comes out to stick my vein.
Once they've got the liter of my blood they approve a fifteen
minute pass to get through to the settlement. The blood loss
and the arak have really messed me up but I think I can
manage getting to the next gate into the Quarter in time.
They're usually pretty good about getting the blood back
in once you're there depending on the line, though once or
twice I've gotten someone else's liter. Probably healthier than
whatever I've got going on, probably might have saved my
life. I don't know.

The settlement civic center looks the same as always.
Clean and stupid. The glass looks terrible and it never lasts.
And they've ruined all the landscape work they made us do
in Ansar too, synthetic olive trees on every fucking corner
like a postcard. And the synth poppies look as sad as I

knew they would. I stop and bend down to feel them, the sickly genetic smell. None of the settlers know how to grow anything real here and none of the Palestinians have the resources even if they did know which they don't.

Before the settlements when this was just empty planet it was so possible, just crammed to the brim with possible. It was going to be free and we were going to learn the land and find God again and all that bullshit. I believed it so deeply I left everything behind on Earth. The people who couldn't leave I cursed and tore from my heart. I was stupid and I thought things would be different. And when the settlers followed and they liked the wide open planet so much they left the old land behind, they declared any flora from Earth contraband and put me away. Now we've got a provisional government I don't know or care about and my brother's been living in Reunified Palestine for years while I drink myself to death, which reminds me my brother is here for me, and I want to just pull up everything with roots on this fucking planet, just salt the ground and then salt myself too. But I've only got a few minutes before the blood loss passes me out so there's no time for being angry or anything else.

At the other delineation gate there's a protest on the Arab side. They're holding signs in Arabic I can't read. Somebody took down one of the hasbara drones and they're passing it around like a football though it doesn't really roll. People are dancing and something's on fire. I don't know what they want, not sure I can even guess anymore. Some days I'm sad about losing the language, but most days I don't mind it. Ansar policy is to reprogram prisoner consciousness with Hebrew once they wipe the Arabic which serves me fine. I like not understanding things.

The blood bot gives me my liter back and I stand a little straighter. I'm looking at the faces of all the Arabs through the light-meshed gate and I hear myself thinking they're idiots, they're evil, we ought to just shut up and die and float out into space, cold and empty as every day here, all we deserve. Sometimes I don't know what's my voice and what's the guards at Ansar VI and what's the drones and what's the

drink and what's Farah and what's God. All I know is when
the protesters make space for me to stumble through their
anger, when they touch me and tell me to join them, I loathe,
I loathe every cell on my body that feels and I loathe every
second I'm breathing and the pit opens up in me and I want
something more and I don't know what it is. So I push them
away and while they're yelling and spitting at me *collaborator
coward fucking drunk* I drain the last of the arak and I say thank
you to the drone when it passes out an Arab in front of me
and I can pocket a few loose coins that spill out from her
hands like petals.

❖

WHEN I GET to Abu Khaled's he's curled up on the floor and
I can tell he's soiled himself. Touch his forehead and it's hot
as an iron. Probably he'll last a few more days and then go. I
wonder if he has papers for the house or if it'll go to the settlers.
Last place I ever felt decent was in this front room of his—
curled up a lot like he is now and crying nonstop while I tried
to dry out for the first time in years. His hands on my head.
His hands. Remembering feels terrible so I dig a nail into my
palm until the pain brings me dull again. I need to get him
stable and then ask for some cash. That's it. That's all.

I get his pants the rest of the way off and drag him into the
tiny bathroom and into the tub. While I rinse him off and
he's groaning, eyes floating open-closed like a camera shutter,
I look at him. Skin used to be brown but now it's some sick
grey blue. Bruises everywhere. So thin you could think he
was just pastry.

When I'd stumbled in, that night I was trying to be good,
he was patient. I cried and he just sat there and touched me,
just a little, just to show he was there, and eventually I slept,
and the next day he fed me and we didn't say anything to
each other since he only spoke Arabic and I didn't. I was
close to dead from trying to stop drinking cold, but he kept
me alive and I got back to normal. I'd hated him for how
kind he was and how it made me feel okay for a moment so

one night I drank enough so that I knew I'd do something cruel, and I did, and so I left and knew that it was my fault that I was leaving, which was right. After that I didn't see him again, but I went back once, late at night when I knew he was asleep, and I worked for hours until the sun was just coming up, sweating and freezing and pissed myself but couldn't stop until it was right, until I'd made him these long wooden planters with bell peppers growing in them, real ones, part of the stash of seeds I'd hidden, or at least I hoped they were growing, but they were definitely there. I felt good, so I went and loitered near the border fence until the OSP spotted me and did what they do, and I fell unconscious feeling nothing.

Now he's shivering in the tub all wet. It takes me a while to get him out and into the bedroom because I'm starting to shake from not drinking since the arak a few hours ago. The room is nearly empty. Only things around are socks and his paintings and cigarette butts. Get him on the bed and pull the sheet over him and it pretty quickly gets soaked in his sweat, and a little after it's got some of mine on it too. Abu Khaled is shaking and I'm shaking and I can't think straight, and I'm trying to ask him how he is, or if he can hear me, or if he has any money he can spare, but I can't get the Arabic out though I really try and remember. So for a few minutes the two of us are just making sounds at each other, groaning a little like birds. He starts to sound like he's in a lot more pain, and I don't know what to do or say so I start crying and just touching him, his head, his neck, the soles of his feet, shoulders, stomach, just putting my hands on him the way I would put them on soil, just getting to know what it is. He starts trying to say something, and I'm listening harder than I ever have.

"Law samaht," he's saying, over and over, "law samaht, law samaht." I don't know what he means except that his voice sounds like he needs something. And I'm remembering what he did and what I've done and didn't do, and I can't fucking understand what he's saying and I'm a sorry excuse for flesh so I take some deep breaths and I leave him there

crying out like I was an angel who turned away. And in the
front room I find a few crumpled up shekels and stuff them in
my pockets. Hold down some puke and try to stop shaking.
Hear him still in the room saying what he's saying, needing
what he's needing, and I walk out and I shut the door, and in
the yard the wooden planters are empty.

❖

NEXT MORNING I'VE got a few ribs broken. Last night I took
Abu Khaled's money and went to a bar in the civic center.
Wasn't enough money to settle my tab at Farah's, so I figured
it was worth it and besides some settlers might beat me
bad enough that I'd be passed out until my brother's gone
back to Earth. No such luck obviously as I'm awake now.
Neighborhood drone picked me up walking toward the bar
and put me on the municipal timeline, so some settlers came
by and I hit one of them kind of half-hearted but enough to
get beat. It felt alright. I actually think one of them might
have served as a guard at Ansar VI, but I couldn't be sure,
passed out too quick and besides I can't remember much
from those days. This morning the money's gone and I still
haven't had a drink, so things are pretty bad. Can't even
puke. Can still feel my insides breaking down. I'm willing
them on.

Out of options, so I get up from the civic center street
and limp through the delineation gate. Nothing left to do
but go to the house. My head is killing me and something
in my side is aching, in addition to the broken ribs. Maybe
they're poking some organ, something fragile in there, just
puncturing it with every step I take back toward the house.
Or maybe that's just all my fuckups talking.

The breath scanner at the front door is busted, stripped
for parts by someone since I've been here last, so I muscle
down the door and get inside. Most of the inside's been
stripped too. I stopped caring about it a long time ago so I
let it happen, even encouraged it sometimes. Not much left
inside the wooden walls, most of it synth wood but a few

planks here and there real that I brought with me on the first rocket. Standing inside it's still, empty like the remnants of a ghost. A reminder of what gets left when I try, which is nothing. A wave of something hits me and I feel sick, really sick, a new level of pain and nausea. Get on my knees to wait for the puke to come. I know what to do in my throat to coax it out and I do, little burps and swallowing, and soon enough there's a new puddle of bile on the floor, some arak smell and more blood than usual. Something in me knows there can't be much of this left. I rest my forehead on the floor. Red dirt tracked in by looters mixes a little with my sweat and I rub it around a little: Mars makeup. Almost pretty again. Don't want to get my head up from the floor or open my eyes so I crawl with my forehead pressed to the synth wood floor like some protracted migratory prayer. Feel my way around to the little closet I used to keep seeds in. Check first for the liquor compartment—found, broken, and emptied. I figured as much. But I reach behind and underneath and open up the second compartment, the one nobody knows about, not even Farah when we shared this place as lovers and comrades and fools. Eyes closed I'm fumbling around in the dark trying to find the last part of the person I was and then I do. I stay still for a little, and feel the blood pump in my body and around my rotten organs and through to my bruised and broken and reset arms and into my fingers and then somehow a little bit into the soil that my fingers are feeling, and through the soil into the roots of the last real poppy on Mars, the last remnant of the place I thought this planet could be.

When they took me to Ansar I'd already started drinking. Already just a shadow and welcomed the Palmach vehicles, the shackles. Farah already gone even when he was with me, the country on Earth already reunified, free. I knew I'd missed whatever a person's life could be that was good. The ship had flown. I gave up everything and let myself conceive of the life held in the imagination of Ansar VI and that was all. But still I kept this plant. Sometimes, in that sweet spot when the drink loosens my mind but doesn't wipe it, I

remember the little poppy and get wistful, swear to myself
I'll find a piece of land for my own and get things going, start
over, eke out home through the sweat and the tears, and then
I take another drink and it all just seems too hard so I let go
again. But here it still is, rare as all hell, almost impossible to
keep alive on this planet. My last resort.

My hand still stuck in the compartment and illuminated
by the artificial sunlight bulb I installed, the misters come
on. Wet fingers, a little caked up blood or dirt washing off,
and when the sound is done I can hear somebody behind
me in the room. I try to yank my hand out and turn around
and get up off the ground all at once and do none of them,
somehow end up hitting the ground face first. When I can
open my eyes and lift up my head a little some things swim
into view, two pairs of feet, one big, one heartbreaking small,
and I know.

"Hi, Fathi," I say, trying to push up onto my hands and
knees but not quite getting there. Suddenly my arms feel like
spun sugar. Nobody says anything while I keep trying to get
up, scoot over to the wall and sort of push up against it to get
some leverage. Eventually I give up and stay on the ground.
I shut my eyes and move my face so they're pointed where
I know Fathi's face will be and then I open them and I keep
them trained only on his face. I can't look at her. I don't want
to see how she's seeing.

Fathi looks older but then he always did. People always
used to guess he was the older one of us and sometimes I
thought they were right. I was born first but Fathi was born
smart. Born good maybe. He's dressed in nice jeans and a
yellow collared shirt and I start counting the hairs in his
beard to avoid looking at her.

"I'm here to take you home."

Looking right in his eyes I try to smile a little. "Like that
British song. Remember that? *Pack your things I've come to
take you home.* Something like that right? Only I don't have
anything to pack."

"Farah told me you're sick. Dying."

Fucking Farah.

"*Solsbury Hill*, that was it. Gabriel. You remember? Every time we'd play it Dad would tell us Peter Gabriel was pro-Palestine. Remember?"

"I don't want you to die."

My eyes are locked on Fathi's face like a leech but I can hear her breathing, I can feel her here with us seeing me and I don't know why these memories are coming to me now but I need Fathi to remember them with me. I know I smell like alcohol and blood, probably other things more vile and sick, but he's looking at me without any pity, without any anger even, and for once I let myself sit in that non-judgement, in that love, and I don't run away this time.

"Do you remember that? Fathi? The song?"

"I remember that. Of course I do." His eyes are soft and blue. I can feel one of my ribs poking into my skin and I wonder if it's bleeding but I can't look down to check because I might see her. "It's been a long time, habibi."

"Yeah." My mouth feels like brick and dust. "How have you been?"

"Good. Things are good."

Fathi used to cover for me when I came home late back on Earth. When the soldiers were looking for me after throwing rocks. When our parents were looking for me after boys. Fathi was my anchor and I've only been able to drift so long because I didn't have him here with me.

"You know things are different now, back home. There's a place for you there."

"I don't know. I don't know about that."

"I do."

Fathi and I playing football. Trying cigarettes together. The way he held me when my heart got broken. The way his face looked when I left him in the morning, asleep like an angel, and I took my bag of seeds and crawled through miles of tunnels to get to the rocket and held Farah's hand while we sobbed and the land got smaller and smaller and then gone.

"I left. I gave it up. It doesn't want me back."

"It doesn't want you dead either."

"I left you there. I left you all alone and I went away."

"Yeah, you did. So you're a piece of shit. What else is new."

Even sick as I am Fathi gets a laugh out of me. But the laugh hurts my ribs which remind me I've got ribs which reminds me I'm a person and so on. I try to avoid thinking those things because they hurt so I say something to get this to stop.

"I'm glad I left. And I'm glad I didn't take you with me." I don't feel anything when I say it, because I'm staring at the corner of Fathi's mouth and praying he'll get hurt and leave. I don't want to do this. Fathi's eyes I can't read and he comes forward, leans down to me and touches my forehead. Like some insect landing on a bloom. I'm blinking hard and he's wiping off the sweat from my brow. Fathi speaks soft to me while he holds my hand.

"I will forgive you no matter how hard you try to stop me. B'hebbek. Remember? B'hebbek. You can still come home."

The Arabic doesn't process in my brain but it does somewhere else. And I know he's telling the truth. His mouth is in that little curve it makes when he's being sincere. It used to make me annoyed that his body was bad at lying and mine was too good. I want to shake him and tell him to lie for both our sakes, for her sake.

"I don't have papers. They've got me on no-transport. There's no point in trying."

"One of the port employees agreed to get you off planet. They'll get you papers and a ticket on our return flight and you can live with us. You can come home."

"How much?"

"Sixty-five thousand."

His words are sieving through me like water, and the drink-guards-God-me voice is saying *You could get that for the poppy, easy. This is it. This is the moment. This is your soil telling you to come back. This is goodness finally coming to meet you where you are.* Trying my hardest to listen. To believe that this is my voice and that it's telling the truth.

"I'll try to get the money."

When I let myself say that my eyes almost waver, almost drop down to meet her gaze and let her see me. But I don't. Fathi looks down at her, and then at me, and his eyes get harder, sadder. I watch the muscles in his arm tighten, relax, tighten.

"The flight leaves at 11. Meet us there."

He turns to leave, tugging at his daughter's little arm so gently, just the way I used to tug at his when we were kids.

"Fathi?"

He stops and looks back.

"How's the soil?" I say. He smiles.

"Lush," he says. "Waiting for you." Between the three of us, Fathi and his daughter and me, something almost begins to grow, something almost claws its way to taking hold. I close my eyes, and as they leave the little one says "Buh-bye" but I hear it for a moment as "alive."

Alive.

❖

Now everything's a blur. The blood bot a blur. The still-raging protest a blur. Hasbara drones projecting blurs as I get close to the Import/Export and Contraband Office in the civic center, hands obsessively going to the little package of soil and life hidden in my crotch, making sure it's still there and I didn't break it. Now the IEC guard checking my papers and getting ready to jail me. Now whispering into their ear what I have and who I need to see. Now the higher up. Now the little room and the surveillance bots blanked for a few minutes. Now I'm taking out the poppy and now the higher up's eyes going wide and now "Name your price" and now I hear somebody's voice saying "Sixty-five thousand" and now one of the times I can't hear if it's me or God or drink or death or love but now the cash in a discreet little tote bag and now the poppy leaving my hand and now the last chance I had at what I'd dreamed of gone into the hands of a bureaucrat who'd sell it for more than I'd ever dare to dream. But, now, I don't care. I have what I came for. I know where I'm going. And all the way back through the civic center it's like I'm floating like the gravity's gone out again though it hasn't. And I get my rotten blood back and I keep walking and as I walk I'm shedding so much weight: the poppy, Ansar, the drones and the blood bots, the IEC, the beatings and the OSP, the settlers, Abu Khaled, the protest, the Quarter, hope, home, hope. And then I get where I'm going. And I'm silent as I push over the tote bag of money. And I speak in the voice of somebody too stupid and too wrong to do any different and I want to say so many things but instead I say "This covers the tab and then some. I'm going to sit here and drink and I don't want you to ever try and stop me" and Farah looks at me like the way you look at something that's not there anymore, like the way you look at where a plant used to be or a vase or a building, and then something in his eyes changes and he pours me something clear and unknowable and that's the end of it, and I drink until I can barely speak, and then when I'm ready I go to the port.

❖

CAN BARELY STAND. Make it to the viewing section and find the hole Farah and I hacked into the lightmesh fence years ago. Sneak through and collapse onto the bit of shadow on the edge of the takeoff platforms and find the one rocket gearing up for a launch. Where Fathi is. Where she is.

Pain in my back and in my stomach. I don't care. I take a swig from whatever I brought from Farah's and things quiet down. Just my rot and the settlement's rot and the planet's rot all communing, all sharing a body. I'm blissful knowing I did exactly what everybody with any sense thought I would do. I'm already somewhere floating outside anyone's jurisdiction. And then I look over at the rocket and my eyes roam to one of the windows and there she is.

It's too late to look away, I've already seen her and I swear she's seen me even though I know that's not possible, I'm too far away and it's dark. But I believe we're looking at each other. She's plain looking and sweet, a brown curtain of hair

and her eyes like two onion bulbs, little I mean, and light.
If anything was left of my heart she would break it. I can't
remember her name, if anybody ever told me in the letters to
Ansar or on the bulletin or maybe Fathi said it or fuck maybe
she told me herself once but I can't remember. The ship's
starting to lift off and I send my soul with it. I touch my
empty knee and I whisper like she can hear me.

I tell her they're right about me. They always were. I'm
bad and I'm a criminal and a threat and I tell her it's okay,
that she doesn't have to be that way, that people disappear
from your life and you can forget who they were or what they
did to you or what they looked like drunk, I tell her she's
home and she should know that she's home, that her dad is
good how I'm not, I tell her that God loves her and the land
loves her and I tell her that poppies need lots of sun and
not too much water and she just has to care for them until
they're gone, and I tell her that they self-seed so beautifully
that she'll forget about them for years and then, so suddenly,
like heartbreak or hope or pain, just so fucking quick, they'll
come back, and she won't even remember they were ever so
far gone.

Twenty Thousand Last Meals on an Exploding Station

Ann LeBlanc

ILES YALTEN HAS approximately thirty minutes before
she dies, and that's just enough time to try the new
gravlax place on level sixteen. She ducks through a
staff-only hatch and slips into the swift cold waters of the
maintenance access canal. Up in station engineering, her
team is probably just starting to panic, having found the
impending failure she so carefully hid.

Down on level sixteen, the gravlax joint looks promising.
The owner stiffens when he sees her. His eyes slide up and
down her body. First: her hairless head, mucus-slick skin, and
black-metal smart-nose. Second: her gilled and wattled neck,
the bio-metallic utility-tentacles that take the place of hands.
Finally: her backward knees and flippered feet.

She is dripping wet from the canal, making a mess of
his floor. A pause stretches between then, a mere second
lengthened by adrenaline. Then he goes to the closet and
pulls out an aug-friendly seat, setting it at the counter. Riles
smiles, and notes in her review that this place is aug-inclusive.

She orders one of everything, knowing she won't have
time to finish it all. With hope, she can at least try each dish
and cross this place off her list. If she doesn't, she'll have to
come back next loop.

The cured salmon—locally sourced from the station's aquaponics rigs—is creamy and salty, the perfect companion to the crisp of the knäckebröd. This one has a dab of mustard-dill sauce, that one has a bit of roe and lemon zest. She notes everything—texture, taste, plating, ambiance, and so on—in her mem-aug.

As she takes a bite of the last plate—new-potato with roe—the station lights flip from calm blue-white to fearful red. The shop owner's eyes widen, stuck in panic response, before he starts packing up his little shop—in violation of protocols; he should evac immediately.

"Don't bother," Riles says over the howl of the sirens. "Station reactor's gonna blow. Anti-matter containment failure." She takes another bite. "So you might as well try to enjoy the next... three minutes. Your food is astounding by the way."

His eyes flicker between fear, anger, and confusion. He points at the emblem on Riles's wetsuit. "Aren't you station engineering? Why aren't you up there helping?"

She starts to respond, but all that comes out is a slurred, "Oh, blarghle." Her emergency mem-backup flenses her brain like a nictitating membrane made of fingernail scraping across her consciousness. By the time it's done, the owner has fled.

She wipes the drool from her face, takes one last bite of potato, and waits for the end. She wanders out into the promenade, to an observation window, and watches ships flee through the speckled black of space, trying to escape their inevitable antimatter annihilation.

All but one. She gasps when she sees it. A ship emblazoned with the logo of the Pan-Aafaras Insurance Agency, burning hard *towards* the station. Had she not noticed it before? Or was this something new?

Before Riles can frantically update her mem-backup, the reactor fails. One moment she is alive, and the next she is bathed in a glory of white hot plasma. She dies, along with all the station around her.

❖

THREE DAYS EARLIER, Riles Yalten awakens, immersed in the warm waters of station engineering. The memory backup activates, pumping three days of memories into her brain. And then another three days, and another. More than two-hundred iterations of the three days before the reactor failure, all the way back to the first loop.

In this iteration—like the several hundred preceding—she pushes off from her work station and swims down to the emergency backup hub. An alarm tolls in time with the blinking lights, indicating a mem-backup from the future has arrived.

"False alarm," she lies on the engineering staff groupchat, after disabling the alert. "I'll look into it once I'm done checking the S4 baffles."

They don't need to know they're going to die. If Riles tells them about the fatal flaw in the newly installed magnetic baffles, they'll spend three days stressed beyond bearing, working nonstop with no sleep, to save a station that cannot be saved.

Instead, Riles slips out—taking a sick day—while her team meets to discuss the latest round of department budget cuts. It's time for her next meal.

❖

THEY SAY BELLAYN station has a restaurant for every planet, every culture, every taste. There are over twenty-six thousand restaurants on the station. Every year, a quarter of those restaurants close—competition is fierce, and rents are high—and are replaced with new ones. Thus, even if someone did nothing but dine out, it would be impossible to eat at every restaurant in the station, before churn rendered the task endless.

Impossible—unless you are trapped in a time loop.

Riles Yalten lost hope of escape more than a hundred iterations ago. Now, she has a new goal: to eat at every restaurant on Bellayn Station, and to review and record each dish (along with notes on service, ambiance, and accessibility).

This loop is dedicated entirely to a single restaurant, The Lab Wisteria. Specializing in Neo-Minimalist cuisine, they are consistently rated one of the top ten restaurants on the station. Getting a reservation can take months. Riles only has three days.

She pauses at the door of the restaurant, her date, Ina, standing beside her in a lavender halter-dress. Ina squeezes Riles's bicep, then intertwines her fingers in Riles's tentacles, unbothered by their writhing.

What Ina doesn't know is that Riles is only on a date with her because—in a previous loop—she'd scoped out that Ina fit the narrow criteria of both already having a reservation *and* being willing to go on a date with a merp-aug. Riles is the reason why Ina's original date flaked on her. Does Riles feel guilty about that? She would have, in the times before the loops, but now she has grown accustomed to knowing the consequences of her actions will be wiped away in hot plasma at the end of each loop.

Through the door, and the maître d' smiles, unaware that Riles considers him her nemesis. She sees the exact moment he notices her augs. She is deeply familiar with the transition from friendly to formal, relaxed to tense, open to guarded. He is about to declare that a reservation is required. He will say that the waitlist is months long. He will *not* willingly offer any opportunity to add their names to the list. He will be exceptionally polite, overtly kind in tone, but the subtext will be as obvious as it is deniable.

Riles's date—bless her—does not let him say anything at all.

She has a reservation, she says. She asks if the owner is in, her words and tone implying a personal relationship. Throughout this exchange, her arm is draped across Riles's back, her hand resting at the top of her hip, holding Riles close under her protection.

They are not seated at Ina's usual table—near the windows that look out over the restaurant's flower garden—but in a table nestled in the back corner. Riles doesn't care, she's here for the food. In the time before the station began exploding, she would've been frozen with anxiety over the semi-polite glances and hostile stares of the other diners. Current fashion only accepts augs if they're discreet, and only if the owner is polite enough to be mildly ashamed. Riles is not discreet, but she has learned not to care for the opinions of those who will shortly be atomized. Not only will they forget, but she has practice of hundreds of iterations at ignoring her own internalized hatred.

Despite the ambiance, the food is excellent. An interesting take on Neo-Minimalist cuisine utilizing specially-bred flowers acting as light counterpoints or accents to the simple flavors of each dish. The decor—a much celebrated commentary on the color of wisteria flowers—does nothing for Riles. She prefers the plastic tables and bulkhead walls of an inner-station hole-in-the-wall. Or—even better—one of the few waterlogged canteens that serves the station's merp staff.

The first course is a spoonful of black-cream, topped with spinach foam, and a single nasturtium blossom.

After that is fried skate—wild-caught, imported at great expense—with a caper-citrus sauce and a borage blossom dressing. The best part of being trapped in a time-loop is not having to worry about blowing a years salary on a single meal.

While waiting for the third course, Riles feels a familiar itching and excuses herself to the bathroom. It's as bad as she feared: recessed lighting, trendy gargle-pop music, hanging vines, and no hookups for a waste port. Twice, someone walks in, sees her emptying her waste-tube into the sink, freezes, and then ducks out again.

So she's already in a bad mood when—making her way back to her table—she hears her sister's voice yelling her name. Which is impossible because Milla is light years away, and the station's loop-bubble is only three light-days in radius.

Yet here she is, power-suit clad, face angry behind her plex-bubble helmet.

"Why aren't you in engineering?" she asks, stomping towards Riles.

Riles opens her mouth, but her brain is too busy screaming confusion to provide any words besides, "Ummm..."

Milla gestures at Riles's body. "Does mom know about this?"

The screaming in Riles's head transitions to horror, shame, anger. She wishes the station would explode right now.

"I... no. We don't really talk." Riles and her mom have been no-contact for five years now. Riles has been careful to only talk to her sister briefly, vaguely, and with no video.

"Whatever." Milla rolls her eyes. "We can deal with your bad decisions later. I need a debrief *now*. Station computer says your mem-backup's active, so don't play games with me."

"I'm in the middle of something." Riles tries to edge her way back towards her table.

"Not any more you aren't. Debrief. Now. What's causing the backup system to engage? And why haven't you fixed the problem already?"

The nerve of her. "You think we haven't tried? You want to know why we're still stuck in a loop? All of the replacement magnetic baffles—every single one—is tainted." Riles is up in her face now, breath fogging Milla's faceplate. "Our department has been defunded over and over again. Forced to use a cut-rate supplier, and now, here we are, with an antimatter containment system that will always—"

Milla interrupts, "But haven't you tried—"

"Whatever you can think of, we tried. Nothing worked. Nothing. Which is why—"

Milla tries to grab Riles's hand. "Then what are you doing here? You should be—"

"Let me finish! One-hundred and thirty iterations me and my team tried to save this station. Over a year of subjective time." Riles gestures to the diners. "These are the people we were trying to save. Do you think they'd do the same for us? These people voted to defund engineering, voted against merp accessibility measures, voted to make it harder to aug new merps. One-hundred and thirty iterations I tried to save them, and these people have no idea. I couldn't let my team keep dying like that."

"What did you do," Milla's voice is flat, eyes like she's going to hit her. Riles remembers that look. Riles thought she was free from that look.

This time though, Riles doesn't back down from the implied threat. "I disabled the backup system for everyone but myself. And now I'm taking some me-time."

Riles starts telling Milla about her plan to eat at every restaurant on the station, but only gets halfway through before Milla's armored fist crunches into Riles's nose. Ina rushes to her side, butter knife brandished against the power-armor wearing stranger.

The station lights go red, alarm wailing. Riles laughs, blood streaming down her face, as the mem-backup painfully yanks all the threads from her brain.

Her nose hurts worse after the backup. "Your team must've messed up," she says. "Been there. See you next—" and then they are bathed in fire.

❖

RILES AWAKENS THREE days earlier, knowing she is doomed. Her sister—acting on behalf of the company that insures the station—will not stop until the station is saved and the loop is cut. Even if it's impossible; she's the sort that will grind herself to dust to meet her superior's expectations.

Riles has to prevent Milla from making the situation worse, but she also has to eat. She can do both right? Fight her armed and angry sister, while dining the full breadth of Bellayn Station.

Two days later, Riles is enjoying the smell of the trees and open water at a lakeside cafe nestled in one of the station's larger parks. She's slurping broth from a bowl of spicy braised beef noodle soup, so she doesn't see Milla coming. An armored hand knocks the bowl from her tentacles; hot broth goes everywhere, chili-oil stings Riles's sensitive mucosal skin.

"You have loop-psychosis," Milla declares, grabbing Riles's arm and clicking a shackle onto it.

Riles tries to twist away, but the chair and table get in the way. "I'm *fine*. I wouldn't be enjoying a nice meal if I still had—"

Milla grabs Riles's other arm, hard. "LP is inevitable if you've been in a loop too long." Milla's arms—assisted by her suit—are too strong to pull away from. "You're obviously suffering from delusions of grandeur." She drags Riles out of the cafe, into the park.

"No. I *had* loop-psychosis. I know what LP feels like. "

"If you were fully sane, you wouldn't have disabled the mem-backups in order to go on some hedonistic mission." Milla pulls the shackles, dragging Riles down the path that winds towards the lake. The shackles are rubbing raw the part of the wrist where arm transitions to tentacle.

"You have *no idea* what we went through. My sabotage was a mercy. And my restaurant reviews? How I saved myself. Staying focused on an achievable goal is exactly what the regulations say to do when loop-stuck."

Milla scoffs. "You can't evaluate your own condition. The fact you thought becoming a merp was a good idea tells me you weren't in a good place mentally to begin with." A low blow, but Riles *really* doesn't want to talk to Milla about her transition. She needs to focus on getting free.

Milla pulls harder. "My team's on its way to disable your mem-backup." She laughs when she feels Riles flinch. "I would've preferred your help, but we'll handle this without you. You don't have to suffer anymore."

The lake spreads out before them, the water mirror-calm. Riles waits till the path takes them alongside the shoreline, then she strikes. Milla's mistake was thinking of Riles as-she-was—a non-aug with hands larger than her wrists—and not as she is—a merp-aug whose utility tentacles hold within themselves a multitude of tools useful for deep-space engineering.

The shackles fall, clattering on the sidewalk. Milla tries to grab Rile's arm, but Riles pushes off her, twisting and falling off the path, down into the water.

A splash, and she is away. Moments later Riles feels the

vibrations of Milla's plunge into the water, but now they are in Riles's element. Milla's powered suit—fast on land—is heavy in the water, and she isn't familiar with the water-based layout of the station's core. Slipping away into the maintenance canals is trivial. Stopping Milla's team will be harder.

Swimming down the spine of the station, Riles searches the station's cam-feeds. Four suits, all non-aug humans, float outside the engineering office hatch, scrabbling futilely at the door controls. Fools probably didn't bring any water rated equipment. Not surprising; there aren't that many old merp-built stations left.

Their stun-sticks don't work underwater either, as they discover when Riles comes up behind them. Her equipment works just fine, and after she stun-locks their suits, she locks the hatch behind her.

❖

RILES AWAKENS, THOUGH the water doesn't feel as safe as it usually does. She thought she had escaped her family. When she was a child, Riles mother told her stories about Bellayn. The people were rude, fast, and unrepentant thieves. It was a hub of moral decay, the sort of place people went to make money or buy their own debasement.

The reality was stranger, bigger, and kinder. Riles couldn't help but stare at the first merp she saw, wet-slick seal-skin, metal head-plate inscribed with concentric circles of sea creatures and ships and constellations. He was eating nopales tacos with a confident ease, and none of the diners in that cramped commissary paid him any mind.

Riles had no idea a person could have a body like that.

❖

RILES IS TRAPPED, and the walls are closing in.

The station's vast antimatter stores—released all at once—are capable of reverting time three days—enveloping a three light-day wide sphere. Milla's fast-response ship would've been caught in the loop as soon as they crossed the reversion line, but it's equipped with its own chrono-reversion system. Only able to revert one-hour at a time, it took her ship more than seventy iterations to make it to the station.

Every iteration, Milla arrives earlier. More and more of Riles's time is spent setting traps, finding new ways to thwart her sister. It is never enough.

"Why are you even here?" Riles asks, over comms, as her sister chases her from a mussels-and-fries joint.

"PAIA insures Bellayn—we're contractually obliged."

"No, why are *you* here?"

She doesn't reply. Either the question caught her off guard, or she found the lamprey-drones Riles set in wait for her.

Or, she's preparing her own ambush. Riles hides behind a decorative shrubbery along the promenade. The afternoon crowd is thick with slow-walking tourists, loud kids, busy locals. Milla could be anywhere in the stream of bodies, waiting for Riles to make a run for the canal access hatch.

A scream cracks across the noise of the city, and the crowd ripples. Milla hurtles past, an electric lamprey-drone stuck to her neck. She goes down, eyes locked to the ceiling, lamprey writhing, debilitating current locking her suit.

"You being here isn't an accident," Riles says, foot on Milla's shoulder, keeping her down. "It has to be mom. She pulled strings."

Milla tries to reach up to Riles, and fails. "Loop... psychosis," she grits out.

Riles presses harder into Milla's shoulder. "Mom interfering isn't farfetched. Remember when she got me fired from the remediation job on Mintilla?"

"No. You lost that job because you were obsessed with saving those clams."

Milla wouldn't stop struggling, so Riles uses her utility tentacles to weld her suit to the floor.

"Is that what mom told you? I'm thirty-eight and she's still treating me like I can't make my own decisions."

"Is she wrong? You had such a promising career. And you
threw that away because you wanted to be a fish? Why can't
you just be normal?"

Riles's chest swirls, a mix of rage and fear. But instead of
cranking the lamprey's current to max, she says, "You sound
just like mom," and walks away. She probably has enough
time to try the caldo verde joint before Milla's team cuts her
loose to continue the chase.

❖

ITERATIONS BLUR TOGETHER, accreting in her memory like
a mollusk building the layers of its shell. In one memory
she slurps mint ice-cream, in another she swims up and up,
her sister screaming below her, the station falling to pieces
around them.

How many iterations pass this way? Riles loses track. She
could look it up with a thought, but she'd prefer not to know.
It's easier to live in the moment, and the only number that
truly matters is how many restaurants are left to review.

6,452 restaurants still on the list. She hides, jianbing in
hand, wedged trembling in an electrical shaft. The canals
aren't safe anymore, Milla started poisoning the waters five
iterations ago.

5,978. Station security hunt her through the corridors,
shock-sticks humming a deadly tune. Each iteration Milla
and Riles struggle to convince security that the other is an
existential threat to the station. Station security is loop-
locked, and thus predictable, but it's yet another way Milla is
tightening the possibility-space Riles operates in.

5,722. Riles and Milla wrestle on a kitchen floor, pizza
ovens baking the air around them.

"Why are you still fighting me?" Riles asks, pinning her to
the ground. "You don't have to make yourself miserable for
Pan-Aafaras. Do you know how much they charge Bellayn
for insurance? They'll pay you a pittance of that, then send
you on another mission. Stop fighting; take a vacation for
once."

Milla's writhes below her. "Give up? Like you did? I have an actual career, and I won't let you derail it with another of your weird obsessions."

But Riles is already gone, leaping up and back, out through the door.

5,255. Riles flees, mouth full of acorn-squash dumpling. The restaurant explodes behind her, throwing her into the air. She's been planting explosives, sacrificing parts of the station she's already dined.

Riles loses count. She floats in the void, stars all around her, body swelling, moisture evaporating, mind drifting.

She remembers the day she started her transition. A small pink pill, a glass of water, the table spread with potluck snacks, her merp friends there to celebrate. She mostly doesn't remember the surgeries. The pain of recovery is small compared with the feeling of fear and hope transitioning into certainty and peace—the glorious *rightness* of her new self. Nothing more right than the cool water on her gills, nothing more perfect than knowing she could live within the water forever and ever.

Eternity swells out before her. She returns to the present, sitting across from Milla. Smoke hangs between them. The station is burning, a small fire compared to the impending antimatter flame, but no less deadly to the station.

"Riles," Milla tries to sit up, slumps. "I... can't do this anymore. My team... we all have LP. I held them off as long as I could, but..."

"You're going to kill the station." Riles knows about the railgun on Milla's ship. She knows that Milla could have done this at any time.

A titanium slug, fired precisely, piercing the station's heart. Milla might get lucky; it might only kill a few hundred souls between the outer hull and the engineering office. It might only disable the mem-backups. Riles would awaken at the start of the next iteration—no memory of her struggle to save the station, her failure, or her culinary salvation. All her reviews, so carefully compiled, lost forever.

There is also a chance the titanium slug hits the antimatter reactor—or any of the subsystems that keep it stable. The emergency reversion system *might* fire, or it might not, depending on exactly where the slug hits, and what it damages. The station might be annihilated instantly. The loop would end. Nine million lives would be gone, forever.

Riles has lived so long within the safety of the loop. A gamble like this is unthinkable. Nine million souls. Her own sister. Though perhaps the thought of destroying Riles's merp body is a plus for Milla.

Riles slumps, "You always were stronger than me."

"You lasted longer loop-locked than I did. You're tougher than I thought. Your team—I've never gotten them to betray you. They trust you so much—respect you, love you. I didn't know—"

Mem-backups hit them both at the same time. Riles will have one last iteration, one last chance.

"I'm sorry. Mom was... a lot, and I should have stood up for you. I should've listened," Milla says, her voice cracking from the smoke, or perhaps the pain of that admission.

Riles is stunned. "I'm sorry too. I should've let you try to help when you first got here," she says, then pauses. What else can she say? There aren't words that will revert the damage between them, and they've already been backed up, so neither will remember this conversation.

"I wish..." one of them says, and then they die, hope being no match for antimatter.

❖

RILES AWAKENS THREE days earlier, knowing this is her final loop. She has maybe five hours before Milla's ship can take the shot.

One last meal. Riles sits on a chair at the center of Bellayn's Hexagonal Gardens. Here amongst the reeds, in the transition between water and ground, below the stars, is the best merp-food joint on the station. Passed down from master to apprentice for five generations, it has existed in one location or another since Bellayn was a tiny merp-run entrepot.

This place—wet and full of life, smelling of comfort food—is her favorite on her station. Riles had been saving it for last, and now—with her work unfinished—she is here for her final meal.

She greets the owner with a kiss, as she has done many times before. They've prepared a multi-course meal, a full exploration of Bellayn's merp-cuisine. Around her sit her friends, merps and non-merps, co-workers and lovers. They all came when she called.

First course is a pureed cauliflower dip, accompanied by raw cucumber and broccoli. Second course is a beet and leek soup, seasoned with dill. In the early years of Bellayn, the station was mostly water, the crew mostly merp. They couldn't afford fancy imports, and ate a simple diet of what they could easily grow in rickety aquaponics rigs.

Third course is tilapia, poached in a ginger-tomato broth. Tilapia is a hardy fish, hard to kill, like the community Riles found on Bellayn.

Fourth course is boiled brine-shrimp, with a basil and sweet-vinegar dipping sauce. Riles's comm pings, Milla telling her she has just two hours left.

Five courses later, and Riles is full. Thirty minutes until the end. She spends ten minutes writing her last review. Above her, Milla's ship's drive-plume flares orange-bright through the plasglass. One last sip of rice wine, and then she activates the program she wrote.

Her mem-backup rips her brain apart, preserving her memories. It only takes a moment, just a few hours of her favorite foods and her favorite people.

When it's done, she slumps in her chair, sliding lower and lower until she's fallen into the brackish water. She floats, watching the stars, waiting for what will come next.

Deep in the station, her program runs. It compiles her memories, all of them, all the way back to the first loop and all her life before that, and it sends them to Milla's ship, along with a message.

This is Riles's surrender. She tells Milla she won't fight back, and she'll do what she can to help her fix the station.

She's attached all her notes from the year of hell, everything they tried and failed. Maybe Milla's team and the equipment they brought can solve the impossible, maybe not. Riles asks for a few hours each iteration to work on her reviews, but this isn't an ultimatum. Riles is placing herself at Milla's mercy. There's no going back from this. Milla could disable Riles's mem-backup and work without her. Or she could take Riles's hand and work towards healing the damage to the station and their relationship.

But whatever happens, it will be an end. And after thousands of loops, Riles could really use a vacation.

❖

TWO YEARS LATER, Riles and Milla share a meal—their first together since the loop ended. Fried crawfish, smothered okra, dirty rice, laid out on a scuffed plastic table in a cramped commissary wedged between two bulkheads. Milla's only passing through, a few hours before her ship departs.

Riles attracts a few glances from the other diners. She has a sort of local fame: from saving the station, from her almost-complete restaurant guide, from her newly-won spot on the city council.

The last two years were rough for Bellayn. They never did fix the reactor. Fifty-three iterations they tried, till even Milla admitted defeat. Desperate, they used parts from the railgun in Milla's ship to launch the reactor as far from Bellayn as possible. Three-hundred people died. The station survived on emergency power for over a month, during which another thousand died. The PAIA inquest lasted a single week; the agency absolved all parties—including the original faulty baffle vendor. The rich fled, taking their neo-minimalist cuisine and seats on the city-council with them.

Riles tells all this to Milla, who mostly stays quiet. They've been messaging each other across the light-years. Their relationship still awkward, but Milla is listening, and Riles has hope that something new will grow between them.

Riles never did finish her restaurant list. In her spare time she eats, filling in the gaps, but she's made peace with the fact that she'll never truly finish. She knows that her and Milla's relationship will never be what either of them truly wants. Instead, she'll try to enjoy the infinite space between here and there, one meal, one conversation, at a time.

Blood in the Thread

CHERI KAMEI

"TODAY," SHE SAYS, "we are women who are actually cranes." Her hair is loose and her face is bare. Off to the side, her wedding dress lies strewn across an entire hotel room bed, train trickling down, a stream of white silk shot through with crimson ribbon. "Do you remember?" she asks.

You remember. You hated that story when you were younger: the molting feathers, the discovery, the betrayal, the abrupt, unsatisfactory conclusion.

"Hey," she says. The engagement band on her delicate finger gleams in the light. "It's only a story. And today we are cranes because I say we are beautiful, beautiful cranes." She tips your chin and her kiss is a resolution, not a promise. You shouldn't have agreed to see her before the nuptials, but she asked, and you can never say no.

"Okay," you say. You unpack your bag, lay out the tools of your trade, the colors and powders and stains. While her face is still naked and true, you reach out, cup her cheek, whisper, "Marry me." You will never tire of saying it.

Everything from the fading stars to the hotel Bible holds its breath. She beams. She breaks into helpless laughter. She gestures at the wedding gown and presses your hands to her tired face.

You nod and pull yourself together, stretch her arm out toward you, and begin to dream of wings.

❖

Once upon a time, there lived a man who found a wounded crane upon his doorstep. Deep in the bird's breast lay a fletched arrow. A slick spill of blood stained her feathers a furious shade of red, the exact shade of a poppy gone to rot. The man pressed his hands to the wound and, beneath the squelch and gore, he felt a heart that still fought, pounding back against his palm. He had no obligation to the crane, but its beauty, its tragic majesty, moved him. "I will care for you," he told the crane. "I promise, I promise, I promise."

❖

IT HAS ALWAYS been the two of you, ever since you were both jam-handed and pulling the fat, flowered heads of roses off of the bushes in your front yard. You do everything together and never question it. In high school, when she stars as the lead in a few musicals, you attend every show. You fill sketchbooks and canvases with your waking dream: the same girl aging in real time, standing, singing, smiling, in repose; yours, kept pressed between the pages. When junior prom comes around, you get ready together in her bedroom, zipping up dresses, surrounded by tubes of lip gloss and a rainbow of eye tints. The night is perfect and she looks so lovely. She closes her eyes and tilts her head for the touch of a blending brush, and so you kiss her.

It is no surprise, then, that you follow her into the city for the auditions and part-time jobs, the two-bedroom shit apartment you share with one bed made up for show and the other rumpled from two bodies curled close. By day, you attend beauty school and ache with her absence. By night, you dream of the lives you could have together, all the scripts and wardrobe decisions, together, entangled. "Marry me," you practice whispering as she sleeps. Anything feels possible with her body warm next to yours.

Neither of you feel the world shift the day she books a job, a shoot in the same city where you tear ticket stubs and buy your groceries and make love and exist. You do her makeup for her, at her insistence; for good luck, she says. She leaves in the morning and comes home at night and so you go on. Absolutely nothing changes until everything does.

The movie premieres. Her face is in subways tunnels and on billboards, lovely and large as the moon.

Suddenly everyone wants to stake their claim.

The night before her first televised interview, she sits in bed, breathing into a paper bag. She clings to you and you hold her together with your own two hands. "Come with me," she insists. "Tomorrow. We'll tell everyone that only you can do my makeup. It can't be anyone else. Please."

It's how you end up backstage in a small dressing room, murmuring encouragement as you stain her eyelids purple and gold. Turning her face this way and that, you lift the apple of her cheeks with a blush soft as plum blossoms. You rouge her lips into a pink slick as a sliced peach. You hide away the little girl who used to scribble on sheet music and eat too many jam sandwiches and give her a mask to hide behind instead. When you watch her smiling and chatting nervously on the television monitor later, you know you are the only one who can peek behind this version of her. Only you have held her face between two hands and seen the truth of her, brilliant and terrified and beautiful. You think, *I am going to marry that woman.*

And then her costar walks out to thunderous applause. As he answers questions, he keeps touching her forearm, resting his hand on her thigh. Only you seem to be able to see the way her smile goes rigid. As they depart, he draws her close. She disappears into his embrace, cut from sight like a bird shot from the sky.

❖

THERE IS NO question, then: The man takes the injured crane into his home and tends to it with great patience and care. The crane seems to understand his intent, and so allows the touch of his rough hands, the stink of wood smoke and musk that stings. She bears it as best she can. Eventually, she recovers.

There is no question, then: The man must release her. He has no use for a crane, no matter how beautiful. He takes her out of the woods. The sky stretches out. The crane flies far.

But that is not where this tale ends.

The very next evening, a woman appears at the man's door, beautiful and majestic. She gives no indication that she is a changeling, once a crane. And what reason would the man have to believe in such magic? No version of the story will say.

In any case, it is always the same: The man falls in love.

(Does the woman?)

In any case, they marry.

❖

"I DON'T UNDERSTAND," she says. Her manager has called her in for a discussion. They want photos and flirting and more, playing things up to build buzz for the film. The handsome lead and the beautiful ingénue: It is a story that writes itself.

She looks to you for an answer. You will not be the one to hold her back. You tell her, "I have an idea. Trust me."

You get out your growing sprawl of cosmetics. For her first awards show, you send her out covered in shimmering camellias and barbed butterflies that spiral down her bare arms, fading into the faint lines of her blue, blue veins. You saturate those delicate petals and wings with all the venom in your heart. You line her eyes sharp as spears. You leave a giant golden flower, bulbous with poison, where her costar is most apt to smack wet kisses. If you cannot show that she is yours and you are hers, then you can at least make them all realize that their touches will be rebuffed, profane and unworthy.

He doesn't lay a hand on her. (Not that night.)

From then on you give her everything in you: labyrinthine shapes like magic runes, drawn in neon for a fashion show; poetry that curls around the shells of her ear, creeping down her exposed neck, wrapping like a gauntlet round her elbow; a splash of cherry blossoms connected by branches that become swollen stitches, lines becoming giant centipedes, white and delicate as lace, curling protectively around her jaw, for a dinner out she cannot avoid.

You shield her from what you can, but her face is in every magazine and newspaper, and her costar is right there with her. You follow her dutifully and remind yourself that this was your dream. (Somewhere between the shifting planes of each transformation, you buy a ring, deep gold, diamonds and devotion.) But people can only reach out for so long and the barricades you build together stretch only so high. Their touches begin to land, and there is only flesh beneath the fantasies you sear into her skin.

The first time it happens, you are waiting to prep her for some industry event. She comes home and won't look you in the eye. She is already crying and you don't understand until she removes her coat and you see the ring of bruises around her biceps. "Don't be mad."

"Who did this?" you ask her—can't look at it, start to reach out, think better of it.

"I told them I didn't want to do it anymore." She shakes her head. "They're going to ruin everything if I tell. The things they said..."

(You think about the ring hidden in a shoebox under your side of the bed.)

That night you don't bother color correcting the indigo and violet smudges that form stepping stones around her arm. Instead, you smear on black body paint, thick and angry as an oil spill. From shoulder to fingertip, you turn her skin unrelenting and then pull from it shining galaxies, deep and dark as lost strength, swirling with all the sadness in your veins. You waft a nebula against the expanse of her forearm. You fill the spaces beneath her puffy eyes with glittering stars fallen.

When you kiss her, it is not a proposal, but it is a promise and a lie all the same.

"It's okay," you tell her. "We're going to be okay."

❖

HERE IS THE crux of the tale. The man is poor, so his new lady love, this mysterious woman, this maybe crane, offers up her one skill: She can weave the finest silk, but only in secret. She makes her new husband promise never to set eyes on her work, not even a peek. What else can he do? The man agrees. He buys her a loom. He keeps the doors tightly shut. Soon, the house fills with the endless creak of the warp and weft.

When the woman emerges, hours later, she carries with her yards of gorgeous silk, light as air, soft as cream, every inch dyed a bright vermilion. Taken to market, each yard sells for the highest prices. Soon the couple are able to live comfortably.

(Do not ask: How did the man earn his living before this miracle?)

After so many months of weaving day and night, the woman's pallor sinks to gray. She can never seem to keep warm. She does not eat. Still, she churns out the silk to take to market. Whenever she is not working, she sleeps and the house falls silent.

(Do not ask: Does the man ever offer to help?)

The man wears red silk slippers. He furnishes the house with fine food and rare jewels. When buyers praise his wife's work, he tells them all how he is desperately, deeply, achingly in love.

(Do not ask, ever: Would the crane wife be able to say the same?)

❖

"TODAY," SHE SAYS, "make me something far away." You brush her skin gray and wash her out, turning her flesh to television static. You push her behind all the noise and let her stay there, somewhere numb with pins and needles. Above it all, you overdraw her mouth and paint it a magenta so garish that no one can see the split lip she sports beneath. She still draws it tight in a perfect smile.

"Today," she says, "remind me how it used to feel." You grow fat-headed roses around the sunken curve of her right eye and layer on foundation so heavy that the page of music you shade into her eyelid has the exact texture of aged parchment. The shiner beneath only adds a depth that no one else can seem to replicate.

"Today," she says in a rasp, but can say no more because of the ring of bruises like sapphires around her neck.

You reach beneath the bed for the shoebox one night because you cannot stand it. You know it is the wrong time. "Marry me," you say, fumbling the ring. You have only one free hand. The other holds a bag of frozen peas to her swollen rib cage. "We'll go away from here. We'll start over."

There is a moment when her eyes slide away to the magazines and bundled script pages, the view from the new apartment, the billboards and city beyond. It is just a moment. Her gaze returns to you, red and puffy as a poppy gone to rot.

"Marry me," you ask again. When you try to smooth away her tears, you only manage to rub the salt into her skin. It is then that she shows you the unsigned contract that came with the diamond and platinum monstrosity that has taken your place on her ring finger. Through your tears, she is someone you cannot recognize, bare-faced and broken.

❖

THE MAN GROWS curious or he forgets or he ignores the consequences or he simply doesn't care. The point is: Eventually he disregards his wife's one request. He looks.

This is what he sees: The woman he claims to love, wasting away, yet, still, she weaves. Rummaging beneath the fabric that conceals her hunched flesh, she seems to pull. Extracting part of herself, she jams it into the loom. The blood drips from her fingers. (Is it her feathered body plucked raw? Is it her thin human skin sliced open?)

Inch by inch, red silk emerges. The finest in the land.

(The result is the same: She stitches herself into the silk. She tells her husband to sell it to make him happy.)

The woman turns to look. She knew he would be there someday. Perhaps her human face falls away and the crane appears, blood trickling from its breast, a wound reopened. Perhaps her human face remains—attached to her human body, her human destruction—for no reason at all except so that she can finally say, "My love, where are your promises now?"

❖

"TODAY," SHE SAYS, "we are women who are actually cranes."

The crane wife is supposed to fly away in the end, never to return.

"Today we are cranes because I say we are beautiful, beautiful cranes."

Did you stop to wonder how the crane came to the man's doorstep in the first place?

"Marry me," you beg.

Did he shoot her out of the sky himself?

❖

YOU WALK HER down the aisle in matching white dresses like when you were children. The wings down your bare arms are identical to hers, pearlescent white tipped with coal black. (It is just a story, but you can feel the spill of blood down your chest, the damp forest floor at your feet. The fletched arrow came from nowhere and now you are looking up at the sky.)

Her costar stands at the altar. Her manager peeks out from the front row. Frankly, you want to rip your own skin to shreds, but this is the story she has chosen to weave with her own blood and bone and tears.

(Cranes mate for life.)

You walk down the aisle together, like it was always meant to be. (You support her weight as she works off her veil, one-handed.) There are freesias everywhere. (You keep her balance as she tugs at her dress, leaving it behind, molted feathers.) You feel the heat of tears hit you. (She walks with her beaten body on display, blues and greens that swirl into yellows, her ribs and thighs and back.) Her costar pulls nervously at the knot of his tie. (She scrubs her arm across all the makeup you've carefully applied.) They stand next to one another, face-to-face.

The camera flashes go off like an enchantment.

(Tomorrow, the photos will drop, the record you've taken of the damage over time, feathers plucked from her own raw and battered flank, woven into the story she never truly owned.)

The entire congregation hushes.

(Half-naked, winged, bleeding, she drops to one knee. "Marry me," she says. And you say, "Yes.")

YOU FLY AWAY into the sunset, like a movie, like a fairy tale, like another pretty story of love and sacrifice and freedom. You weave your feathers into the loom, the warp and weft and pattern, your blood adding punctuation to each lie, crossing out every single truth. You look over your shoulder for the betrayal. You tell yourself, "I will care for her and she will care for me, and we will live happily ever after." The creak of the loom echoes, "I promise, I promise, I promise." These days, when you pull your skin apart in the name of love, you do not even feel the pain. You weave your story. You set it free.

Sutekh:
A Breath of Spring

SHARANG BISWAS

RESURRECTION WAS NEVER comfortable. Os's lungs had been perfectly content in their laziness, with nothing to do but decay peacefully. Now, they wanted air again. But there was no air: just thick, clinging fluid and a bitter, metallic taste.

Heave—gasp—choke.

Now his lungs were on fire. It took a minute for his brain to start up again before he could claw at the sides of the tub and haul himself up.

His face broke free of the surface. Blessed air.

Gurgle—splutter—BREATHE.

No matter how many times he died, his body never seemed to remember the particulars of resurrection.

Fresh blood clogged his throat. He coughed, forcing the last of it out of his lungs, before launching into one of his usual lines. "Isn't a tub of blood a little theatrical?"

"I don't make the rules of magic," a voice replied.

Os froze. The voice was different. Deeper. Sharper. Masculine.

He scrubbed blood out of his eyes.

A stranger stood before him, regarding him skeptically. A slim, young man with skin the colour of the desert sands and scalp-tattoos so dense they could be mistaken for hair.

"Os, hurry up out of the tub, or it'll congeal," the stranger said, his tone bored. He bent over and began gathering the snuffed-out candles that ringed Os's tub.

Os hesitated. They were in the familiar, rectangular ritual chamber at the back of Isis's cave, with the tub in the centre. Oil lamps on hooks lit the stone walls and their painted reliefs. Shelves were directly carved into the southern wall, filled with papyrus scrolls and stone tablets. Sculpted into the eastern wall was the false door his soul had entered through, lured by the—he glanced down and yes, it was there—plate of fresh fruit on the stone floor next to the tub.

The plate had gained a new offering. Nestled among the berries, dates and figs, there appeared to sit a raw hunk of meat. No, not just meat: a bloody heart. Os wrinkled his nose at it. But the chamber smelled of incense, which, while cloying, was also familiar.

Os realized he'd been dumbly gazing around the room.

"Where's Isis?" he ventured.

"Who?" The man looked up. His eyes were blue-green chips of faience, much like Isis's. "Isis? The witch? Are you her brother or...?"

The man stood up, hands still full of candle. He was dressed like her: white linen skirt, gold bracelets, nails varnished a deep red. He wore no tunic though, and his bare chest was lightly muscled.

"Os, I'm pretty sure you were mauled by a Sacred Hippo on your last delve in the Pyramid. So why are you acting as though you bumped your head on a rock and went nuts?"

His voice turned gentle, patient—condescending, even— as though he were speaking to a five-year-old.

He continued, "I'm Amu-Aa, the witch who drags your sorry ass back to life every time you die. Now will you please get out of the tub? It's very hard to clean congealed blood."

❖

GURGLE—SPLUTTER—BREATHE.

This time, as soon as he caught his breath, Os leaped out

of the tub, narrowly avoiding the food offerings.

"You're back!" he said, eyeing the witch.

Amu-Aa scowled.

Os shivered, naked and drenched in rapidly-cooling blood as he was.

"Os, seriously, are you playing some kind of idiot prank?" Amu-Aa asked, handing Os a towel. "Or did Ammit the Devourer chew up your brain as well as your heart?"

The towel wrapped snugly around Os's waist. Its warm softness seemed almost alien to Os, who had grown used to the hard edges and blistering heat the Pyramid offered. And it was certainly more comfortable than anything Isis had ever given him.

"I thought..." Os tried, but didn't know how to finish the sentence. Amu-Aa clearly had no idea who Isis was. Must be a witch thing. Maybe Isis had bespelled the man, at the behest of the Gods, or something.

The pause stretched awkwardly between them.

"Congratulations on your first thought?" Amu-Aa finally said, though he sounded more confused than mean-spirited.

"Never mind," Os muttered, blushing. "Could you pass me my armour?"

Amu-Aa lifted the leather-and-bronze affair off its shelf in the southern wall.

"I polished it for you," he said.

"Yeah?"

It showed. The bronze glowed a comforting red, as though lit from within. Os could smell fresh wax. "You didn't have to."

Amu-Aa shrugged.

"You're the only one idiot enough to repeatedly venture into the Pyramid. Not many other mythic heroes for me to care for, and the villagers like to leave me alone. You're the most exciting thing around here."

Os considered this as he donned his armor. He'd never really thought about Isis growing bored, or how she spent her free time. Well, he'd actually thought about how he'd have liked her to spend her free time, specifically with him—

"Os, you're blushing again."

"What? No, I'm not!"

"You have green skin, Os. A blush shows up pretty well."

"Just give me my sword!"

❖

—SPLUTTER—BREATHE.

"How do you keep getting new armor?"

"What d'you mean?" Os asked as he toweled the blood out from under his arms. It had the unfortunate habit of clinging to his hair.

"You always have new armor," Amu-Aa said, holding a breastplate up to his face. "See? This one has carvings of Lord Anubis in it. And more straps. More straps than metal, really; don't know how that's supposed to protect you against anything..."

"I—err—" Os stammered, unused to answering questions about himself. Isis had never seemed interested. She had been all smoky-eyes, lingering looks, and husky comments about his battle prowess or the size of his muscles. Though he was sure there was at least one time it wasn't his muscles she had been referring to—

"You'd never find something of this quality in town," Amu-Aa continued. "And I can't believe the Pyramid just happens to be stocked with fresh armaments for any self-important jock trotting inside!"

"I mean, I slew Ammit the Devourer this time..."

"This is Ammit the Devourer's armor?" Amu-Aa spluttered. "What, you just thought, 'Oh here's the fresh corpse of a demon-god I just killed! Why don't I strip off its armor and don it myself!'?"

"She wasn't in it!" Os snapped. "She doesn't wear armour! She's not even human! More like a crocodile...lioness... thing..." he finished lamely, gesturing vaguely in the air. "Can I have it, please?"

"Not really an excuse," Amu-Aa muttered, but brought it over anyway. He cleared his throat noisily. "Turn around."

"Huh?"

"I need to help you get into this, you himbo! You're never getting into all these straps and buckles by yourself!"

❖

—BREATHE.

"Don't you get tired of it?" Amu-Aa asked as Os scrubbed his chest with another impossibly luxurious towel. He sat cross-legged on the floor, popping figs from Os's offering plate into his mouth. Os noticed that Amu-Aa didn't seem to mind the flecks of blood that had dripped down from the heart and onto the fruit. Where did he find all these fresh hearts, anyway?

"What d'you mean?" Os asked absently.

"Dying all the time? Isn't it—I don't know—tiresome? I mean, you just got pecked to death by a Dire Heron! How embarrassing is that? And I know the resurrection process isn't pleasant."

Os dropped the towel and regarded Amu-Aa. His expression was puzzled, even as he daintily placed a ripe fig between his lips. Dried blood stained his skirt, no doubt from preparing the tub for Os's inevitable arrival. And he'd forgotten to snuff out the candles.

"Amu-Aa, have you just been watching me all this time?"

"What?"

"You haven't even begun to clean up like you normally do..."

Amu-Aa scowled and scurried over to the candles, snatching at one before he had even blown it out. As he touched it, the flame grew white hot, stretched upwards, and hissed, sending sparks fizzing. Amu-Aa yelped, dropping the candle onto the stone floor and hastily sticking his fingers in his mouth.

Os reacted without thinking. Reflexes honed for dodging plague-mummies and jewelled death-crocodiles surged into action. Like a scorpion sting, he leaped towards Amu-Aa and stamped out the offending candle.

The witch, unprepared for the violence of Os's reaction,

yelped again and stumbled backwards into a stone shelf, sending papyrus scrolls flying.

"Are you alright?" Os asked.

Amu-Aa's eyes were wide. He merely nodded.

"Show me your hand!"

"I'm fine, Os. No, really! It's a minor burn! And besides, I'm the one who's supposed takes care of you!" He smiled to show Os that, yes, he really was fine, picked himself up, and began to retrieve his scattered papers. It was somewhat of a weak smile.

"What was that?" Os demanded.

Amu-Aa shook his head. "Nothing! I forgot to discharge the candle, that's all."

Os hesitated, then nodded. Amu-Aa was a witch. He knew what he was talking about, didn't he? "Just...be careful," Os said. "If something were to happen you...I'm not the one who knows resurrection magic..."

Amu-Aa did not respond, seemingly busy with his cleanup. His sandals clack-clacked against the floor as he continued to tidy the chamber. Presently, he made his way to Os's equipment. The sword had been replaced by a crescent-shaped battle-axe.

"I do, yeah," Os said suddenly.

"Hmm?"

"Get tired of it. But that doesn't mean I don't have a duty to do. I need to vanquish Set. And if that means I die a thousand deaths, to be pulled back from the Duat a thousand times, so be it!"

Amu-Aa made a funny noise in his throat as he retrieved a breastplate from the shelves.

Os nearly winced. Even to his own ears, the words sounded trite and rehearsed.

Isis' conversation had never been deeper than, "Have you sufficiently recovered for your next venture, Lord Osiris?". More than once, he'd wanted to say "No, I'd like to rest for a bit!", or "Would you care to join me?" but he had never felt brave enough to actually speak the words.

He was supposed to be brave.

Os stood there, naked and helpless, a peculiar new feeling rising in him like the waters of the Nile during the flood season.

Amu-Aa, armour and axe in hand, froze when he caught Os's expression. He stood perfectly framed by the false doorway behind him, a vision of magic and mystery.

"Os, what's wrong?"

Os bit his lip. Murderous two-headed jackals he could dispatch with ease. Flesh-burrowing beetles were old hat. This...this was new territory.

"Amu-Aa, can I—could I rest here for a bit? Before venturing back into the Pyramid?"

"Oh...sure? I need to clean up, anyway..."

"No, I mean—" Os floundered, "—I mean would you like to...talk? For a little while?"

"Talk?"

"Yeah."

"You want to delay your epic, tomb-delving quest for a chat?"

"...yeah?"

Flickering lamplight glittered off of Amu-Aa's polished scalp, almost animating the tattoos. His brow creased as though he wrestled with some internal dilemma. Finally, he nodded.

"All I can offer you is goat's milk," he mumbled.

❖

OSLOVER616 | DEC 20, 2020, 2:28 AM
GENDER-SWAPPED ISIS MOD

Hey Folks! It's finally here, V1.0.0 of my mod! It was inspired by @osisboss's fan-fiction about a gender-swapped Isis. Let me know what you think? Special thanks to @PyramidPenny for her amazing 3D rendering and animation work!

I haven't touched the actual game mechanics. You should be able to plug this mod in even if you're in the middle of a run.

(I tested it with all three difficulty levels just to be sure).

NOTE: The original developers wrote a MASSIVE amount of text for this game, so there might be a few plot-continuity errors here and there. File a bug report here if you spot anything weird!

XOXOXO

❖

"WHAT DO YOU mean, lava?"

"I mean the floor is literally made of lava."

Amu-Aa looked up from whatever mysterious animal he'd been busy dissecting. He looked skeptical.

He'd added a table and two stools to the Ritual Chamber a few resurrections ago, modest, wood-and-leather affairs. He would work while Os talked.

Os had begun to learn something about himself: he liked talking. He didn't really have much of an opportunity within the Pyramid: monsters tended to be more "eat first, ask questions later," and the Gods left behind only short messages to accompany the blessings they bestowed.

And Isis had been...beautiful, yes. Intriguing, yes. But an interesting conversation partner? Well...

Amu-Aa was easy to talk to. In fact, when the fangs of an Acid Asp sank into Os's flesh, a plume of flame from a Trumpeting Camel spiraled towards his head, or whenever a mortal blow reared up from somewhere in the Pyramid, he found that he was looking forward to his death. He was looking forward to the impatient orders of "Hurry out of the tub, you himbo!" Looking forward to relaxing on a leather stool while Amu-Aa pretended not to pay him any attention.

"Why did Lord Set decide that lava was appropriate construction material for any part of the Pyramid?" Amu-Aa asked, his left eyebrow quirked so high it disappeared into his scalp tattoos.

"I don't know, Amu! Why does Lord Khepri push the sun around every day? Why does Lady Sakhmet only drink beer when it's dyed red and poured into pools in front of her? Why do the Gods do anything?"

Os brought his hand down on the table, but only lightly, not wishing to disturb the carcass that constituted Amu-Aa's work.

Amu-Aa's mouth quirked. "Himbo," he muttered, turning back to the dead creature. Bone-tweezers whirred as he expertly removed the corpse's vital organs and placed them in a precise pattern on an inked papyrus sheet. Os noticed feathers. It might have once been a bird.

"What are you working on, anyway?" Os asked, fully expecting a sarcastic joke about his own intelligence. Amu-Aa was always fiddling with something bizarre. With Isis, apart from the tub of blood, it had always been lotus flowers, chrysanthemums, and honeyed potions. Amu-Aa favoured things like beetle dung, baboon intestines, and on one memorable occasion, the half-digested remnants of a man regurgitated by a pregnant lioness. ("A very potent ingredient," Amu-Aa had solemnly intoned.)

"A present for you," Amu-Aa replied, without looking up. He was doing something extremely delicate and extremely disgusting with the bird's eye.

Os paused. He had never seen Amu-Aa blush; his skin was always the colour of the swirling sands. But he tended to clear his throat noisily when embarrassed. Like he was doing just now.

"A present for me, Amu?" Os said softly.

Amu-Aa grimaced. "Shut up, Os. It's a prophecy to help you in your next delve. So you don't die as quickly. And so you stop bothering me by letting bathtubs of blood congeal."

He wouldn't meet Os's eyes. The sounds he was making from his throat might have suggested that he'd swallowed a whole frog.

"Err, thanks?"

A small smile curled on Amu-Aa's face as he placed a dismembered beak onto his papyrus diagram. "And you have my permission to continue," Amu-Aa added.

"Continue what?"

"Continue calling me Amu. Since you've done it twice already without asking."

Os, on the other hand, could blush deeply and profusely.

❖

ActionKilla212 | Dec 24, 2020, 10:23 PM
PANDERING?

So I love Amu-Aa as a character. He's WAY more fleshed
out than Isis. But is the flirting between him and Os a bit
much? There's never a hint that Os is into dudes. He's
always been (if I read between the lines) kinda into Isis, or
even Bastet. Forcing this gay element onto Os seems to
be pandering to the LGBT?
　I'm not homophobic or anything, but is this the
representation gays really want? Isn't this kinda like
bullshit tokenism?
　Or AITA?

GirlPhreak | Dec 24, 2020, 10:31 PM
RE: PANDERING?

@ActionKilla212 Yes, you are the asshole.

❖

"Os?"

"Yeah…?" Os opened one eye. Arms crossed behind his
head, he had been happily dozing against the eastern wall,
next to an image of Lady Bastet painted in greens and yellows.

Amu cleared his throat. "Come help me with something?"

Os opened his other eye. "You want my help? With
witchcraft?"

Amu shot him a withering look. "It's about the Pyramid,
himbo. You're the only one I know who's been inside it."

"Really?" Os asked, picking himself up. "No-one from
town has ever been curious?" He stretched lazily, feeling his
muscles pop. It was good to spend time outside his armor and
clothing. He thought Amu might be watching him but when
Os turned to look, Amu was bent over a sheaf of papyrus,
swallowing audibly.

"Well, the only one I know who's still alive," Amu mumbled. "Are you coming?"

Os sauntered over. "I'm only alive thanks to you, Amu," he said, leaning over the witch.

Amu kept his workspace neat. A single sheaf of parchment, a few reed pens nestled in a case, and an inkwell. The leather surface of the table shone, as though oiled recently. Os braced himself with one arm near the edge.

Amu's eyes flickered up at Os looming over him before returning to his hieroglyphs. "Yes, well..." he murmured, gesturing dismissively with a hand. "Have you seen these glyphs anywhere in the Pyramid?" he asked, stabbing at a string of symbols with his pen. "In one of your lava-rooms or something?"

Hovering above the witch, Os smelled...lilies and cinnamon, with a touch of honest sweat. Smiling, he allowed his eyes to rove the papyrus scroll. He was hardly a scholar, but he'd seen some unusual stuff in the Pyramid. This however, escaped him completely. It started familiar enough, but then grew strange, as though a different language altogether, letterforms spiky and ominous.

ERROR 504
UNDEFINED VARIABLE:
"AMU-AA"

"The hieroglyphs refer to Set," Os said, frowning. "But I don't know whatever that is after it."

Amu nodded thoughtfully, while his fingers traced the strange writing. "I recognized Lord Set. Which is why I wanted to ask you. Due to your, err, connection to that particular deity..."

"You mean my blood-sealed oath of vengeance?"

"You took the words right out of my mouth."

Os shook his head. "Honestly, it looks a bit like Greek? Or maybe Latin?"

Amu's head snapped upwards so fast Os had to jerk back to prevent being struck on the chin.

"What?" Os asked, excited. "Did you figure something out? Did I help?"

Amu's eyes were wide. "Himbo, you read Latin and Greek?"

A twinge of hurt wriggled up from Os' belly. It must have shown on his face because Amu's expression instantly changed from surprise to dismay.

"No—Os, I didn't mean—just—I wasn't saying that you're stupid or anything."

Os turned away from the table. It was about time to head back anyway.

"Os, I—that was—"

"Don't worry about it," Os muttered, reaching for his breastplate.

"Os, please don't go!"

Something new in Amu's voice tugged at Os, yanked his head around to look back at him. The witch had stood up, hands balled at his sides. He looked upset.

"Os, please stay?" Amu pleaded, no trace of acid or barbs in his voice. "I'm sorry."

Os smiled, his ill-feeling melting away under the brightness of Amu's obvious consternation. He trotted over and placed a conciliatory hand on Amu's shoulder.

"Well, if you insist," he began, "But only because it's really fun to bother this one witch I know while he tries to work..."

"Please don't make me regret my decision."

Os's laugh was luminous and rosy, like the dawning sun.

❧

An excerpt from Fags, Fandoms, & the Future: How LGBTQIA Modders & Amateur Game Designers Imagine a Queerer Videogame Multiverse
Arundhuti Mandal

Rather than simply accept the bland excuses or weak attempts at "diversity representation" touted by mainstream corporations, these passionate fans are taking the future of their favourite properties into their own hands. Fan modifications to existing videogames are nothing new, and mods focussed on exploring sexual interests are arguably some of the most popular. However, it is only recently that queer-themed mods have been garnering widespread attention. Indeed, entire storylines featuring queer content are being retrofitted into popular AAA titles by amateur designers.

The significance of this phenomenon cannot be understated. A legion of young, queer, justice-oriented gamers are essentially saying "We want gay art, and if you won't make it we will!" Queer gamers are demanding positive representation in a hetero- and cis- normative world, and actively creating the change they wish to see. The resulting new, Frankenstein-artworks are experiencing a wave of popularity comparable to the original games themselves.

A poetic soul might wonder how the videogame characters themselves might feel. What would Super Massimo say to reading "Your Prince is in Another Castle" instead of the usual Princess? How would grizzled monster hunter Gustav of the Riviera react to being hit on by the legions of attractive male barmaids and sorcerers?

❖

IT TOOK MORE than two dozen resurrections before Os dared look through some of Amu's things. While Amu bent over the bloody tub clutching a coarse, camel-hair scrubber, Os rifled through the scrolls ensconced within the shelves that were cut into the southern wall, expecting to uncover ancient and terrible hieroglyphs to steal the breath of men, to strike down crops with the plague, to blind, burn, and bewitch...

"Amu, is this a recipe for Tiger Nut Cakes?"

"What?" Amu looked up. Pearls of perspiration glinted rather pleasingly on his chest. Os noticed Amu had blood in his eyebrows.

It suddenly struck Os that Amu was very, very attractive. He'd seen it before, certainly, but never really...internalized it?

"It's a historic recipe, himbo." Amu snapped. "I have other things to occupy my time besides constantly raising you from the dead, you know. I have other clients!"

That statement was jarring enough to pull Os out of pleasant thoughts about Amu's chest.

"Wait, you do magic for others?"

Something in Os's voice must have sounded off, because Amu straightened and raised an eyebrow quizzically.

"Yes?" he replied, gesturing to the tub. "The hippo blood doesn't pay for itself you know..."

That...made perfect sense, of course. Amu wasn't there solely for Os's benefit. Of course Os hadn't believed that. Of course not."I thought you were bored? That the villagers left you alone?"

"Yes, well..." Amu cleared his throat and unconsciously picked some dried blood out from under his fingernails. "I didn't want you growing a big head, did I? Travellers and such often ask for me." His voice softened a little at the end of his sentence, almost as if he was embarrassed by the statement.

Standing by the shelves, Os took in the information. Travelers came in search of Amu, to ask for his advice and his magic. Was Amu famous? It dawned on Os that bringing a warrior back to life time and time again was possibly a rather complicated feat, something only a master witch could achieve.

Amu was really hot.

Despite the banter he had engaged in with Isis, Os had little experience with actual romance. He was a warrior. He had a mission. Everything else had always been secondary.

Os glanced back at the recipe. The glyphs were cut into an old slab of stone, instead of painted on papyrus.

"What were you doing with this recipe?"

The momentary embarrassment had vanished from Amu. He relaxed, folding his arms, and leaned jauntily against the tub. It was rather fetching.

"I'm glad you're taking an interest in reading, himbo," he said wryly. "That was actually a request from the Pharoah. A feast for her birthday featuring historic dishes." Amu's voice had taken on a hint of pride. "The Pharoah gifted me twenty debens of ivory for it. Good pay. And for work that's far easier than rubbing your corpse down with antelope grease before hauling it into the tub, let me tell you!"

Os' thoughts, which had veered towards interesting avenues regarding Amu, crashed at the image of being rubbed down by the witch. He opened his mouth dumbly.

"Huh?"

"It's one of the preparations I have to make to your body before your Resurrection. Pain in the ass. I have to massage you with camel grease and rare herbs. It's partly why the blood comes off your skin so easily."

Os's brain was now steeping in several pleasant images of Amu making expert use of his hands. Letting this happen turned out to be a bad idea. What with Os being naked.

Amu's eyes widened as he looked down

"Os—are you—?" Amu stuttered, his voice breaking.

Lady Hathor, heed my plea!, Os prayed desperately. He had already resolved to be brave around Amu, hadn't he?

"Amu?" he ventured, keeping his voice low. "Can I kiss you?"

Amu stepped back. His brow furrowed. He cleared his throat before hesitantly answering, "No...?"

❖

BEYOND A CURSORY, "Thank you," Os barely said a word to Amu the next few resurrections. He avoided even looking at the witch for too long.

Finally, Amu rounded on him as he clambered out of the bath, splashing blood all over the food offerings.

"Are you done sulking, himbo?"

Os grabbed the proffered towel and grunted something indistinct.

"Os, you can't just spring a question like that onto me, and then get upset when I refuse! What's even the point of the question, then?"

Os stared down at the bloody towel in his hands. Something was curdling in his stomach.

Amu continued to scold him, "...and if you had paused a minute before huffing off, or even tried to talk, I might have said 'let's share a meal and talk about this first'..."

Os looked up, but Amu's brow was still wrinkled in anger.

"...but instead you decided to act like a child, and honestly, I have better things to do than date immature, self-important, petulant wannabe-heroes, thank you very much."

Os opened his mouth.

Os closed his mouth.

He was not a child. He was Osiris, divinely sworn to defeat Set. Within the Pyramid, he had faced hordes of unspeakable monsters, dodged innumerable traps, overcome countless dangers. He had died and lived and died again, a hundred times over.

He deserved this, didn't he?

He was not a child.

Was he?

He said nothing.

❖

GURGLE—SPLUTTER—BREATHE.

Os did not open his eyes. He remained in the tub, basking in the viscous warmth. He had penetrated further into the Pyramid than ever before, into a cold, alien level with jagged teeth of ice thrusting from the ceiling.

He fought, he died, he returned. There would be no respite from that. There was nothing else, not until he defeated Set.

Amu had said—

Amu.

It didn't matter what Amu had said.

Amu would normally be snapping at him by this point, complaining about congealing blood. Had he finally given up on Os?

He began dragging himself out of the tub, runnels of dark, red liquid spilling everywhere.

"The blood becomes you, my lord."

Os froze. His eyes snapped open.

Jet black hair hanging long and loose. A crown shaped like a throne. An enigmatic smile.

Isis.

"My Lord Osiris, are you ready for your next venture?" Isis asked, her voice smoky like frankincense. "Pardon my forthrightness, but the flex of your muscles is rather more pronounced than last time. It would seem you are deepening not only your strengths but your handsomeness..."

Os sprang up, not caring that he knocked over an offering plate of enormous dried chrysanthemums and splashed blood onto Isis' white linens. His gaze darted around the room.

The furniture Amu had installed was gone. The man was nowhere to be seen.

"Lady Witch, where is Amu-Aa?" he croaked.

Isis' delicate brow furrowed. "My Lord? To whom do you refer? Is that perchance the demon that slew you this time? Rest assured, no demon can puncture my spells!"

"No!" Os cried as he continued to whirl about the room, hoping to find a trace—any trace—of the tattooed witch with the sharp tongue. "There was another witch. A man— named Amu-Aa. Where did he go?"

Isis stepped softly towards him. "There is no other witch," she said in a silken voice, "Only me. Perhaps my lord is upset from his last visit? Perhaps you desire...something more of me?"

Os's eyes finally snapped back to Isis. She was very close to him now. Her skin, sandstone brown, was smooth and flawless. Her lips were parted and moist, her eyes large.

"Err...What?"

In response, Isis smiled as she ran a red-lacquered finger gently down his arm. She hadn't offered him a towel. He was still soaked in blood.

Okay...

Isis had never been this...this...blatant, before, had she?

Isis' eyes travelled down from his face. Down the length of his body, down, down, until her gaze paused and her smile deepened.

"You appear eager, my lord," she crooned.

Os stepped back. He felt betrayed by his own anatomy.

"Err..Isis, I...I barely know you..."

"What is there to know, Lord? We need not talk. Only indulge in earthly delights." The sway of her hips hinted that the delights would be very earthly indeed.

But where was Amu? Os could not think. His brain fizzed with Isis's curves, Isis's softness, Isis's honeyed voice.

"Come, Lord. Let me show you what a witch truly knows..."

Os's world melted into mist.

❖

SUTEKH: THE LONG WINTER - REVIEW
BY MELODY CHAN
RATING: ★★★★★

The first expansion to blockbuster roguelike Sutekh does not disappoint. With the addition of winter themed levels, the khopesh as a brand new weapon, and tonnes of new story content, S:TLW delivers a potent dose of Sutekh goodness in one inexpensive package.

Players will even get to see a deepening of the Os-Isis romance, complete with a fade-to-black sex scene between the two slow-burn lovers.

Unfortunately, developer HyperLilliput has announced that they have no plans to ensure the expansion's compatibility with fan-made mods (I had to uninstall three in order to launch the game).

❖

—SPLUTTER—BREATHE.

Resurrection was never comfortable. But it was never like this.

Os knew what a spear shoved through one's skull felt like. An instant of jagged pain, followed by peace. This was the same, except there was no relief. Again and again, the pain stabbed into his head, like the battle-roar of a lioness, like the vengeance of Lady Sakhmet. The blood in the tub grew hot, begun to boil. He tried to cry out but scalding blood flooded his mouth as unknown, alien symbols burst into his brain.

ERRORAMUAA.EXENOTDEFINEDERROR
AMUAA.EXENOTDEFINEDERROR

His fingers scrabbled for purchase against the rim of the tub but he couldn't get them to do what what he wanted, couldn't get them to work—

Hands. Someone's hands had grabbed his and were pulling pulling pulling him up and out. But Os slipped against the slick sides of the tub, splashing blood everywhere and they weren't strong enough weren't strong enough—

ERRORAMUAA.EXENOTDEFINEDERROR

A bite of cold around his ankles. The world turned upside down and Os felt himself being yanked out of the bath by his feet. Blood sluiced off him and he spluttered, dangling upside down from the ceiling.

The pain still hammered in his head but he could see again. Amu stood before him.

Hope erupted in his chest, star-bright.

There stood Amu, arms outstretched, sweat pouring down his chest. He was chanting something. A look of intense concentration gouged lines into his forehead. His scalp—

The tattoos that normally adorned Amu's scalp like a skullcap had somehow broken free of their two-dimensional prison. Writhing, black forms, they twisted around his head like a monstrous crown. Inky chains reached out from them, towards Os's feet, holding him up above the bath of churning blood.

But the pain wouldn't stop. The pain still pierced his skull, the weird symbols still thrust into his brain. This had to end. He couldn't stand it for much longer.

"Amu," he managed. "Kill me!"

Amu's eyes widened, even as he continued to chant.

"Please!" Os begged. "Before—"

Twin javelins of darkness shot out of the mass of crawling tattoos, straight towards Os' heart.

❖

OSISBOSS | SEPTEMBER 21, 2021, 3:03 AM
ISIS GENDER SWAP & TLW

I removed all my mods before installing The Long Winter expansion, and then tried to re-install @oslover616's gender swapping mod. The game now crashes every time I boot it up. Does anyone know of a fix for this? I love the features of TLW, but I NEED #OsAmu!

OSLOVER616 | SEPTEMBER 23, 2021, 9:42 AM
THE LONG WINTER BUG

Hey folks! As you're probably all aware, my Amu-Aa mod hasn't been playing well with TLW. I've tried to figure out where the problem is, but honestly, I don't really have the time to devote to it.

Looks like you'll have to play TLW without the mod. Or if you really want to finish Amu and Os' storyline, you can keep your save file before installing TLW in a separate folder, and like, return to it later after finishing the expansion.

Sorry folks, but I just don't have the spoons for this right now!

xoxoxo

❖

—BREATHE.

Os scrambled out of the tub faster than he had ever before. He stood there, naked, shivering. Blood cooled on his body.

There was no pain in his head. In fact, he felt curiously light.

A warm towel settled over his shoulders.

"Os?"

Amu was worried. Os could tell from the quaver in his voice. But hearing Amu filled him with a giddy happiness he'd never thought possible.

He turned and regarded the witch. Normally tough and thorny like a desert plant, Amu now looked small, anxious, fragile. His hands were clasped around his elbows, his eyes large with worry.

"Os, how are you feeling?"

Inside the Pyramid, Lady Hathor had once left Os a gift of a poem, a token to think upon as he battled his way to Set. In the chaotic hellscape of the Pyramid, he had clutched the words to his chest, held on to them tightly, treating them like an amulet against all the horror around him.

Now, he released the words gently in song.

"Your form revives my heart.
It is your voice
that makes my body steadfast..."

Amu didn't say anything for a moment.

Os held his breath.

"Himbo, if you're trying to woo me, at least try it without using a plagiarized poem."

Os's breath escaped in a great guffaw as he fell back onto the floor, the towel sliding off his shoulders, his back hitting the tub. Tension rolled off his body in great bellows of laughter. He couldn't help it. Amu's gentle stings were some of the most exquisite sensations in the world, he realized.

Once his laughter subsided, he looked up. Amu's worry had dissolved into skepticism.

"I feel good, Amu. Really, really good." And he did. He

was bright, buoyant.

Amu nodded, but didn't take his quizzical eyes off Os.

"I had sex, you know."

If Amu had been expecting anything, it wasn't that. His jaw didn't exactly drop, but his lips did part in surprise."Oh!...how was it?"

"Honestly? It was...really adequate? Fun. But... mechanical?"

"Ah."

Amu coughed.

Os got up. He walked to his armour, neatly placed on the shelves. His fingers played over the worked leather and metal. Curiously, he felt no compulsion to don any of it, no burning desire to dive back into the Pyramid in search of holy retribution.

"Amu, would you like to go on a date?"

He turned, and looked directly at Amu.

"Os—"

"To get to know each other better," Os interrupted. "To talk things out. You said you would've liked that."

Amu paused to regard him. He cleared his throat.

"What do you mean by 'go on a date'?" Amu asked.

"I mean outside!" Os gestured around him. "I've never really been outside your ritual chamber, outside your cave! And you know, I think I'm going to take a little break from Pyramid-delving!"

Amu's brow creased. "Os, is this you trying to have sex with me?" He looked down Os's body suspiciously.

Os made a dismissive gesture. "Yes, obviously. But not right now. After we hang out a bit more. I think it'll be better that way."

It took a while, but Amu finally smiled. "Okay, himbo."

Ancient Egyptian Love poem adapted from "THE CAIRO LOVE SONGS," translations by Michael V. Fox, excerpted from the Journal of the American Oriental Society.

To Rise, Blown Open

Jen Brown

You should know: when Calamity sundered the skies, I was minding my business. Loading groceries into the car; rock-paper-scissoring with Mr. Marvelous and Watrella, to see who'd drive home. Mundanity. Polyamorous domesticity. All the stuff you'd encouraged me to do, while on so-called sabbatical these months.

Now, the sky is breaking.

It buckles, dripping entrails from another dimension, which feel out of place above our grocery store. You're probably seeing this from Union headquarters; I'd pay good money to watch baby-supers, with their budding powers and frigid idolatry, quaking as seventy-three-year-old Dawn Obsidian—majestic, telepathic heroine—chews out blackening skies. Though, at least you're inside; I experience the full brunt of what follows.

First, gravity uncoils with what I can only describe as a dry *snap*. Dropping grocery bags, I drift skyward, and downtown Los Angeles lurches, its skyscrapers and construction cranes rippling between darkened realities. The distant, snow-capped San Gabriel Mountains tremble— groan, really. It's like I can hear them; as if five hundred fault lines shudder before a darkened maw overhead. Like a stain, it spreads: black devouring blue, flaying the sky to reveal worlds unknown. A lavender gas giant—that definitely isn't Jupiter—fills the foreground. Through the terror addling my mind, I realize it's pulling us, like ants in orbit.

Now, I can't recall any of your emergency drills. It was my job once—one I'd really like back. But hurtling toward unknown space makes curd of my insides; plus, I'm still pissed at you. Instead of remembering, I stretch toward those I love. Toward Marv, who swims against air, grasping for his prosthetic gauntlet; toward Watrella, who activates her Union-provided implant, probably to reach you—right before a voice interrupts, crashing through our minds.

My implant flares, and I can't hear myself scream. Soon, that ringing gives way to laughter, nasally and hollow.

Dr. Calamity's laugh.

Every good hero needs a nemesis.

You joked about this decades ago, when I was still a gangly teen upset at the world. I'd felt jagged, ill-fitting. Both too much and never enough. You said we bore generations of rage, that it was buried beneath our melanin, stoked through centuries of subjugation and supremacy. *Now Mindstress, gon' ahead and get mad*, you'd say. *But, sooner or later, rage'll eat you out of house and home.*

Your teachings return to me, while I careen skyward. Toward a sky broken by my nemesis, no less. I've long realized something, Dawn; a benefit of living limned with rage. Anger fuels, too. And right now?

I'm fucking furious.

❖

WITHIN HOURS, SEVERAL things happen: scientists at your lauded International Union of Heroes pull a lever somewhere, temporarily righting gravity; meanwhile, you call in the best—augmented and naturals alike. Needlerella arrives by helicopter, donning aug-appendages tapered to terrifying points. Tankheart and Bolt Boy, nats both, arrive with their innate powers readied. In fact, you call in every super comprising the Greater Los Angeles Ass-Kicking League, except for me. Disappointing, but expected.

After all, I've come to change your mind.

"Now, babe," Watrella begins. She's parked us near IUH's headquarters, and watches me warily. "You're taking the car straight home."

"Agreed," Marv adds, before the sharp planes of his face soften. "Though... given who's stirring the shit this time, we're here, Kendra; to listen. Support. Whatever you need."

It's sweet, but not Watrella's brand of sweet. She cuts lovingly, fiercely through the suggestion with one of her own: "We'll talk once Calamity's captured. For now, nothing else needs saying." Her fingers twine through mine and Marv's, connecting us. "Go home, love."

Wait for us, she implies. Shit, that's all I've done since our last Calamity-showdown. So, and I mean this kindly, *fuck that*.

They mask up; Marv fits his prosthetic gauntlet into place, securing it just below his elbow, and Wat tosses me the keys. I kiss assurances into their knuckles; sell the ruse by starting our car while they head inside.

Fifteen minutes later I've stolen through the mail room (stacked packages provide excellent cover), doggie-paddled through another gravity fluctuation, and reached the tenth floor (where, blessedly, my keycard still works)—all before you've finished briefing everyone.

You've gathered the Ass-Kicking League in a closed meeting room at the end of a frantic, paper-strewn hallway. I pace just outside, ignored by staff busily gesticulating at the windows, their mouths agape. Once the meeting's over, everyone streams out—my former teammates; my friends, really. Their expressions shift upon seeing me, but you? You just snort, while a *good Lord* expression deepens your frown.

"Kendra?!" Tankheart says, rushing over. I wink at my partners, enjoying Marv's impressed smile and Wat's flattened glare, before the lanky super crushes me into a hug. "Oh shit," they exclaim, eyes alight. "Does this mean the band's getting back together?"

Before answering, I'm swarmed with more hugs (forcing

me to dodge one of Needlerella's wayward limbs), and more questions.

"That depends." I catch your eye. "But don't count me out. I'd make a good roadie, at least."

Chuckling, Tank herds my former squad into nearby elevators, leaving you and I to an awkward silence. I wait for its departing *ding* before stepping into your path.

It's time for a truce.

"You may not want to hear this," I say, "but you need me."

"I need a break from your incessant shenanigans. *That*, I know."

Here we go.

I fall into step with you. "And yet, I'm the best super for this job." It's simple: Dr. Calamity controls bioorganic and machine tech, and I'm the nat who psychokinetically controls technology.

"Need I remind you what happened two months ago?"

No, I want to say, but it sounds pouty. I settle for: "She kicked my ass. Trust, I remember."

"Correction, Kendra: she embedded genetic malware inside your cells." Waltzing into your office, which still brims with leafy plants and creamy neutrals, you pin me with a glare. "She tricked your organs into—almost—destroying themselves. Baby, that's more than an ass kicking."

Suddenly, your telepathy spiders my body; like woven netting, sinking below skin. I sense kindness—*you survived*, I feel you say. *Let that be enough.*

Yet, surviving isn't living.

"It's been months. I've trained. My movement's improved, and my timing's back—"

I don't finish that thought, because—so fast that it startles me—you retrieve a cellphone from your desk. It *thumps* against the wood grain, glossy screen landing face-up.

"All right. Move that." You shrug. "It's got some of Calamity's malware on it; same as before. Show me this new and improved Mindstress."

Suddenly I'm a fish, plucked from comforting seas. "I only work with e-waste now. It's safer that way."

I don't say *for everybody*, but your grim expression tells me you understand.

I expect derision. Disbelieving laughter, maybe. Instead, you search me again; sift through my anger. Desperate, I allow you this glimpse; hope, foolishly, that you'll unearth whatever trust you need to grant me field work, again. It's awkward, staying silent while you probe, so I fixate on magazines framing your walls. There you are, proudly occupying one 1968 cover, garbed like a Black Panther power ranger. In '77, your slick cat-eye's just visible beneath an ornate mask. Everywhere, you loom; gigantic. Triumphant, even.

Unscathed.

By the time your telepathy abates, your frown could level cities. "Kendra, you're not seeing active squad time. Though, if you really want to help?" You toss me a clipboard. "Bring your tactics to the desk."

For fuck's sake.

"I owe Chantel—" I stop myself; *correct* myself. "Calamity. I owe her."

Decades of practice, and one name undoes you. Your telepathy unfurls, growing thick enough to wring truths from the walls. "You'll have to get in line."

We're kindred when it comes to power. Telepathy and telekinesis go hand-in-hand. It's why I found myself in you, all those years ago; why I accepted your guidance the moment you offered it. Still, we aren't kin; I once loved Calamity boundlessly, but you still do. No matter what she's become, she'll always be your granddaughter. But to me: she's the one who sundered us.

You sigh into the silence; thread words through my mind: *I won't risk losing you again.*

We should face her, together. Break beneath the weight of shared bonds, if it comes to that. But you'd rather cleave us with distrust and empty declarations. Ain't that some shit.

On my way out, I fling you one last thought, and I mean for it to hurt: *You already have.*

❖

Two weeks pass. Two weeks filled with a brand of chaos only Calamity could conjure. Fourteen days of reeling, clawing at the question: What the hell do I do now?

Planning's difficult, given the circumstances. For starters, we can't distinguish between night and day anymore, courtesy of Not-Jupiter shining through the sky-tear. Worse, Calamity's dredged up another distraction: re-wired delivery bots. Now, the squat, cooler-sized couriers terrorize shin bones across the country. Sprinkle in continued gravity fluctuations and you've got a world under siege—but for no clear reason.

This is all a feint. It has to be. There've been a few serious injuries, but nothing's barrelled through the rift. Frustrated, I wrack my mind for answers; wait, powerlessly, for Marvelous and Watrella to amble home beneath the gas giant's light. Sometimes, they're bruised, but they're always exhausted.

When you return them to me, they remove their masks; take refuge in an inner world of our making. A world without distinctions between "hero" and "self." There, our touch is fevered; our lips, hungry. Anxiety deepens everything: sharpens caresses into claws, and guides teeth through flesh. I lose myself in them; drown beneath Marv's delicious gasp, and pry Watrella's thighs apart while she trembles.

Yet, your hold never lessens.

Always, you summon them back; preach that the world needs their bodies. Do you see the rash climbing Marv's residual limb, left in the wake of his gauntlets? Have you noticed Watrella ghosting about, forgoing food the second her implant chimes? You deny me justice, and claim the people I love most.

I should be out there with them.

"Just—let me come along," I beg, one morning. "I'll avoid our body cams; I can use e-waste to make debris storms—"

"Too risky," Marv interrupts.

Watrella scoffs, but it lacks her usual fire. "Yeah, out of the goddamn question. We're not letting her near you."

They silence me with kisses, but I'm fuming by the time I report for work. "Work" being retail hell, of course.

Months ago, I found a gig selling furniture at an upscale department store. It's not saving lives and the pay's shit, but my bills aren't on sabbatical. As I pull up, a wholly different—yet oddly comforting—kind of chaos greets me. Slick SALE signs, featuring "end-of-the-world" deals, span from kitchenware to gardening. Marco and Daniela, college-aged morning shifters, smile tensely at me while ringing up customers. I've barely hit the sales floor before an elderly woman trundles over, arguing for steeper discounts over a "dented" spatula she found.

Woo, sweet mundanity. (No, you're not mistaking my lack of enthusiasm.)

Hours after helping her and organizing product, I join Marco at the cash register.

He nudges me. "You good?" There's a lull in customers thanks to LA's newly implemented gravity fluctuation alarms; they're louder than tornado sirens and use satellite data to predict when Fake-Jupiter will destabilize gravity. As the one outside our store blares, Marco's springy, dark curls float. He yells over it: "It's the end of the world and stuff, so I get it if you aren't."

"I'm fine," I grumble.

When gravity stabilizes and we've righted ourselves on the sales floor, he sighs. "I feel... powerless. The League's saving everybody. Meanwhile, I'm just ringing up rich people who love a deal."

I clutch mocking hands to my non-existent pearls. "But where will their children sleep, if not on llama-fur, three-thousand-thread-count sheets?"

He laughs a little. "Well, I'm studying comp sci. You'd think I could do something. Stop the stupid bots, at least."

Maybe it's the lurch in gravity, but Marco's words trigger a physical, full-body response—a thought, reckless and wanton; a scheme outside your protocols.

"Maybe you can." I slide closer. "Could you hack... stuff? Systems, and such?"

Calamity works digitally; she's got to be leaving trails, entering and exiting systems. Nodes. Computer-y shit that, just maybe, this kid knows about.

"Define 'hacking,'" Marco laughs. When I don't, he trails off. Squints. "Why?"

I lower my voice. "Because, bots aside, the person who started all this could be traced, found. Could you pinpoint Dr. Calamity's whereabouts?"

His hands stiffen where they grip the register. "The government hasn't even found her yet—"

I don't have time for timidity. Grabbing Marco by his apron, I drag him to the storeroom, then lob my best heroic speech at him. "You want to help? Now's the time. Don't ask me how, but I'm close to people in the Ass-Kicking League. Believe me when I say: they're struggling." I shake him for added effect. "Real heroes don't hesitate."

For a second I think he's going to shout—for security, maybe. Instead, he nods shakily. "I-I can't do much, but my brother's a security engineer." Marco rids the tremor from his voice. "I'll talk to him."

❖

SO, THIS IS what it's come to: lying. I've become a big, fat, civilian-endangering liar.

Marv and Wat think I'm home ordering takeout after a hard shift. Who knows where you think I am; I've denied your calls all week. For five days, I've mostly shut out Calamity's chaos; focused on rediscovering myself. On becoming a new kind of hero.

The kind who faces genetic malware and wins.

Tonight, I park on a nondescript block, just outside of Long Beach's deserted shipping yards. I ignore obvious energy sources, thrumming with current: darkened telephone poles; towering traffic lights. Instead, I don a Halloween skull mask—alabaster, set atop my russet cheeks; incisors hitting my full, brown lips—and get into character.

You'd hate this look. But my old mask was frilly, designed to resemble circuit boards superimposed atop butterfly wings. (IUH Directorate insisted it "played better" on broadcasts.) Sure, this new mask's a touch dramatic, but it suits me; suits what I'm about to do.

Ahead, an e-waste shop looms, lonely and quiet. Sign says it's closed, but my lock pick disagrees. I'm inside within minutes, scanning the store's square footage, the number of side rooms, and derelict goods lining the shop. There are boxy, wood-lined televisions, broken light grids, degraded SIM cards, abandoned VHS tapes. No live batteries humming with electricity, save for a desktop powering the cash register. No genetic malware, waiting to strike. Only solder, long cooled; grime, accumulated over decades; trash turned treasure.

Telekinetically, this room tastes of circuitry. Probing connections, I extend my power; surge electrons through forgotten nuclei.

I bring the dead back to life.

Heady, I grow dense; a planet, in my own right, pulling keyboards, laserdisc players, and rotary phones into orbit; I summon every broken, abandoned thing until a cyclone rages around me; until the storm grows a throat and howls. As my braids snatch against the swell of it, I fade, indistinguishable from the tempest.

It feels good, but delicious as flexing is, Calamity doesn't fight fair. Not when we were little, playfully one-upping each other, and certainly not now. If Marco finds her (admittedly, a big *if*), I'll have to be ready.

Gingerly, I withdraw a chip from my pocket. Thumb-sized, it doesn't seem capable of ending a person. Yet you pressed it into my palm months ago; told me what lurked inside. Licking sweat from my lips, realization hits: I need to let go. Let the storm take it. Then, bulwark myself as the malware senses me; as it deploys.

Repel it. Maintain the cyclone, and repel it.

I wonder, Dawn: when you were little, did you ever spin in circles, faster, and faster, weightless and light and free, before

they told you our city would live or die on your watch? I lean
into a dizzying kind of weightlessness now, just like that;
loosen my grip as Calamity's chip sails into my storm.

You are magic, I tell myself. It's your refrain, after all—we're
excellence, manifested. Beautiful and brilliant and proud.

Between wires and plastic, the chip disappears. Still,
I brace myself. Tighten my core; plant my feet; steady
my breathing. I wait. And wait. Then—*there!* Something
undulates, backwards-scuttling through my will. It dances;
sings, jubilantly, refusing to hide.

Hold it! I try to conjure your tenor, your tenacity;
pretend this is a live mission, like the days of old, where you
supported from the sidelines. But it's too fast. It races, zig-
zags and darts; nips at my ankles, then my eyebrows, before
sticking barbed, binary tongues into the hollow of my neck—

I can't do this.

Doubt snaps my kinetic tether, and debris goes flying,
striking glass, clattering against the concrete walls.

There is only silence, sweat, and the light pressure of food
climbing my esophagus. I take off, legs and arms pumping,
skull-mask slipping. My car peals from the curb, and before
long, I've reached home, snot-mouthed from hiccup-sobbing.
Inside, Marvelous and Watrella await, their expressions
puckered by my betrayal. Clearly, I *wasn't* home enjoying
takeout. Still, their anger flees once they get a good look at
me.

"What happened?" Marv demands.

"Where were you?!" Wat sobs.

They're at my side in seconds. All I want is to peel out
of my sweat-slick clothes; to have a hot bath and scour
the weakness from my skin. To return to the unstoppable
Mindstress of old, cloaked in debris storms dark as pitch.

Instead, I tell them everything.

❖

FOR A BRIEF, terrible moment I worry that they'll tell
you—about my enlisting Marco, and training with genetic

malware outside your auspices. Instead, my partners remove that ridiculous skull mask, clean the snot from my lips, and listen. Wat picks plastic from my tangled braids. Marv holds us, both. When I've regurgitated what feels like a year's worth of anguish, Wat whispers: "Whatever you need, we're with you."

"Always," Marv adds.

Turns out, it's that simple—to love one another, past duty. Amid their touch, I forget the e-waste shop; remind myself that, together, we're unstoppable. I'm not Calamity; I don't abandon my loved ones.

Now tangled in their sleeping arms, I stare at my phone; consider calling you. After all, I led the Ass-Kicking League because I forge paths, and find allies to walk them with.

I miss you. Though it won't reach you, I conjure this thought before exhaustion takes me; pull it from the gristle in my chest. *I miss you, Dawn.* But morning comes, burningly bright, and Marco texts: *Found her.* It seems there's no time for middle ground.

Marv, Wat, and I concoct a plan: they'll keep up appearances at your morning briefing. I'll race into work, pass on what Marco's discovered; the League will then be free to converge, outside your command. Dressing quickly, I crawl through surface-street checkpoints, avoid stray bots roaming the store's parking lot, and find Marco inside.

"Were you followed?" He asks, leading us into the storeroom. "Does anybody know you're here?"

"The League knows." I frown, hesitant. "They're ready to act on whatever you've got. Where is she?"

Marco averts his gaze, and I realize that something's off. Not his nervous energy, because finding an infamous supervillain would make anyone jittery. It's the terror-stricken expression he wears while reaching into his backpack, retrieving his laptop, and opening it.

Inside that bright screen, Calamity smiles.

"She found us," Marco says, setting his laptop on the ground. I hardly hear him over my pounding heart. "Said we had to show you this."

He doesn't say *I'm sorry*, but it's etched into his retreat.
Now, the room feels smaller; my chest, tighter. Below, my
nemesis sits tall before a digital backdrop—a vast, open
sea, bracketed by her broad shoulders. Pixelated gulls seem
caught mid-soar, trailing behind her pink twists. Trembling,
I press "play."

"Hey, sis." That *sis* conjures up memories of all the times
she'd said it, endearingly. Now, Calamity sounds gleeful; like
she's spun a web, and I walked right into it. "Good to 'see'
you."

Activating my implant, I open a private channel with
Marv and Wat. "We have a problem."

While they wring details from me, Calamity prattles. She's
fervent; salivating over her shorn sky.

"Am I to understand," Calamity begins, "Granny
benched *the* incomparable Mindstress, which forced you to
work retail?" She laughs, sharp and hollow. "Tell me how it
feels, Ke. To lose the things you love."

I reel as something viscous thuds inside my ears, thicker
than blood; it crowds out sound, stifles my breathing.

"Still, it's nothing compared to losing people." Fury
limns her words, skewering me through pixels and glass.
Then, she whispers like we're twelve again, trading secrets
in Dawn's backyard: "I found her, Ke. It took breaking the
sky, but I found her. This time, I'll fix what you and Granny
destroyed."

Ringing assaults my ears; I choke around memories
clawing to the fore—antiseptic hospital rooms, searingly
white beneath fluorescent lights; staggering to and from the
ICU, hunched and wet-eyed; listening numbly as doctors
declared your daughter— Chantel's mother—brain dead.

Everyone goes, yeah. But for some, it's painful. Erin
suffered.

Calamity snorts, sounding just like you. "Now, leave me to
my work. Especially since you've got bigger problems. Let's
see if you find it before it finds you."

The screen goes black.

"Kendra, talk to us!" Wat's pleading returns me to myself;

to the dim storeroom, and the dark computer screen and a roiling stomach. "Marv, *we need to move.*"

"Already on it," Marv chimes. "Ken, we're coming. Hold tight."

Words die beneath my tongue. *I love you both*, I want to say. *If I go, take care of each other.* But I refuse to go, painfully or otherwise, today.

Running, I emerge from the storeroom, caught between two worlds. In one, I roam the sales floor, rounding customers and overpriced throw rugs, eyes peeled for Calamity's threat. In another, I'm years away; huddled inside a private hospital meeting room. It's overly large, meant for families discussing end-of-life care. Only Chantel and I pepper it, empty-eyed, as you decide Erin's fate.

Marco gestures from my periphery, calling out, but something—small, many-voiced—snatches my awareness, and there's no time for updates. Something's coming, but I can't tell from where; still, I knew back then. The moment Erin's chest stilled, and Chantel wailed, I knew she'd ask me to will current through those machines; to breathe life into her mother once more.

"Dammit." I spin desperately, telekinesis surging. Nearby, shoppers stare. My frantic mind conjures an old mantra, one that got me through Erin's funeral: Death comes for us all. *I am not the reason she's gone.*

Then I sense it; malware, odorous and pungent, surging from someplace, many-tongued and single-minded.

Think—*think.* That which I can't see; that which surrounds me.

Wifi. It's pinging through the connection; searching out the node my implant uses when producing telemetric data. Trembling, I've got seconds and few choices: disable a router somewhere, or succumb. You used to drill us with manufactured scenarios; split-second judgements based on crisp, unrealistic binaries. Black or white; life or death.

I can stretch across two floors to find the source, or repel it.

Shouting, I extend my awareness; grasp at malware spidering wifi along the drywall and glass storefront. Cash registers careen toward me, light fixtures twist from overhead sockets, and wayward cellphones rush toward the event horizon of my will as I reach, *reach* for the thing coming to end me.

Then, I break.

❖

WHEN THE DEED is done, and I've wrung the last bit of malware from my pores, my throat is raw and there's little left standing inside the store.

Air rushes through what were once windows; customers and staff are strewn across tables, overturned couches, and jarred dinnerware. Nearby, Marco lies unmoving, save shallow breaths expanding his chest.

Gape-mouthed, I stagger; *hear* the powdery press of my foot stepping into something.

Tech. I'm stepping into all the wifi-covered objects I culled. They surround me now, soft and vaporized, confectioner's sugar tinged with acrylonitrile.

I did this. Destroyed things I've only ever been able to move; to summon. Not break.

Everybody changes, right?

Not like this, you'd probably say.

❖

STANDING BESIDE YOU now, inside your plush office, I feel strangely calm. Or, maybe comatose. They're hard to differentiate.

You haven't spoken since I arrived, hours ago; since Marv and Wat pried worried fingers from my scarred flesh (turns out, vaporizing things burns pretty bad), and let me come to you. Instead, you stare at a sky that's begun to mend. Clouds knit. Birds retake their domain.

"There was another world through that thing," you say, so quietly I almost miss it. "Another Earth."

"She found Erin then."

Your nostrils flare, and whatever secret force held you up all these years, flees. Suddenly, you look your age. "She asked her to come here. To come home."

I have so many questions, but they're sap-sticky; hard to grab amid the muck. I settle on: "Is she? Coming home?"

Your silence is answer enough, but you say, "Dr. Calamity has turned herself over to the Union."

I should feel exuberant. Triumphant, like all those Dawns, splashed across the magazine covers surrounding us. *I won. We won.*

"I vaporized tech today," I croak. "My telekinesis—it's changed, somehow."

It isn't a thing that lifts or commands; now, it decimates. I want to ask, to beg: *Did you ever feel this way?* Did someone hurt you enough to give your scar tissue teeth?

"I worried as much." You direct your words to the window, hardly blinking.

In moments, the last sliver of black disappears; blue skies, unending, stretch on. I'd ask you what comes next, because you've mapped a version of the hero's journey along your weathered palms, thwarting challenge after challenge.

This, though? This raw, unknown is our new map, splayed wide.

"I'm coming in, on Monday." Tentatively, I wrap my arms around you; squeeze, while you shudder into my shoulder. "Okay?"

Your telepathy blankets me, but you don't send a thought. Instead, you speak with your arms; you cling to me. You let your breaths harshen and your façade fall.

You cry. I hold you.

And I give myself permission to brokenly face the unknown, by your side, no answers needed.

To Exhale Sky

Shingai Njeri Kagunda

Kila has always been able to turn grief into tiny little things.

When Dimples, the family dog, dies at age five, Kila pulls all the sadness inside her and breathes out a cowrie shell. A small greyish cowrie shell that shimmers when the sun shines on it from a certain angle. Her grandmother makes her a necklace while singing a song about how the cowrie shell—such a small thing—became the totem of her tribe—such a big tribe. Every time Kila breathes something new, her grandmother sings a different version of this song.

Years later, after getting off her stage at Kencom, Kila runs into a man in a deserted alley near Kenyatta Avenue. He has a gun and tells her to run, but only after she gives him all her money. It is just after 6pm and the Nairobi sun is starting to set, the darkness taking over the space the light has left.

The man grabs the shell necklace Kila's grandmother had made for Kila. "Please no, tafadhali I beg."

The man hits her. "Shut up!"

Kila holds her purse up, her eyes squeezed shut. The man freezes when Kila opens her mouth and screams out stars. Two bright balls of fire the size of pupils float out into the air between them. He drops the necklace and runs away, blinded by their light, but they follow, penetrating his skin, burning into his core. Kila places the necklace back around her neck and takes a shaky breath in.

A few years after this, Kila falls in love with Tam, who she first saw on a Tuesday morning grabbing a coffee across the room at the Java on Mama Ngina street before work. Tam makes her inhale big, beautiful things into herself. Brown eyes, slightly slanted, small, locked dreads, dimples that accompany a smile, and two nose piercings, one on each nostril.

All small things attached to this big love which tumbles and unfurls over a glance, two numbers exchanged, first coffee date where dawa is spilled onto white pants with yellow daisies, hand grabbed to prevent a tragic death by accident on the of course crazy busy streets of Nairobi—laughter—so much laughter about everything and anything and nothing, and bathroom kisses in restaurants between whispered secrets of big love.

When Kila dreams of Tam and their secret big love that carries pasts and presents into the spaces between them, she feels herself inhale buildings, taste cities, and swallow continents. With Tam, Kila forgets what—if anything—is big and what is small.

Tam loves looking up at the sky, pays attention to the clouds, constantly contemplates the sun, and sighs at the moon and stars. Maddening as a wordless poet.

"Tell me," Kila teases her love, gulping down the picture of Tam's eyes. Tam is the shape of the world within Kila.

"Everything looks so small from down here," Tam says, "so far away. While up there, it is this whole expanse. Yani, we can't even imagine how large and fierce those balls of fire are." She kisses Kila's neck softly. "And in our little humanness, we have the audacity to sing, *twinkle twinkle little star.*"

Kila touches the cowrie shell attached to the necklace on her heart. That night she dreams of swallowing the sky. The little big thing for her little big love.

Cancer is the thing that steals their time.

"Who are you?" Tam's family asks.

"A friend," Kila responds, as she holds in her crying. *A love,* she thinks as she tries not to exhale, scared she will breathe out things instead of air.

And with the chemo comes a world of brown eyes, still slightly slanted, now with tired wrinkles, small-locked dreads that fall one at a time to the ground leaving parts of scalp visible—vulnerable—dimples that never go away—thank god they never go away— accompanying a smile that these days leaves for extended periods of time without notice.

At night, Kila throws up continents. Coming out of her, they slice her open from the inside out until they are in the toilet bowl and they become tiny things again. Only totems of bigger things. She holds on tightly to the sky within her chest, refusing to let it go.

Kila is scared that if she throws up the stars, she will lose Tam; she convinces herself it is the only thing that keeps her tiny big love alive.

One day Tam is coughing up phlegm stuck with tiny specks of blood on her hospital gown and says to Kila, "Let us go see the sky."

Kila wants to say, "It is in my chest. I have saved it for you," but instead she says, "You are not allowed to leave your room this late at night."

And there is a little twinkle in Tam's eyes but Kila is not fooled. She knows it is a ball of fire. "Live a little."

When Tam laughs—and Kila will do anything for that laugh—she says, "If we get caught, they will have more pity on you, so I am going to say I tried to stop you."

Tam says, "You are going to blame the patient. How cruel!"

And they are both holding in their laughs and sneaking through hallways and past nurses falling asleep on desk duty until they are at a balcony on the east wing under the night sky.

"We're not all the way outside." Tam sighs.

"Close enough." Kila wraps her love in her arms and inhales Tam's scent.

Tam touches skin, turns around and lifts fingers to the necklace around Kila's neck. "Tell me again of your grandmother's song?"

As Tam touches the cowrie shell that Kila breathed out when she was five, it glows. Kila does not know if Tam can see it, but the warmth seeps down her neck into her shoulders. "There are so many versions of it."

"We have all the time in the world, baby."

Kila laughs and stops pretending she can hold in her tears. She starts telling the version of the story of the big tribe being protected by a small spirit that lives in the cowrie shell. How the spirit taught the big tribe that time doesn't exist in the conjunction of big and little things.

Tam looks at the stars in the sky. "I think I am going to be a big ball of fire pretending to be a tiny twinkling star."

And Kila thinks *time doesn't exist at the conjunction of big and little things,* so she inhales her tiny big love in and exhales the sky.

About our Contributors

Cherae Clark is the author of *The Unbroken*, the Nebula-nominated first book in the Magic of the Lost trilogy, and is a BFA and Locus award winning editor. She graduated from Indiana University's creative writing MFA and was a 2012 Lambda Literary Fellow. She's been a personal trainer, an English teacher, and an editor, and is some combination thereof as she travels the world. When she's not writing or working, she's learning languages, doing P90something, or reading about war and [post-]colonial history. Her work has appeared or is forthcoming in *FIYAH, PodCastle, Uncanny,* and *Beneath Ceaseless Skies*.

Laurel Beckley is a writer, Marine Corps veteran and librarian. She is from Oregon, and currently lives in northern Virginia with her wife, fur creatures and a collection of gently neglected houseplants. She can be found on Twitter @laurelthereader, and links to her works are on her blog, thesuspectedbibliophile.home.blog.

Sharang Biswas is a writer, artist, and award-winning game designer. He has won IndieCade and IGDN awards for his games and has showcased interactive works at numerous galleries, museums, and festivals, including Pioneer Works in Brooklyn, the Institute of Contemporary Art in Philadelphia, and the Museum of the Moving Image in Queens. His writing has appeared in *Lightspeed, Strange Horizons, Fantasy Magazine, Baffling Magazine, Eurogamer, Dicebreaker, Unwinnable,* and more. He is the co-editor of *Honey & Hot Wax: An Anthology of Erotic Art Games* (Pelgrane Press) and *Strange Lusts / Strange Loves: An Anthology of Erotic Interactive Fiction* (Strange Horizons). Find him on Twitter at @SharangBiswas.

Jen Brown (she/her) weaves otherworldly tales about Black, queer folks righteously wielding power. An Ignyte Award-nominated writer, her stories have appeared in *FIYAH Literary Magazine, Tor.com's Breathe FIYAH anthology, Baffling Magazine, Anathema: Spec From the Margins, PodCastle,* and was recently translated for Crononauta's *Matreon* publication. She tweets at @jeninthelib, & you can find more of her work at jencbrown.com.

Aliette de Bodard lives and works in Paris. She has won three Nebula Awards, an Ignyte Award, a Locus Award, a British Fantasy Award, and four British Science Fiction Association Awards. Her most recent book is *Of Charms, Ghosts and Grievances* (JABberwocky Literary Agency, Inc., forthcoming June 28th, 20222), a fantasy of manners and murders set in an alternate 19th Century Vietnamese court. She also wrote *Fireheart Tiger* (Tor.com), a sapphic romantic fantasy inspired by pre colonial Vietnam, where a diplomat princess must decide the fate of her country, and her own. She lives in Paris. Visit aliettedebodard.com for more information.

Shingai Njeri Kagunda is an Afrosurreal/futurist storyteller from Nairobi, Kenya with a Literary Arts MFA from Brown. She has work in or upcoming in *Omenana, FANTASY magazine, FracturedLit, Khoreo, Africa Risen,* and *Uncanny Magazine.* Her debut novella *& This is How to Stay Alive* was published by Neon Hemlock Press in October 2021. She is the co-editor of *Podcastle Magazine* and the co-founder of Voodoonauts. Shingai is a creative writing teacher, an eternal student, and a lover of all things soft and Black.

Cheri Kamei (she/her) is a Japanese-Okinawan American, queer writer. Her short stories have previously been published on *Tor.com* and in Scott J. Moses's horror anthology, *What One Wouldn't Do.* She resides in Honolulu, Hawaii with her wife, plants, and a corgi named Charlie. She can be found online at cherikameiwrites.com or Twitter @cheri_kamei.

LA Knight is a biracial Black, queer, disabled, chronically ill, autistic author of fantasy and sci-fi. She's a huge fan of portal fantasy, mythology, fairy tale & lit retellings, anime, and Broadway. This is their first work that openly and defiantly celebrates autistic joy, and the beauty of and beauty in autistic stimming. She is active on Twitter at @LA_Knight89, and their previous work has appeared in Combat Magazine, Foliate Oak Magazine, The Young Adult Reader, Tomorrow's Cthulhu, and New Legends of Fantasy: Caster*Castle*Creature. She lives with her husband, two life-partners, and their cats in the Sonoran Desert.

Ann LeBlanc lives in the forest with her wife, where she writes about queer yearning, culinary adventures and death. Her stories have been published in *Fireside Magazine, Escape Pod, Apparition Lit,* and *Baffling Magazine.* She can be found online at annleblanc.com or on twitter at @RobotLeBlanc.

Sam J Miller's books have been called "must reads" and "bests of the year" by *USA Today, Entertainment Weekly, NPR,* and *O: The Oprah Magazine,* among others. He is the Nebula-Award-winning author of *Blackfish City,* which has been translated into six languages and won the hopefully-soon-to-be-renamed John W. Campbell Memorial Award. Sam's short stories have won a Shirley Jackson Award and been nominated for the World Fantasy, Theodore Sturgeon, and Locus Awards, and have been reprinted in dozens of anthologies. He's also the last in a long line of butchers. He lives in New York City, and at samjmiller.com.

Watson Neith is a writer and multimedia artist. Their work has been published in *Corvid Queen* and *Translunar Traveler's Lounge.* @watsonneith on Twitter.

H. Pueyo (@hachepueyo on Twitter) is an Argentine-Brazilian writer of comics and speculative fiction. She's an Otherwise Fellow, and her work has appeared before in *F&SF, Clarkesworld, Strange Horizons, Fireside,* and *The Year's*

Best Dark Fantasy & Horror, among others. Find her online at hachepueyo.com. Her bilingual debut collection *A Study in Ugliness & Outras Histórias* is out by Lethe Press, and can be found at hachepueyo.com.

Alexandra Seidel writes strange little stories often turn out darker than she thought, unless they turn out funnier than she thought. Follow Alexa on Twitter @Alexa_Seidel or like her Facebook page (facebook.com/AlexaSeidelWrites), and find out what she's up to at alexandraseidel.com. As Alexa Piper, she writes (very queer) paranormal romance books which have been rumored to make people laugh out loud in public. Such rumors please this author.

Bogi Takács (e/em/eir/emself or they pronouns) is a Hungarian Jewish author, critic and scholar who's an immigrant to the US. Bogi has won the Lambda and Hugo awards, and has been a finalist for other awards. Eir debut poetry collection *Algorithmic Shapeshifting* and eir debut short story collection *The Trans Space Octopus Congregation* were both released in 2019. You can find Bogi talking about books at www.bogireadstheworld.com, and on various social media like Twitter, Patreon and Instagram as bogiperson.

Fargo Tbakhi (he/him) is a queer Palestinian-American performance artist. He is the winner of the 2018 Ghassan Kanafani Resistance Arts Prize, a Pushcart and Best of the Net nominee, and a Tin House Summer Workshop alum. His writing is published in *Strange Horizons, Foglifter, Hobart, The Shallow Ends, Mizna, Peach Mag*, and elsewhere. His performance work has been programmed at OUTsider Fest, INTER-SECTION Solo Fest, and has received support from the Arizona Commission on the Arts. He is currently a Halcyon Arts Lab Fellow and works at Mosaic Theater.

STORY ACKNOWLEDGEMENTS

"The Captain and the Quartermaster" by C.L. Clark originally appeared in *Beyond Ceaseless Skies*.

"A Study in Ugliness" by H. Pueyo originally appeared in *The Dark*.

"Mulberry and Owl" by Aliette de Bodard originally appeared in *Uncanny*.

"The Lake, the Valley, the Border Between Water and Wood, and the End of Things" by Watson Neith originally appeared in *Translunar Traveler's Lounge*.

"Let All the Children Boogie" by Sam J. Miller originally appeared in *Tordotcom*.

"The Hidden Language of Flowers" by Laurel Beckley originally appeared in *Misspelled: Magic Gone Awry* edited by Kelly Lynn Colby.

"The Art and Mystery of Thea Wells" by Alexandra Seidel originally appeared in *Diabolical Plots*.

"To Rest and To Create" by LA Knight originally appeared in *FIYAH*.

"A Technical Term, Like Privilege" by Bogi Takács originally appeared in *Whether Change: The Revolution Will Be Weird* edited by Scott Gable and C. Dombrowski.

"Root Rot" by Fargo Tbakhi originally appeared in *Apex*.

"Twenty Thousand Last Meals on an Exploding Station" by Ann LeBlanc originally appeared in *Mermaids Monthly*.

"Blood in the Thread" by Cheri Kamei originally appeared in *Tordotcom*.

"Sutekh: A Breath of Spring" by Sharang Biswas originally appeared in *Unfettered Hexes: Queer Tales of Insatiable Darkness* edited by dave ring.

"To Rise, Blown Open" by Jen Brown originally appeared in *Anathema: Spec from the Margins*.

"To Exhale Sky" by Shingai Njeri Kagunda originally appeared in *Baffling*.

About the Editors

L.D. Lewis is an award-winning SF/F writer and editor, and publisher at *Fireside Magazine*. She serves as a founding creator and Project Manager for the World Fantasy and Hugo Award-winning *FIYAH Literary Magazine*. She also serves as the founding Director of FIYAHCON, Researcher for the (also award-winning) *LeVar Burton Reads* podcast, and pays the bills as the Awards Manager for the Lambda Literary Foundation. She is the author of *A Ruin of Shadows* (Dancing Star Press, 2018) and her published short fiction and poetry includes appearances in *FIYAH, PodCastle, Strange Horizons, Anathema: Spec from the Margins, Lightspeed,* and Neon Hemlock, among others. She lives in Georgia, on perpetual deadline, with her coffee habit, two very photogenic kittens, and an impressive LEGO build collection. Tweet her @ellethevillain.

Charles Payseur is an avid reader, writer, and reviewer of speculative fiction. His works have appeared in *The Best American Science Fiction and Fantasy, Lightspeed Magazine,* and *Beneath Ceaseless Skies,* among others, and he's a six-time Hugo Award finalist and two-time Ignyte Award finalist. His debut short fiction collection, *The Burning Day and Other Strange Stories,* was published by Lethe Press (2021). He currently resides in Eau Claire, Wisconsin, with his herd of disobedient pets and husband, Matt. He can be found gushing about short fiction on Twitter as @ClowderofTwo.

About the Press

Neon Hemlock is a Washington, DC-based small press publishing speculative fiction, rad zines and queer chapbooks. We punctuate our titles with oracle decks, occult ephemera and literary candles. Publishers Weekly once called us "the apex of queer speculative fiction publishing" and we're still beaming.

Learn more about us at neonhemlock.com and on Twitter at @neonhemlock.